TWO RIVERS

BY ZOE SAADIA

Two Rivers
Across the Great Sparkling Water
The Great Law of Peace
The Peacekeeper

Beyond the Great River
The Foreigner
Troubled Waters
The Warpath
Echoes of the Past

Shadow on the Sun
Royal Blood
Dark Before Dawn
Raven of the North

The Highlander
Crossing Worlds
The Emperor's Second Wife
Currents of War
The Fall of the Empire
The Sword
The Triple Alliance

Obsidian Puma
Field of Fire
Heart of the Battle
Warrior Beast
Morning Star
Valley of Shadows

TWO RIVERS

The Peacemaker, Book 1

ZOE SAADIA

Copyright © 2013 by Zoe Saadia

All rights reserved. This book or any portion thereof may not be reproduced, transmitted or distributed in any form or by any means whatsoever, without prior written permission from the copyright owner, unless by reviewers who wish to quote brief passages.

For more information about this book, the author and her work, visit
www.zoesaadia.com

ISBN: 1535096454
ISBN-13: 978-1535096454

AUTHOR'S NOTE

"Two Rivers" is historical fiction and some of the characters and adventures in this book are imaginary, while some are historical and well documented in the accounts concerning this time period and place.

The history of that region is presented as accurately and as reliably as possible, to the best of the author's ability, and although no work of this scope can be free of error, an earnest effort was made to reflect the history and the traditional way of life of the peoples residing in those areas.

I would also like to apologize before the descendants of the mentioned nations for giving various traits and behaviors to the well known historical characters (such as the Great Peacemaker, whose name I changed out of respect even though it was translated into English), sometimes putting them into fictional situations for the sake of the story. The main events of this series are well documented and could be verified by a simplest research.

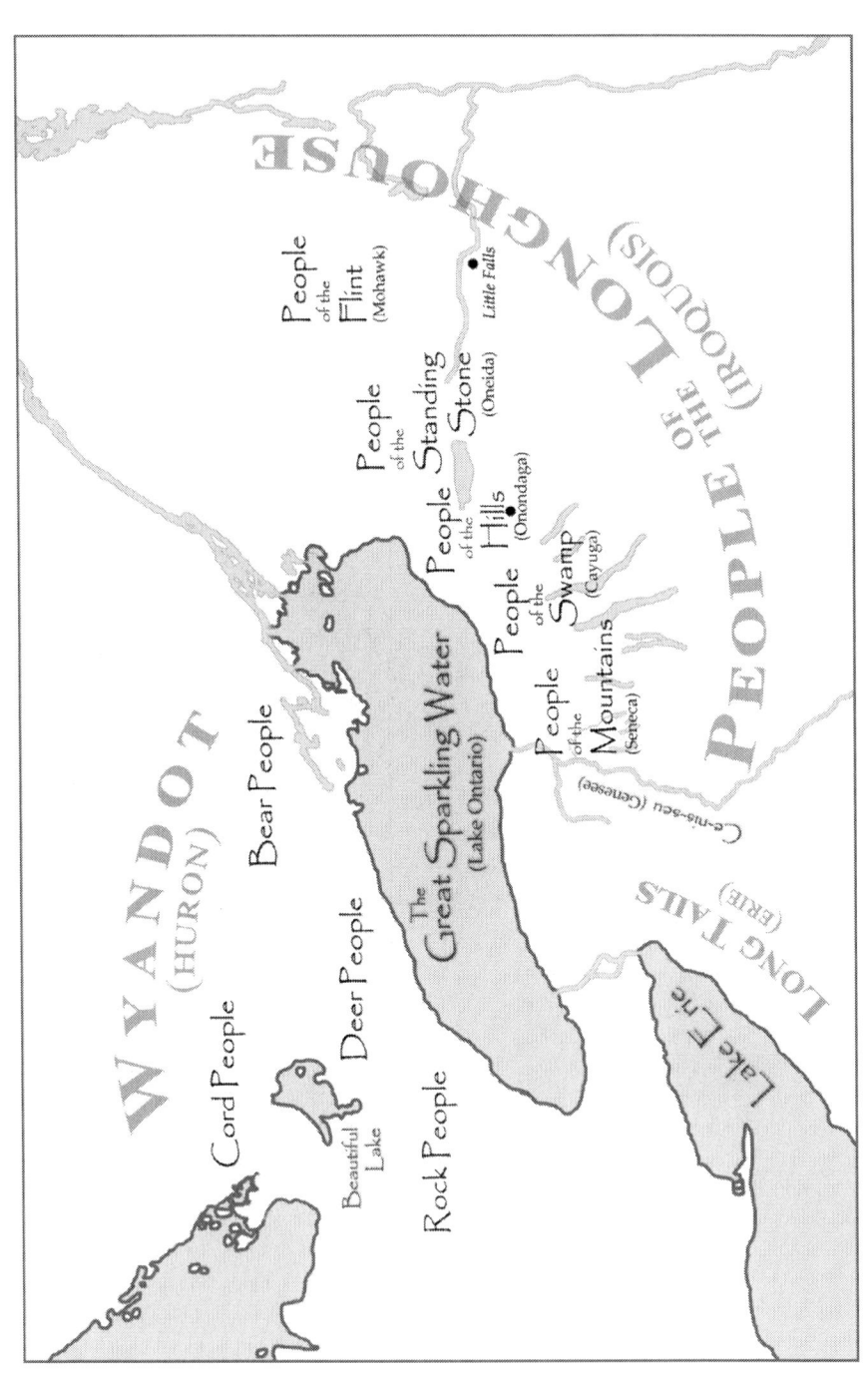

PREFACE

The Great League of the Iroquois existed for centuries before both Americas were discovered by other continents. Composed of five nations known to us under the names of Mohawks, Oneida, Onondaga, Cayuga, and Seneca, the Iroquois Confederacy occupied most of today's upstate New York, from Delaware River north to the St. Lawrence all the way to Niagara Peninsula and Lake Erie with its surrounding areas.

What made this confederacy special was their amazingly detailed, well-defined constitution. Recorded by a pictographic system in the form of *wampum* belts, the league's laws held on for centuries, maintaining perfect balance between five powerful, warlike nations. Many modern scholars believe that USA constitution was inspired by the Iroquois constitution. To what degree, this is another question, but Benjamin Franklin, John Adams, and some other Founding Fathers were, undoubtedly, very well-versed in the laws of the Great League, with Franklin advocating a federal system akin to that of the Iroquois and Adams leading a faction that favored more centralized government but still citing many of the Iroquois laws in the process.

So what was this remarkable constitution, and how did it come to life? This work of historical fiction attempts to recreate the remarkable events that happened more than eight centuries ago.

CHAPTER 1

Southeastern Canada, near Lake Ontario
1141 AD

The ball sprang into the air, glowing dully, making its way toward the edge of the field, determined, resisting the wind coming from the lakeside.

A good throw, reflected Tekeni, leaping forward along with the rest of the players, his shaft grasped tightly in his sweaty palm, ready to pounce. Squinting against the glow of the afternoon sun, he followed the path of the ball, calculating fast. It was coming down, nearing the other side of the field, the opponents' side.

Pushing another player out of his way, Tekeni leaped ahead, seeing the momentarily clear path. His shaft shot forward, as his eyes estimated the distance. Oh, yes, he was going to trap this ball, to catch it safely in his net, to make a run for the opposite team's gates, and maybe, with a little luck, to score.

Racing on, oblivious of the cheering crowds, he turned sharply without slowing his step, catching his balance, ready to face the descending ball. It was coming down fast. For a fraction of a moment, he could see it clearly, a coarse, round thing made out of a stuffed deerskin, heavy enough to inflict damage if one wasn't careful. Blocking the sunlight, it made its way toward his outstretched arm, making it unnecessary to get into a better position, not even to tilt his body. It was going straight for his shaft. He caught his breath and felt the silence as the watching crowds went still, holding their breath, too.

Then, as the ball was about to land in his net, his arm shot sideways, driven away by a force he could not comprehend for a moment, the pain in it paralyzing, making him gasp. As the heavy body of another player slammed into him, he felt the grass slipping under his feet, jumping into his face, revoltingly damp, permeating his breath. From the corner of his eye, he could see the ball crashing into the earth just outside the field, cumbersome, powerless upon the ground.

People were yelling, their words gushing above his head, as he pushed himself up, his arm numb and not reacting properly. The taste of the earth was nauseating, and he spat violently, glad to find something to do before trying to make sense of what happened. All eyes would be upon him now, that much he knew – *Seketa's eyes, too* – yet the fresh earth clogging his nostrils was his most immediate concern.

Someone picked up the ball and was carrying it away. To put it in its place upon the middle of the field, he knew, to await the announcement of yet another round, because when the ball fell out of the field, the whole move was canceled.

"You will be out of the game before you know it!" shouted someone angrily. Recognizing the voice of Ogtaeh, a player from his team, Tekeni wiped the mud from his face, blinking to make his vision focus.

"It was an accident," answered Yeentso smugly, a thin half smile twisting his lips. He was a tall, broadly built man of twenty or more summers, the best player of the opposite team.

"It was no accident!" fumed Ogtaeh. "I saw it all!" He turned to the surrounding players. "You all saw it, didn't you?"

"Well, it might have been an accident," murmured someone. "The slippery ground and all."

"The slippery ground in your stupid dreams!" Spitting the remnants of the earth from his mouth, its taste mixed with the salty flavor of blood, Tekeni came closer, trying to pay no attention to the pain rolling up and down his arm. "He collided with me on purpose!" He took another step, glaring at Yeentso, seeing the hated face so very close, every scar, every speckle, every bead of sweat upon it. "And you hit me with your shaft to make sure I did not catch this ball, you dirty piece of excrement."

The high cheekbones of the man took a darker shade.

"You better watch your tongue, wild boy," said Yeentso, leaning forward.

It took Tekeni a conscious effort not to take a step back, tiny waves of alarm running down his stomach, making it twist. Yeentso was a seasoned warrior, strong and dominant, renowned for the shortness of his temper. And yet, and yet… The ball game had very strict rules, and while the players were always ready to sustain injuries on account of the heavy ball and the frequent collisions with each other, one had no right to hit his rival with his shaft, so very openly at that.

For another heartbeat, they glared at each other, but a glimpse of his doubts must have been reflecting in Tekeni's eyes, as his rival's lips twisted into another derisive grin.

"Wipe your face and go away, boy. Learn to talk properly before you address your elders and betters." Yeentso straightened up and looked around, eyes glittering. "You hit me, you dirty excrement," he mimicked, doing Tekeni's accent quite well. "Go away, you dirty foreigner. You will never be one of us."

The wave of rage was so sudden, so overwhelming, he found it difficult to breathe. Eyes fixed on the man's smirking face, he felt the sounds receding, disappearing, melting in the choking cloud of fury. People murmured, but their voices reached him barely, coming in waves. Still, he tried to control his temper, his palms going numb from the force with which they clutched onto the handle of his playing stick.

"Stop talking nonsense, Yeentso," said someone calmly. "You did enough for one afternoon. Let us proceed with the game. They are waiting for us to resume."

Indeed, the people crowding both slopes were still silent, watching with curiosity, but the elders' stony faces showed disapproval.

"I'm willing to proceed if the wild boy is willing to stop whining." Shrugging, Yeentso began turning away.

"You played dirty, you coward!" cried out Tekeni, hardly able to control his voice. It was trembling badly.

The tall man whirled around, moving with surprising speed. One heartbeat, he was turning away, the next, his wide body was pressed against Tekeni's, the large, weathered palms grabbing his throat.

"Don't you ever call me that, you slimy piece of foreign dirt. If you want to enjoy a little more of your worthless life, keep very quiet, and away from me." The hands grabbing his throat fastened. "You are nothing but a dirty foreigner from across the Great Sparkling Water, and why you were given a chance to live I'll never understand. They should never have adopted you, but killed you along with your stinking, worthless people."

This time, the wave of rage was too forceful, impossible to control. Struggling to stabilize himself, Tekeni found it easy to squirm out of the strangling grip the moment his foot connected with the man's shin, the vicious kick making his attacker waver. The shaft, still grasped tightly in his hands, came up as though acting on its own accord, crushing against the man's temple, sending him sprawling into the damp grass, to lie there motionless, just a heap of limbs.

Wavering, he struggled to get grip of his senses, his heart pounding, trying to jump out of his chest. The silence was encompassing. No one moved, no one seemed to breathe even.

Then the collective gasp escaped many chests, and the murmuring went up and up, gaining strength, turning into a loud hum. People were running from all over, and women were screaming. Strong hands grabbed his arms, tore the heavy stick away from his sweaty palms. He didn't try to resist, too numb to think straight just yet.

"He killed Yeentso!"

The voices were all around, surrounding him like raging water, when one's canoe would overturn in the rapids of the river. This had happened to him once, when a young boy of no more than ten summers old. He could swim well, but the rapids were vicious, raging around, splashing over his head, the current strong and pulling, impossible to resist. He had panicked immediately back then, thrashing his limbs and breathing the splashing sprays, until Father's strong hands grabbed him, pulling him out of the lethal grip, making the world right again.

Well, now the feeling was back, the helpless sensation of fighting for one's life, mindlessly, if need be. And there would be no Father to pull him out, because Father had been dead for two summers and three moons, killed with one single arrow on that day, when the world turned upside down again.

He tried to break free, but the grip on his wrists tightened, turned unbearable. Biting his lips, he suppressed a groan as they fought to slam his hands behind his back. The clamor around was deafening, this same raging water, climbing higher and higher, threatening to drown him. The panic was back, the mindless, desperate efforts to break free.

"Let the boy go. What do you think he'll do, kill you all?"

The same even voice of the man who had suggested getting back to the game earlier was familiar, calming in its tranquility. He remembered him vaguely, from other ball games and from some heated arguments with the Town and Clans' Councils. His name was Two Currents Flowing Together, but everyone called him Two Rivers. He belonged to the Turtle Clan, residing in the longhouse next to the one Tekeni had grown to regard as his own. Everyone talked about this man and his peculiar opinions that he never bothered to keep to himself.

Kneeling beside the crumbled form of Yeentso, the man put his ear to the wounded's chest, then straightened up and inspected the bleeding head.

"He is breathing," he informed the stunned crowds, straightening up and pushing his hair off his sweaty face. "Maybe he'll live."

"If he doesn't, the loathsome brat will pay with his worthless life!" cried out a tall woman, dropping beside the wounded. "And it won't be an easy death, either. The despicable murderer, the filthy foreigner! I'll make sure that..." Her voice trailed off, turning into sobs.

"This will not be your decision to make," said Two Rivers, unperturbed. "The Clans Councils will deal with this youth, or maybe the Town Council." He stood the woman's glare, his prominent, well spaced eyes unreadable. "But you can make yourself useful by asking the medicine man to see your husband, the sooner the better."

"He is coming," volunteered another woman. "And the elders of the town. They were watching, anyway."

"Good." Two Rivers got to his feet briskly. "Give him some space, so he can get a gulp of fresh air. Bring water and clean cloths. And let the boy go. He won't make any more trouble. Not this afternoon."

"Who put you in the lead?" demanded one of the men whose hands were still pinning Tekeni's arms, their grip painful. "You are not one of the council's members to distribute orders. And you are not the leading warrior, either."

"Well, neither are you, Anue." Two Rivers shrugged, still unperturbed. "But while I was thinking about Yeentso and his well being, you've been busy taking your frustration out on a young boy as though he were a dangerous enemy warrior."

"The cub *is* dangerous," murmured someone.

"And he is an enemy!"

"He is not an enemy. He is one of us. He has been adopted into the Wolf Clan, and it did not happen a few dawns ago." Two Rivers' grin twisted, challenging. "And he is no more dangerous than any one of those other young men. But if you are afraid of a boy armed with a wooden shaft, I suppose you should not go around unprotected."

This did not go well, neither with the insulted man, nor with the rest of the crowd. The glares Two Rivers received could rival the ones shot at Tekeni, who peered at his unexpected defender wide-eyed, forgetting his own plight for a moment.

Why would someone want to help him, the despised enemy? Yes, he had been adopted like the man said. It happened more than two summers ago. Still, no one made the mistake of trusting him, not yet, not ever maybe. He was an enemy, a boy from across the Great Sparkling Water, captured while raiding those northern lands, a part of a warriors' party, too young to belong, but still a male child who had seen close to fifteen summers, almost a warrior. He should have been killed with his people, shot like his father, or put through a customary ceremony with those who were captured. A difficult death, but a worthy one. Yet, he was not. He was too young, and one family wanted him, to replace a dead member.

He clenched his teeth against the memories, banishing them with a practiced skill. He had become well-trained in the art of shutting his mind, not letting memories take power until he could not control them anymore, drowning in the black wave of desperation, or succumbing to all sorts of wild ideas.

"Spare your speeches for the councils, Two Rivers," Anue's sharp voice brought Tekeni back in time to make the threatening wave go away. "Let us have one afternoon with no politics and no strange ideas of yours."

For the first time through this day, Two Rivers' eyes sparkled dangerously. "You will not tell me what to talk about and where. My ideas may be strange to you, but they make perfect sense, if only you and your likes would deign to actually listen instead of closing your mind to simple good sense." He shrugged. "And, anyway, I talked no politics. All I did was simply point out that this boy should be treated fairly, as one of us. He has been adopted formally, at the request of the Wolf Clan's Council. According to our laws and customs, which you are so fond of bringing up every time I suggest a slightest change, it makes him one of us, his origins notwithstanding. Had he been a grown-up warrior with rivers of blood of our people upon his hands, he would still be turned into one of us the moment he had been adopted. The tradition of hundreds of summers says so. But while you are passionately defending every one of our old ways, you let your hatred blind you to the point of disregarding them when it's comfortable to you, brushing aside any consideration of humanity. And any sparkle of common sense, for that matter."

The large eyes glowed now with a strange, unsettling fire, making Tekeni shiver, unwilling to hear more. This man, indeed, was renowned for his far-fetched ideas, contradicting some of the old ways. And, while he was not afraid to sound them aloud, his passion was what made people frown and move away. He was a strange person.

"Our laws and customs are sensible, logical, the ones to make perfect sense," declared Anue, stepping forward, his cheeks coloring a darker shade. "Not the strange changes you are suggesting. Those make no sense at all, contradicting our good old ways. Maybe you are right, maybe this boy is to be treated fairly, even though he behaves like the worst of the savages from across the Great Sparkling Water. Maybe he can be turned into one of us one day, if we are patient. I don't doubt the action of the Wolf Clan's Council, but I do wish they had chosen more wisely while selecting new members to replace the mourned ones." The man's eyes glimmered unpleasantly. "Well, maybe they will succeed in the end, and this boy will add to the glory of our people. He is still very young. But you? You are proving to be the real problem, Two Rivers, stirring nothing but trouble, bringing nothing but discord to our settlements and our people, making such tremendous efforts to disrupt our way of life. So, while having no serious concerns about this youth, I do have my doubts about you, a man who has seen more than thirty summers, a man whose ways are settled on disrupting our way of life."

People held their breath, tense, afraid and expectant at the same time. Was one incident not enough? Would these two be reaching for their knives, two respectable, grown-up men this time?

The air hissed loudly, bursting through Two Rivers' clenched teeth, the effort of holding onto his temper evident in the vein pulsating upon his forehead.

"My ways, indeed, are settled, but they are aimed at bettering our people's circumstances, not at disrupting our ways. You should open your ears to my words, instead of shutting them so thoroughly, spending all your energy on doing this. I wish I could say I believe in making you and your kind listen, but, alas, I'm afraid I'm on the verge of despairing."

"I hope you would despair already," cried out Anue, eyes glowing in his turn. "It would make the life of our town so much more pleasant."

The air thickened rapidly, but before any more words were uttered, the elders were upon them, and the crowds parted, clearing the way for the medicine man and his followers as Yeentso began groaning, coming around.

"Make room for him," said the healer curtly, echoing Two Rivers' earlier demand. "Don't crowd around him like that. Move away."

One of the elders knelt beside the wounded. "Better yet, go back, return to the town. The game will not be resumed." He looked up, measuring Tekeni and his capturers with an impartial gaze. "What happened will be discussed between the Town and Clans' Councils. Do nothing until then." The man's eyes narrowed, turning threatening. "And I mean - nothing! No one is to seek justice, or to try to solve the problem by his or her own means." His gaze encircled the crowds, penetrating, making Tekeni shiver. "No one!"

CHAPTER 2

Rounding the corner of a longhouse, Two Rivers hesitated, pondering his possibilities. The darkness enveloped him, welcome in its thickness, protecting, making him feel alone. Craving the privacy it offered, he turned toward the dark mass of the palisade fence and the plots of tobacco scattered along the wide entrance.

What a rotten day, he thought, following the curves of the fence as it twisted tortuously, creating a corridor between two sets of poles. It took longer to get in and out of the town, but the double row of palisade made it more difficult for the invaders to get in, giving the defenders an advantage, and the benefit of time.

How could a pleasant, sunny day have turned into such a mess? he asked himself again and again, squinting against the wind as it pounced on him the moment he left the protection of the fence. It was already midsummer, but the wind was always there, trying to get in one's way, never allowing a person to enjoy the summer to its fullest. The questionable location was at fault, he knew, with the settlement situated on the windiest bay in the whole land, never allowing one to enjoy the true summer's warmth.

He shrugged. This was his town, his homeland, his people. Even if they were stubborn and could see no farther than the tips of their long, aquiline noses, adamant in their opposition to oh-so-very-necessary changes, they were his people, his family.

He sighed. Why were they so opposed to anything new or different, laws or ideas; or people? Like this boy from the other side of the Great Sparkling Water. What a wild thing! But a courageous one, a true wolf cub, baring his teeth, watching the world with his haunted eyes, afraid and daring at the same time.

Of course, the boy was right to hit Yeentso. He was provoked beyond reason. But a wiser person would control his temper better, would not grab the stick so readily. Not when one had no friends and no real protection from one's family. The boy had spent enough time living in the town, but not nearly enough to become one of them. Not with such unwillingness to adapt, to make friends, or to take life in a lighter way.

He frowned, trying to imagine how he might have felt if captured and not killed but adopted into one of the other nations' settlements. There were enough enemies to the east and the west, all those towns and villages spread along their side of the Great Lake. But what if he were captured by the terrible enemy from across the endless sparkling water, this boy's people?

He shuddered, then dismissed this thought as an unlikely possibility. Not in the face of the escalating hatred. If captured, a warrior of his age and abilities would be executed, in a painful way, too, forced to run a gauntlet of striking clubs, on the carpet of glowing embers, maybe. Would he die bravely, showing no fear and no pain? And what if he had been found worthy of adoption, forced to live among his people's fiercest enemies? Would he find it as difficult to adapt, surrounded by a fair amount of hatred and mistrust?

He shrugged. There were plenty of adopted people, but usually women and small children, kidnapped or captured, most of them seemingly with no difficulties fitting into their new lives, welcomed most readily, because no one was adopted unless a clan or a closer family unit needed to replace a dead, killed, or kidnapped member. This was the custom, and it had worked since the time immemorial. The enemies were everywhere, and every nation warred on each other.

But this is precisely what made Two Rivers' skin prickle. Something was wrong with the whole situation, something cried for a radical change. The war was a part of their lives; killing always avenged by killing, blood for blood, and there were enough hotheads to make tempers fray.

Like this afternoon, with the arrogant, short-tempered Yeentso and the stupid foreign boy. If Yeentso died, his family would demand blood. Rightfully so. But the boy from across the Great Lake had no real family, so maybe his death would be the end of it. His adoptive family was more likely to be relieved, rid of the perpetual nuisance the boy had turned out to be, not likely to try to defend him or to demand revenge in their turn. They had hoped for a better person when adopting the promising-looking youth two summers ago, so much was obvious.

Well, even if this particular feud would stop with the death of the boy, the rest of the cases were not like that, with nations, towns, and even clans having more and more things to argue about, more and more causes to seek revenge. And the war was a perpetual thing, not a part of life anymore, but life itself, the main drive of it. Everything was dedicated to this end, every aspect of the daily life committed to the defense of the town, and to the means of sending war parties, as many as the town could equip; and it didn't matter where anymore. Just to raid anyone's settlements, to avenge yet another attack, yet another kidnapping, yet another insult. The life was about war and nothing else, and while in and of itself, it was not such an unacceptable thing, its toll was becoming more and more obvious, with the fields producing less food, with the worsening diet and the spreading winter and summer diseases, with the gloomier mood and general state of mind.

Many people saw the problem, but no one knew what to do with it. They argued and argued, not listening to each other, yet united in their mutual dislike of Two Rivers and his radical ideas. What he said made no sense to anyone.

He cursed silently, then tensed. A silhouette upon the high bank clearly belonged to a woman, a slender form outlined by the faint moon. Leaning on her arms, she just sat there, facing the water not far below her feet, her back straight, head thrust forward, as though enjoying the touch of the cutting wind, or maybe pitting her strength against it.

He neared silently, but she heard him all the same.

"I knew you'd be coming here." She didn't stir, didn't move to make a place for him upon her perch on the high bank.

"Am I so predictable?"

"Oh, yes, you are. You never surprise anyone in this town. Who wouldn't guess you'd be arguing, stirring trouble again? If you let the councils do their work uninterrupted you would surprise many people. But of course you did not."

He kicked a stone and watched it rolling down the bank. "Well, you did surprise me, coming here tonight. It's not safe to wander outside like this. One can never know if there are no enemies lurking around. Fancy being kidnapped?"

"And you?" Her voice tore the silence, openly hostile. "Fancy being killed? Or maybe kidnapped, eh? You might like it, come to think about it. You seem to understand our enemies well."

Turning abruptly, she faced him, her face barely visible in the faint moonlight, mainly the outline of the beautiful cheekbones, high and oh-so-well defined.

"What do you want?" he asked tiredly, squatting upon the cold sand.

"Me? Nothing! I want nothing from you."

"Then why did you wait for me here?"

"I didn't say I was waiting for you!" The fringes decorating her dress jumped angrily as her chest rose and fell. "I came to enjoy some peace and quiet. I was here first."

He snorted. "Peace and quiet? You don't look so peaceful. And you *were* waiting for me here, fuming and getting angrier with every heartbeat."

The hiss of her breath tore the silence. "I just came to tell you that if you will go on defending the dirty whelp that tried to kill my brother, you will regret it dearly."

He didn't turn his head, not surprised. "Your brother is not dead yet. He may heal. And he was the one to attack this boy. I was there, I saw it all. He grabbed the boy by his throat, and he threatened to kill him, after he hit him in the middle of the game. It was quite a blow, and I'm surprised he didn't break this youth's arm. But maybe he did. It was all blue and swollen, but no one paid attention, of course. No one cared for the dirty foreigner. They were busy fussing around your brother, the impeccable Wyandot man." He raised his hand as she tried to say something, glaring at her in his turn, truly angry now. "Well, I did not intend to defend the wild cub. He was certainly guilty of the charges against him. All I did was to tell the true story when I was called by the Town Council to testify. But now, after talking to you, I may very well do that, try to help that boy. He was treated badly enough, this afternoon, if not through his previous moons here. He was adopted formally, turned into one of us. But he is not treated as one of us now, is he?"

"If my brother dies, he'll die," she said stubbornly, turning away and peering at the dark mass of the water below her feet. "Adopted or not, one of us or not. And I'm warning you. Keep out of it. Many people are angry with you as it is. Your attitude is bad enough, without making matters so much worse by helping the dirty cub." She paused, and he could imagine her lips pressing tightly, unpleasantly thin, an ugly sight, although she was a beautiful woman. "The boy is lost, anyway. If my brother recovers, he will not let this incident pass unavenged. He will kill the boy by his own hand."

"He can't take the law into his hands. We are no savages. We have councils to settle such matters."

A shrug was his answer. He tried to keep his anger at bay.

"How is he now?" he asked instead.

She shrugged again. "He is vomiting, and he cannot see clearly. He is murmuring, coming around, and then going back into the worlds of the spirits."

"Not good." He sighed and more felt than saw her doing the same. "But he still may heal. I've seen people recover from head injuries like that. It takes time."

"I hope you are right." Her voice stiffened again, turning freezing cold. "But if he doesn't, this boy will wish he were never born."

The hatred, he thought, feeling the familiar twisting in his stomach. Always hatred. So much of it. And it is ruling our lives, this ever present sense of being wronged, this persistent need of revenge, this hopeless urge to take our frustrations out on something or someone. And always anger, anger, lakes of anger, not a peaceful moment for anyone, harmful, destructive, corruptive, ruining people and nations. Can't they truly see the wrong in it?

"What are you thinking now?" she asked accusingly, voice low.

"Nothing you would care to hear about."

She acknowledged it with a nod. "Thought so."

"Well, we had better go back and see how your brother is."

But her palm shot forward, grabbing his arm as he began to get up. "Not yet."

He hesitated, her touch sending unwelcome waves of excitement down his spine.

"He may have come back to his senses by now."

"He has his wife and the women of her longhouse to care for him."

"And you? Don't you have to go back to your family?"

She measured him with a glance. "Since when are you concerned with me and my family?"

"I'm not." He frowned, uneasy under her penetrating gaze. Even in the darkness, her eyes glimmered like polished flint, as bright and as dangerous. He pushed the memories away. "We should go back."

"Not together, surely." She tossed her head and sprang to her feet, light and pliant, a beautiful vision against the dark, shimmering sky.

For a heartbeat, they said nothing, staring at each other. He watched her breasts rising and falling, the fringes of her dress fluttering with the wind.

The darkness enveloped them, protecting, bringing back memories in force now, how her body felt against his, firm and soft at the same time, dangerous, challenging, even in the midst of the most intimate moments, never yielding, never entirely. But then, when was the last time he'd stepped away from danger?

His arms took hold of her shoulders, pulled her forcefully, his body fitting against hers, familiar, delighted in this touch. She did not resist, but her eyes were upon him, confronting, defying, daring him to proceed.

The wind tore at them, as though trying to push them away from the cliff. Neither noticed. Mesmerized, they stared at each other, but her eyes were still hostile, still daring, flickering darkly, and he knew he would have to take this woman now, no matter the consequences.

It made no sense, taking this risk. Besides being a danger in itself, she now belonged to a man, a prominent warrior. And he knew she blamed him for this, among other of his wrongdoings. He did not come to live with her in her longhouse while he had a chance. He was busy with his life, not willing to commit to a woman. Oh, how she hated him back then.

Her lips were soft, pleasantly dry, tasting of berries. They welcomed him readily, but he felt her anger seeping, even through the kiss, with the force that her lips pressed against his.

It didn't matter. Dizzy with desire, he led her down the small trail, seeking the protection of the rocks against the tearing wind. And against curious eyes.

Doing their best to make themselves comfortable upon the small patch of sand, they clung to each other, exchanging their warmth, oblivious of anything but the touch of their limbs, the feel of their skin, the rays of pleasure running through their bodies, the danger of forbidden contact adding to the sensation.

Half lying, half sitting against the large rock, he took the most of her weight, as she rested in his arms, relaxed, satisfied, a smile upon her lips obvious, even if invisible in the darkness.

"I didn't think you missed me so much," she purred, not

attempting to get up.

He said nothing, not willing to get into this sort of conversation. There was no need to hurt her feelings by pointing out that it was she who had sought this particular contact.

"Feeling quite stupid, aren't you?" she went on, sitting up.

He shrugged. "We can't change the past."

"No, we can't. But when one is busy changing the future, one might miss the present as well."

He grinned against his will. "An interesting statement."

"And a correct one when it concerns you. You are wasting your life in a spectacular fashion, busy with your strange, far-fetched ideas, noticing nothing else." She leaned closer, as though trying to see his face through the darkness, as though attempting to read his thoughts. "Do you enjoy challenging our leaders? Do you really need this perpetual thrill of danger at playing with fire? You are ruining your life so thoroughly this way."

He shrugged again, not wishing to talk about anything of the sort, not with her. His sense of well-being began to evaporate. It was a mistake; he should not have succumbed to this physical need. Why had she always had this effect on him? It couldn't be her beauty. Beautiful women were aplenty, as shapely, as smooth, as tall and imposing, most of them even-tempered and not as wild or as arrogant. What was so different about her? What was her allure?

She kept peering at him. "You should change your ways. It's about time you took your life seriously." There was an unusual ring of sincerity to her voice now. "You will make a good leader, either War Chief or the Town Council member. Think about it. Is it not what you want? Why ruin your life the way you do? Why challenge the elders of the town, or the other leaders of our settlements? Do you really enjoy doing this?"

He pressed his lips tight. "I'm not enjoying challenging anyone. And I'm not enjoying ruining my life. But I can't stand by when they are busy ruining our future."

"No one is ruining our future!" She straightened up sharply. "Our people are living by the way of our ancestors. They did so since the times immemorial, and they will continue to do so."

"Then you are as blind as they are!" He had a hard time trying to restrain himself from jumping to his feet. "The old ways are not good anymore. Not all of them. We are warring and warring, against everyone. There are no peoples who are not our enemies. Not one single nation, think about it! So all we do now is war. We dedicate every resource, every means to this end, spending our energies on equipping yet another raiding party, on fortifying yet another patch of our fence against the attack that will come. This is the purpose of our lives now, and we pay attention to little else, choosing not to think about the crops becoming less plentiful and the winters harder to get through. Think about it!" He could feel her disapproval spreading like a cloud, and it served to make him angrier. "It is not how our fathers and their fathers lived. They raided an occasional town, I'm sure of that, but there was no perpetual war ruling their lives. Their ways were good for their lives, but they are not fitting our life now. We need to adjust; we need to change our ways."

"Oh, what a harbinger of gloom you are," she said, shrugging, not impressed. "You are drawing a horrible picture, but it is not like that at all. Our enemy got stronger with the passing of summers. That is all the change. We need to strike them harder now, and it requires sacrifice. Some of the coziness and the pleasures of daily life are not available now, but this sacrifice is worthy, because we will be successful. We will be." She rose to her feet and began smoothing the wrinkles upon her dress. "Stop doubting your leaders, people of your clan, your town, your nation, your elders, and your betters. Think about your life and how you can help your community to strike the enemy, instead. To strike them, Two Rivers, and not to try to understand them."

Busy retying his loincloth, he made sure to wipe the crispy sand off his limbs.

"What was I thinking?" he muttered. "Expecting you to open your mind, if even for a heartbeat, expecting you to understand. What a thought!"

She glared at him, as he picked up one of her moccasins that had rolled down the slope, its fall stopped by a protruding rock.

"We should go back before they start looking for you," he said curtly, not returning her glare. There was no sense in trying to confront her, to explain or expect her to understand. She wouldn't listen, even though she might have understood had she only been prepared to open her mind. She was a smart woman, even if spiteful and wild-tempered.

The silence was heavy, pregnant with meaning.

"You used me once again," she said finally, her voice growling like a distant thunder. "You used me like the last of the captive females, to satisfy your needs and to wipe your feet on after you were done."

He stood her glare. "You wanted it. You were the one to initiate it. Don't try to make me take the blame. It's an old accusation, and we've been through it."

She snatched her moccasin, scratching his arm in the process. "You are the filthiest lowlife that has ever been born. You should have died summers ago, on your first war expedition. I wish our enemies would capture you, making you die slowly, shaming yourself, screaming and begging for mercy. I will pray to the Mighty Spirits for this to happen yet. Even to the Evil Twin and his underworld minions. I will live to see it happening." She hesitated for another heartbeat, her eyes glowing eerily, sending shafts of alarm down his stomach. "I will dedicate my life to ridding our town of your filthy presence. Our people will be better off without you and the perpetual nuisance you are. This nation will prosper following its old ways, with you dead, and I promise to you, I will not rest until it happens. Then I will be able to start living my life."

She was gone, evaporating into the darkness, her soft-soled moccasins making no sound, as though she had never been there at all.

Heart pounding, he stared at the suddenly empty space, his skin prickling, sensing the evil of her presence still lingering, wishing him dead oh-so-very-badly. Could such a wish come true, hastened by the sheer power of her will? He didn't know, but the thought made him turn his head, look behind his back, the darkness suddenly hostile and not safe anymore.

Pressing his lips, he began climbing the slope back toward his favorite spot upon the cliff, knowing that now it would be vacant, his and his alone.

CHAPTER 3

"Stop staring and make yourself useful, girl!"

Startled, Seketa looked up, meeting a direful frown. One of the older women picked up a bowl full of foul-smelling contents, holding it up, at arm's length.

"Take it out and empty it."

"I… Yes, of course."

Taking the offered cargo, while trying not to wince, Seketa glanced again at the groaning man that was spread upon the lower bunk. After the retching that seemed to last forever, Yeentso actually looked better, some color creeping into his lifeless face, smoothing the distorted features.

"Empty the bowl away from the longhouses," instructed the woman, eyeing Seketa sternly. "Wash it thoroughly, then fill it with fresh water. On your way back, ask the medicine man of the Wolf Clan to accompany you." The frown was back. "And don't linger. Be quick about it."

"Yes, Aunt," said Seketa, trying to sound nice.

Why her? she thought resentfully, running down the corridor, careful to bypass the fires dotting the long stretch, glowing at the center of each compartment, where people were sprawling on the lower bunks, or sitting beside the fires, resting, talking, playing throwing games. Why was it always her who had to be around, demanded to help, to fetch things, to clean? There were enough girls in their longhouse to spread the chores evenly.

She scowled, knowing the answer. The other girls were clever; she was not. They kept away, out of the elder women's reach, while she had been silly, hanging around, her curiosity getting the better of her, ending up running down the corridor with a bowl full of vomit, getting reproachful glances as she went. How frustrating!

The night breeze greeted her, cold and unpleasant, but welcome nevertheless, taking away the stench. She shivered, then rushed on, determined. Just to empty the stinking bowl, wash it, fill it with water, fetch the medicine man, and then, then she'd be smart enough to sneak away and look for something better to do.

Like what?

She thought about the other girls, probably huddled behind the tobacco plots, near the gates, or on the ceremonial ground, now abandoned. She didn't want to spend her time in this way too, gossiping and laughing and talking about boys and men. And although today was different, and they would be, probably, talking about what happened at the game, she still didn't feel like joining this sort of gathering. She needed to think it over, all by herself. That's why she went to see how the wounded was doing. She wanted to know if he was going to die or not.

Why? she asked herself uneasily. Why should she care?

Yeentso was her cousin's husband, not even a person of her clan. And her cousin was much older, a nice woman, but not a friend. So why should she care? If Yeentso died, the wild boy who hit him would die too, and then it would end, and her cousin would find another husband after the appropriate mourning period. The end of the story.

Washing the bowl in the shallow spring that ran along the elevated part of the town, she frowned, remembering the foreign boy. What a wild thing! To try to kill someone in the middle of the sacred ball game? It was inconceivable. Only a savage mind from across the Great Sparkling Water would think of something like this. But the boy was adopted to become one of them. More than two summers he'd lived in their town, treated fairly. Or was he?

She shook her head. Of course he was! He could have been executed along with his people that were caught raiding this side of the Great Lake, but he was not. Instead, he was given food and shelter, and a family to adopt. He was offered everything, wasn't he? Who would expect him to revert to the ways of the savages?

Carrying the heavy bowl, she turned toward the Wolf Clan's longhouse, wondering. He might be there now, huddled in his family compartment. He would surely not be allowed to wander free until the councils decided his fate. Her stomach twisted with anticipation.

"What are you doing here?"

Tindee and another girl sprang from the sheltered façade, laughing.

"Nothing," said Seketa, uncomfortable, as though caught doing something wrong. "They sent me to call for the medicine man. Where are you going?"

"Just walking around, nothing special." Tindee's giggle was accompanied by conspiratorial glances exchanged with her friend. "Come with us."

Seketa hesitated. "I need to bring this bowl back, along with the medicine man." She frowned. "It will not take me long to do that. Wait for me."

"Find us behind the tobacco plots." Tindee stifled another giggle. "But hurry, or you'll miss it all."

Clutching onto a small leather bag and another suspicious looking package, both girls scampered away, still laughing. Shrugging, Seketa went in. She knew what they were up to, no one better. Smoking the old, cracked, badly clogged pipe of Tindee's father was entertaining from time to time, even if it made them dizzy, coughing and choking. Tindee's brother's tobacco was strong, of the best quality. He had grown it himself, lovingly at that.

The Wolf Clan's longhouse greeted her coldly, its corridor almost deserted, with some fires not flickering at all. She looked around, puzzled. Where did everyone go? Passing through the compartments, she saw a few sleeping figures, and a young woman stirring a pot above one of the fires.

"Greetings," she said, knowing the woman well. The Wolf Clan's field was next to the field of her clan.

The woman smiled. "They are all at the council meeting," she related, not looking up from her stew. A delicious aroma came out of the pot, and Seketa's stomach twisted again, this time with hunger.

"Ah, oh, well," she muttered. "I suppose I should go back, then." She frowned. "I was sent to fetch the Honorable Healer."

A flicker of an interest passed through the woman's eyes. "How is Yeentso?"

"He is… well, he is not dead. Not yet."

The woman nodded, pursing her lips. "I hope he survives. It would be a horrible loss for our town."

"Yes. And your longhouse will also not lose its dweller this way."

"My longhouse can do without the wild boy," said the woman, losing her composure all of a sudden. "But Yeentso will be missed dearly."

Seketa hesitated, surprised by her own agitation. "But this boy, he doesn't seem so bad. I don't think he did what he did on purpose. It was very confusing. We didn't see what happened, except that they collided and the ball went out of the field."

"I don't know." The woman was back, stirring the contents of her pot, quiet again. "I wish none of it happened. It was such a good day, with the game coming right after the ceremony. We were so expectant." She shrugged, shaking her head. "Too bad it all happened."

"Well, I'll be going," said Seketa politely, hiding her anxiousness to escape the pointless conversation.

"Go out of the other entrance. It'll save you some walking toward the council meeting. The Honorable Healer is there, too."

Nodding, Seketa rushed on, passing through the last compartment and diving into the darkness of the storage space to find out that the screen covering the entrance was pulled closed, blocking her way.

Why would someone bother to close the stupid screen? she asked herself furiously, struggling to keep the water from spilling, pushing the screen with her free hand. It screeched and refused to move.

She cursed softly, and was about to place her bowl upon the floor, when a figure moved out of the shadows, soundless like a forest beast. Stifling a cry, her heart pounding, she peered at him as he moved the screen, allowing some of the faint moon to slip in.

"What in the name of the Great Spirits are you doing here?" she cried out, her voice still trembling. "You scared me!"

He said nothing, his eyes dark and haunted, peering at her, the intensity of his gaze unsettling. She contemplated just running out and being gone.

"What are you doing here?" she repeated, tossing her head high. If she ran, he might think she was afraid of him, and that would be paying too much honor to the wild boy. He must be feeling good with himself for getting the upper hand with the warrior of Yeentso's caliber.

"Nothing," he said, his voice low, strangled somehow.

"Are you hiding from someone?"

"No."

She peered at him more closely, but in the faint light of the moon, all she could see was the mere outline of his face, the hint of the pressed lips, the blankness of his eyes.

"No one will hurt you until the Councils decide your fate," she said. "You don't have to hide."

"I'm not hiding." An agitated tone crept into his voice, making it sound almost challenging. "I'm not afraid of them!"

"Them? Who are 'them'?"

He shrugged. "Anyone. I don't care."

"You almost killed Yeentso. If he dies, you'll die too. You should care about that."

"Well, I don't."

She raised her eyebrows, trying to make him see her contempt, although the gesture seemed to be lost in the semidarkness. "What do you care about, then?"

He shrugged again and said nothing.

"Well, Yeentso is not dead yet. He is groaning and vomiting, but he is not wandering the other worlds anymore, so he may live."

"I hope he dies!"

She shook her head. "You are strange, really strange. And you are wild, too. How do you expect people to think good things about you when you behave this way?"

"I don't expect anything from your people. They hate me, anyway. They wouldn't care if I behaved nicely or not. They hate me for being the foreigner, the enemy. They were only too glad to see the proof of it."

"No, they are not!" Finding his words impossible to comprehend, she fought for breath. "My people are not like that. Your people are the savages, not mine. You were adopted, and you are one of us now. This is the law. Maybe your people have no laws, but mine have." She glared at him, truly enraged. "We have plenty of adopted people who became one of us. Every longhouse has them. And they all feel good, at home. All of them but you!"

For a moment, they stood motionless, facing each other, breathless with rage. Then he shrugged, breaking the tension. As soundless and as lithe as before, he slipped back toward the cupboards and piles of weapons and dried food.

"Will you sit here through the whole night?" she asked, reluctant to leave for some reason.

"Maybe."

She hesitated again. "They'll be back soon, your family and the other people of your longhouse. You should go to your compartment. They'll be looking for you. What will they think if you are not there?"

"They'll think I ran away and swam across the Great Sparkling Water."

She found it difficult to stifle a giggle. "They might think that, yes."

The darkness was less oppressive, more comfortable now.

"It would be hilarious if you made it."

"Even more hilarious if I made it through the enemy lands until I found my people."

"To what people did you belong before?"

"The People of the Flint."

She frowned. "I never heard of those. Are they at war with the other savages from across the Great Lake?"

"People from across the Great Lake are no savages," he said sharply. "Well, not all of them, anyway."

"Oh, yes? That's not what I heard about them. They kill people, and they eat them, that's what I heard. They cook their captives as though those were hunted deer, and their leaders have living snakes in their hair."

She heard him gasping in anger.

"It's not true!" he cried out, springing back to his feet. "Where did you hear such stupid, rotten nonsense? None of it is true, not a word!"

She held her head high, unafraid. "I heard it more than once. Some of it must be true."

His heavy breathing tore the darkness and, although unable to see, she knew his fists would be clenched now. "Nothing of it is true!"

"You cannot know," she insisted. "Even if your people didn't cook captured enemy, you wouldn't know if the other people, those who you said were also your enemies, didn't do it."

"They did not. None of them eat people, and none have living snakes for hair."

She shook her head. "You are so stubborn. No wonder they say you are wild. Or is that not true, too?"

His shrug was familiar by now. "I don't know."

"What happened today at the game? Why did you hit Yeentso?"

He sank back into his corner, huddled behind the pile of wooden appliances. With her eyes now accustomed to the darkness, she could see it was full of tools belonging to the field workers.

"I don't want to talk about it."

She shook her head. "I couldn't see well. I just saw you two colliding with each other, and then there were people surrounding you all, and we couldn't see until someone began screaming."

"We did not collide." His voice came out of the corner, strained. "He jumped on me, and he hit my arm with his stick, so I would miss the ball." He swallowed loudly. "I was sure to catch it. It was coming straight into my net."

The twisting in her stomach made her angry. *Why should she pity him?*

"Still, you had no right to try to kill him. Those things happen. It could have been an accident."

"It was not," he said in a firmer voice. "He did it on purpose."

"Even so, you can't kill people for such deeds."

"I didn't try to kill him. I just told him it was no accident, and then…" He swallowed and said nothing for a heartbeat.

"And then?" She held her breath.

"And then… then he said things about savages, about enemies, and… and I said things, too. And then, well, he grabbed my throat, and I… I don't truly remember. He was on the ground, and they were all screaming, and breaking my arms." His voice shook. "I don't really understand what happened, but at some point, Two Rivers was there, and he was arguing, defending me for some reason. I don't know why he did this. It was all very strange."

"Oh, Two Rivers is always arguing against something," she said uneasily, trying to comprehend what she'd just heard. If he said the truth, then it was not like he tried to kill a person for colliding with him. He was not that bad. *If he was telling the truth.* "The Councils are probably listening to the people who were there and saw it, even now, as we speak. If it was like you are saying, then they may decide not to punish you."

"Unless Yeentso dies," he said quietly.

"Yes, unless he dies."

She took a deep breath, trying to disregard the knot in her stomach. Sharing the same longhouse with her cousin's husband, she knew the man well. If Yeentso didn't die, he would hunt down and kill this boy the moment he felt better. A seventeen summers old youth was no match for the weathered warrior like Yeentso.

"Well, it all may turn out to be nothing but a bad memory," she said, trying to sound light. "But you should control your temper better next time."

Hesitating, she looked out, into the moonlit patch of the ground before the shadow of the next longhouse made it dark again.

"I should be going. They will be angry with me for taking so long to bring the water."

His nod was imperceptible in the darkness, but she felt it all the same, the desolate gesture.

"I will go back now, but I will try to let you know, the moment it is certain, if he dies or not," she said helplessly.

What would it help? He wouldn't be able to do anything with this knowledge.

"Thank you." His whisper was so quiet, she wasn't sure she did not imagine it. "You are as kind as you are beautiful."

CHAPTER 4

The wind pounced on him, unrestrained, as though angry with him, too. Oh, this place truly hated him!

Turning his face away, Tekeni clenched his teeth. But of course! The Great Spirits watching over the colder side of the Great Sparkling Water were not the same as the Great Spirits of his homeland. Or were they?

He frowned, pushing his way up the trail, anxious to reach the cliffs adorning the shore. This lake was tiny compared to the Great Sparkling Lake, but it was one more obstacle, one more thing to separate him from home, to make the dream of running away impossible.

Had he only been able to steal a canoe and try to find his way back. How many times he had wondered about it, thinking and re-thinking all sorts of plans. Too many times to forget. But the conclusion was always the same. He would never make it, never. He could not battle the odds, a boy who had seen barely fifteen, and then sixteen and seventeen summers.

Even with no warriors lurking everywhere, eager for blood and revenge, he could not navigate his way along the wild currents, lakes, and rivers, all the way to the fiercest obstacle of them all – the mighty sparkling giant. In order to cross it, the warriors would row for a whole day, at the place where the great water basin was narrower according to the estimation of the veterans who had made this journey over and over for summers. Still, some would miscalculate, and the whole groups of people would disappear in the endless mass of dark blue, never to return. Those who had made it would sail two, three men in each canoe, switching places when one would get out of breath. Strong, battle-hardened warriors. No children, no youths. And never alone.

And even if he had managed with the help of the spirits and the Right-Handed Twin himself, he would still not have completed his journey. He tried to remember the lands of Onondaga, the People of the Hills, the favorite landing place. Another fierce enemy. He had traveled there only once, on this disastrous raiding party, with Father and his warriors, when he still had a family; a fascinated boy, thrilled by the honor of being allowed to join.

Oh, but Father should not have taken him along, he knew. He had been too young. The people of Little Falls, his town, argued, and the Clans Councils were furious. Still, his father prevailed. He was a great leader, great orator. Not many tried to go against his wishes, and less succeeded in it. The War Chief decided to bring his only surviving son, and so it was. And the people shrugged and shook their heads, knowing that the fierce warrior had, probably, found it difficult to cope with the deaths of his wife and his other son, victims of winter disease.

Tekeni shivered, having not thought about his mother and his twin brother for moons, the memories going no further than this bright, sunny day, only two dawns after the crossing, when the arrows came out of nowhere, along with the blood-freezing cries, and the warriors wearing long-sleeved shirts, their faces painted in bright unfamiliar patterns, their eyes blazing murder. And then Father, blood gushing out of his mouth, his nose, his ears even, gurgling sounds coming from between his lips, fingers tearing at the feathered shaft, unsuccessful, eyes pleading.

He remembered the paralyzing fear sweeping him, overwhelming his whole being, not because of the attacking enemy, but because he knew what Father wanted. He knew it too clearly. The man needed his son to pull the arrow out, to stop the agony, to hasten the blissful oblivion with no pain. He needed his son to save his dignity, to spare the humiliation of pain. A simple, reasonable wish, but Tekeni's limbs were paralyzed, out of control, as he watched his father wriggling in the sand, and it had been another warrior who had done this for the War Chief, stopping the fighting briefly to mutter a quick prayer, to send his leader into the new beginning.

The wind tore at him with renewed strength, bringing him back to the present and the top of the cliff overlooking the bay. The cold was penetrating, matching the chill gripping his soul.

Why did they build a town on such a windy bay? he wondered, desperate to take his thoughts off the terrible memory. Most of the towns of his new country-folk were situated inland, sheltered by woods, protected from perpetual chill. The winters in these lands were bad enough, long and freezing, but to take away the pleasures of the midsummer moons was the peak of strangeness, in his estimation. Were there defensive advantages to this location?

Deep in thought, he didn't notice the sitting man until the dark silhouette was right in front of him, watching him, silent. Heart pounding, Tekeni stopped dead in his tracks, afraid to breathe, frozen, fear rolling down his stomach, filling it with ice.

"It's a long way to wander the night, boy," said the familiar voice, as calm as back at the game, but filled with a sort of amusement now. "Or were you trying to run away?"

"I... I just... I was just..." He heard his own voice vibrating, high-pitched and strident, and it shamed him, brought him back to his senses. "I was just walking around. I didn't try to run away."

"Didn't you?" The grin in the man's voice was obvious. "Yes, I suppose you are not that stupid." Shifting slightly, he moved, making a space for Tekeni to squat. "Here, have a seat. I wish the moon were more generous tonight. I love the view of the lake from up here. Makes it worth the climb."

Confused by the chatty friendliness of the man, Tekeni hesitated. Like any of the older warriors and other important people of the town, Two Rivers never seemed to notice his very existence before.

"I don't feel like sleeping tonight, but I suppose you must be even more troubled than that." The man turned back toward the wind, peering at the dark mass of the lake far below his feet. "I can understand your lack of sleep." More silence. "I wonder if your adversary is still alive."

"He is alive," said Tekeni, nearing but unable to gather his courage to sit beside the strange man. "Well, he was until recently."

"How would you know?"

"I know."

The man shrugged, amused once again. "So you have your spies in the Beaver Clan's longhouse? Good for you. I thought you were sort of an outcast, with no friends and no companions. But I was wrong, wasn't I?" He shrugged again. "Sit, boy."

This time it was an order. Carefully, Tekeni slipped down, squatting upon the cold earth.

"So, what are you going to do? Your options are few to my estimation, your chances of survival even less so."

"I don't know. I will do whatever the Councils decide."

"If Yeentso lives, he will make sure to kill you, taking a great pleasure in doing this."

"The Councils will not let him do this," gasped Tekeni, controlling his voice with an effort. He hadn't thought of this possibility, concerned with councils and their decision in case Yeentso would die.

But of course! He imagined the broad shoulders and the massive hands of his rival, the narrow, hate-filled face, the squinted eyes. Oh, yes, this man would not let his humiliation go unpunished. He would hunt his offender down, the filthy savage, the uncouth foreigner, the hated enemy, and he would make a show out of the killing.

"Do you think he will listen to the Councils in this matter?" The calm voice brought him back from the pictures his imagination painted too vividly.

"No."

"Me neither."

The silence was strangely comfortable this time, not threatening anymore, but Tekeni's limbs were heavy with desperation, his head empty of thoughts.

"I was thinking of ways to protect you, but they are dismally few." The man was still peering at the water, his voice ringing quietly, impartially. "Whichever way I look, it seems you are a dead man. If he dies his clan would demand your blood, which would be their privilege and their right according to our laws. If he lives, he will not let you live, even if to kill you would be unlawful and against the custom. Unless he decides to challenge you formally, and in this case, you have not much chance either. Maybe in a few summers, but not now." He felt the thoughtful glance brushing against his side. "You are a promising youth, with enough strength and courage, good instincts and a quick thinking. You don't control your temper well, but you are not panicking either. I saw it this afternoon. Your deed was worthy of a warrior, considering the circumstances. Your reactions were good, your aim admirable."

"Do you think I was right in hitting him?" asked Tekeni, finding it hard to believe his ears.

"No, of course not. You lost your temper in the way inappropriate in a good, respectable man. You didn't stop to think. When you called him a coward, you cornered him into harming you. You pushed him into intimidating you, into making a show out of it. You left him with no choice."

"But he called me names, he accused me of all sorts of things I didn't do. He was the one to hit me, to break the rule of the game. Everyone saw it, and I heard Ogtaeh accusing him of the foul move."

"You should have let Ogtaeh and the others sort out this argument. Or better yet, wait for the leaders' decision. There were enough witnesses to decide in favor of your team, to disqualify the whole move. With the ball out of the field, the game would not have proceeded uninterrupted anyway."

He felt the despondency coming back. He knew all about what he should *not* have done – many, many things. It was an old argument. Through the last two summers of his life, he had done mainly things he should not, never doing anything right.

"You should have swallowed your pride and let the others solve this problem."

His stomach tightened painfully. "Would you do this? Would you swallow your pride and let people insult you, beat you, make you feel like filth?" He listened to the swishing of the wind, afraid he had taken it too far, but not caring anymore. "I don't think you would follow your own advice in this."

"Well, no, I suppose not." The man's voice shook with amusement. "Yeentso is the man of my status, so no, I would not have taken an insult from him. But maybe I would have followed my own advice if it were the Head of the Town Council, or maybe the War Chief, the one snatching my ball and then bringing up my dubious origins."

"You are arguing with these people, too," muttered Tekeni.

Now the man laughed out right. "Oh, you do have guts, wolf cub. And lots of insolence into the bargain. I wonder where those came from. Do all the people from across the Great Sparkling Water resemble you, the fierce savages that they are?"

Somehow, the last question did not offend him as it should have. Tekeni shifted to make himself more comfortable upon the cold sand. "They are no savages. But yes, they are fierce."

"Do they eat people like it's said they do?"

"No, of course not!"

A soft chuckle floated in the darkness. "Thought so."

"And they have no living snakes for hair." He remembered Seketa and the way she stood near the doorway, slender, wonderfully pliant, outlined most clearly against the night sky, her long fingers clutching the heavy bowl. So graceful and pretty. So out of reach.

"Oh, I heard that one, too." His companion shifted, leaning his back against the nearest rock. "So, no snakes, and no deliciously cooked human flesh. What else? How different are your people from us?"

The large eyes rested upon Tekeni, and even in the darkness, he could feel the strength they radiated. And the intensity. This was not a question originated in an idle curiosity. He banished beautiful Seketa from his thoughts.

"Well, our longhouses are longer, sometimes. And we have symbols of the clans carved beside the entrances." He frowned. "We have not as many clans as you have. My people have three clans – the Turtle Clan, the Bear Clan, and the Wolf Clan. But Onondaga, the People of the Hills, have as many clans as you. Or almost as many." Kicking a stone that was jutting against his thigh, he frowned, trying to remember. "Some food is different. And the rules of the bowl game."

The man was peering at him, wide-eyed. "Only three clans? How so? Are you such a small nation?"

"No, we are not. We have a lot of towns." He kicked another stone. "But yes, we are divided into three clans, and we are the most numerous people that live on our side of the Great Lake. And the fiercest, too."

"Three clans? It sounds like a very strange arrangement to me."

For some time they sat in silence, watching the patches of the dim moonlight running across the dark water.

"So, actually, what you are saying is that there is not much of a difference between us and our most hated enemy." The man's voice was low, floating in the darkness.

Tekeni frowned. "Well, I don't know. Probably there is enough difference to make us fight."

"Like the amount of the clans or the way you carve their symbols upon your entrances?"

"No, but there must be a reason for the war. It has been going on for too long to have no reason."

He shifted uneasily, almost regretting leaving his longhouse tonight. *What did this man want? What was he after?* Back in the town he was challenged often, but not with difficult questions.

"This seems to be the best of their arguments as well. The old ways. If our fathers did it, then why shouldn't we?" The man turned his head, measuring his company with a glance full of derisive challenge, of that Tekeni was sure. "So, you seem like a youth who can think, although you don't act like that. And I assume you agree with this claim, ready to follow the footsteps of your forefathers. Which can be a good way of living, I'll give you that. But in everything? Give me one good reason why your people and mine should war with each other. One good reason and I may change my mind. Well, maybe not that readily, but I promise to listen, with my ears opened. Tell me why should I join the next raid across the Great Sparkling Water, to lay waste to your former settlements if we are lucky to run into any?"

The wind gained power, shrieking wildly now, as though trying to push them both back in the direction they had come from, as though wishing to be alone, incensed with humans and their persistent interference.

Tekeni narrowed his eyes. "You should join this next raid because you will have to avenge your dead, the people who died at the hands of my people. Their spirits demand that you avenge them."

"And then your people will come to avenge their dead ones, won't they?"

"Yes, they will."

"And then?"

"And then your people will cross again..." He hesitated, thrown out of balance. The old argument made little sense when said aloud in the dead of the night before the flickering gaze of the strange man. Even in the darkness, he could see the pursed lips twisting derisively. Oh, but he should have stayed in the storage room of his longhouse. He could have slept there through the whole night if he wanted to, with no one the wiser. "Well, this is how it works. We can't change our ways."

"So, here we are, back at the old argument with you saying nothing in the meanwhile. This is how it works? Is that all?" The man's laughter rolled down the cliff, but there was no amusement in it. "Don't take offense, wolf cub. And don't be tempted to try to hit me with any of those sticks thrown around here. I was not insulting your intelligence. I'm not laughing at you. You repeat what they say, and most of them can't plead your youth or your naivety. They should have known better, should have been able to make a better argument, to present their claim in a way that would make sense, even if a little. They are great orators, many of them, yet they forget their abilities to make a speech the moment this particular subject comes up. They can orate about laws and ceremonies, about hunting techniques and the way to work the fields. They can talk well, make perfect sense, present our traditions, our duties to the Great Spirits and our creator, the Right-Handed Twin. They know the reason and the cause. They are very wise people. And yet, when it comes to this particular subject, they lose their common sense. All they can do is grow angry, crying out that 'this is how it is done,' disregarding the damage that the perpetual war brings to our towns and villages, closing their eyes to the deepening plight of our people."

"We also worship the Right-Handed Twin," said Tekeni, feeling obliged to say something. The rest of the man's speech was too strange to try to comprehend.

"I would think so." Seemingly not put out with the digression from the main subject, Two Rivers shrugged. "Our creator, the Right Handed-Twin, is too great not to revere."

For a while they sat in silence, doing their best against the wind.

"You don't understand what I am talking about, do you? You think it's a waste of time."

Tekeni took a deep breath. "Well, no, I don't think it's a waste of time. I suppose you know what you are doing. You are a very wise person, and a great orator, too." Desperately, he sought something polite to say. "I don't understand what you mean by saying that the war is damaging your towns. And about the plight of your people. I mean, yes, warriors get killed, but this is the way it is. They know how to die with honor. I hoped to be a great warrior, too. Like my father was. I wish I could be like him."

"Was he a leader?"

"Oh, yes, he was our War Chief for, oh, summers upon summers. He was so very great!"

"How did he die?"

The spasm in his stomach was back, as violent as always. "He died on your side of the Great Lake. He was shot… shot by a wandering arrow." Swallowing, he tried to control his voice, which began trembling again, most annoyingly at that. His father's story was worthy of a sterner voice. "If he had lived, we would win this battle. He always won."

He listened to the wind, now welcoming its unwavering strength. His father's spirit might have been there, in this fierce, groaning force; listening, maybe.

"That was when you were taken captive?"

"Yes."

"How old were you?"

"I saw fifteen summers back then." He swallowed so hard it hurt his throat. "I… I shouldn't have let it happen. I should have died like a warrior. He trusted me to do that, but I failed."

"I wouldn't judge you too fast." The man's voice held no amusement this time, a trace of compassion in it obvious. "You were a mere boy back then, and you are still too young to be a true warrior. You have a long journey ahead of you, and you may still make your father proud."

His vision was blurred, and he felt grateful for the darkness now. If only his voice would stop trembling!

"I won't have this chance. Even if I don't die in the next few dawns, I won't be given the opportunity to turn into a great warrior. No one trusts me here. No leader would be willing to take me in his raiding party."

"Well, it will be more difficult for you, yes. But not impossible. You will have to try harder than the rest, but if you are strong and believe in yourself and your destiny, you will make it." A shrug. "Maybe this incident will do you good in the long run. It might make you grow up, it might teach you to control your temper, it might make you change your ways." The amusement crept back into the deep voice. "But tell me something else. What if one of the leaders invites you to come along, allowing you to join his raiding party? Will you enjoy raiding your former people's lands? Will you feel good laying waste to your father's town?"

He felt it like a blow in his stomach, and for a moment, his heart stopped. "I… I don't know. I didn't think…"

"Can they trust you not to run away the moment you crossed the Great Lake?"

He cupped his face with his palms. "No, I suppose not," he whispered, his heart beating fast.

Oh, Mighty Spirits! But here was the solution, the wonderful, beautiful, perfect solution! How didn't he think about it before? He felt the blood rushing into his cheeks, his heart pumping insanely, as though trying to jump out of his chest. Taking a deep breath, he tried to control his voice.

"Yes, they can trust me. Of course, they can. I would never do something like that. I belong to Wyandot people now. Not to my former people." He took another breath, pleased with the way it came out. "I was adopted formally. There is no way back from this."

Had he taken it too far? The laughter of the man broke the silence, a hearty, amused laughter.

"Oh Mighty Spirits, I'm afraid I just gave you an idea, wolf cub."

Tekeni fought the urge to cover his burning cheeks. "No, you did not. I'm telling you, I would never do this." He peered at the man, seeing the outline of the well-defined profile, the high forehead, the long, aquiline nose, the shaved sides of the head with an oiled hair sticking up proudly, fluttering in the wind. The warriors' hairdo. "You have to believe me," he added, desperately.

"Do I?" The man turned his head, and even in the darkness, the amused spark in the prominent eyes was obvious. "You said I'm a wise person, great orator and all. Do you think you can fool me that easily? Oh no, boy. You are as transparent as the waters of the lake on the fine summer day. It is so easy to see through you. You are almost shining now, your desperation gone. You've been given a plan." His teeth flashing in the widening grin, the man shook his head. "But it's a difficult plan that will require an enormous amount of patience. More than you indicated as having so far. A lot of time, a lot of effort, a lot of convincing to do on your part. A lot of impeccable behavior. Maybe you would be able to pull it through, maybe not. Or maybe you would change with the passing of summers while you go about implementing your plan, and then you will find yourself in a real trouble, torn between two ways of life, with too many loyalties to keep."

"I will not do any of this," muttered Tekeni stubbornly, wishing to be alone more than anything now. He had so much to think about, all of a sudden. "I wish I could convince you of that."

"Oh, you don't have to convince me of anything. I won't be running to the Town Council, informing them of our conversation. You are an interesting boy, and I will be watching you, but not in an attempt to catch you doing something wrong. I'm curious to know what will come out of you now. Should you decide to pursue this goal, battling the odds in trying to turn into a perfect warrior, whether to truly help our people or to make your escape easier, I'll be enjoying watching this story unfold. It will be too interesting to miss, regardless the ending." He sprang to his feet, swift and strong, a slender man of an average height, but a good hunter and warrior, nevertheless. "I will try to help you out with your current predicament as best as I can. You made me curious, wolf cub, whether you represent your fierce former country folk or not. You gave me food for thought. I will repay you for this by helping you out."

Strong and imposing, the man shook his head, turning around and diving into the darkness, his paces making no sound. One moment there, the next gone. A true warrior.

Tekeni let his breath out. His head reeled, and the excitement was bubbling too near the surface, making him want to scream into the wind. Or maybe to whoop with joy. The meaningless existence was over. He had a plan, and he would work hard implementing it. He would not let anything stop him now, anything at all.

It wouldn't be easy, said Two Rivers, and a man of his stature would know. Still, he would manage to do that. He already felt stronger, a man with direction, a man with a plan. Not a pitiful cub of no importance, dragging along purposelessly. Not anymore!

He grinned against the wind. And Two Rivers thought he could actually make it. He said so himself. He said he would be watching.

CHAPTER 5

The heat was unmerciful, softened only a little by the breeze coming from the hills. Seketa wiped her brow. Glancing at the sky once again, she wished the sun would move faster. Today, of all days, she didn't want to be in the field. She needed to go back to the town, to see what was happening.

The Town Council had not arrived at a conclusion last night. They refused to discuss the matter any further until the news on Yeentso and his condition would be more definite. The fate of the Wolf Clan boy would remain undecided until then.

Oh, how furious the Mothers of the Beaver Clan were. Huddling in the shadows behind the corner of her longhouse, trying to hear it all, appalled with herself for doing the unspeakable, Seketa remembered how her heart beat faster and faster, louder and louder, threatening to give her presence away.

Why she had done this, she didn't know. To eavesdrop on the Honorable Mothers of her clan was the peak of bad manners, a terrible discourtesy, behavior screaming against her entire upbringing.

She bit her lips and welcomed the pain, never before suspecting what a horrible person she was. Still, she did not leave, but stayed in her barely hidden place, listening to the leading women talking in anger, about the stubbornness and the arrogance of the men in general, and the Town Council members in particular.

Nothing was said about the savages from across the Great Sparkling Water, but their anger germinated from there, a fruit of their frustration with the despicable enemies and the wild boy who would not fit in no matter how many chances he had been offered.

She remembered last night and the conversation in the storage room of the Wolf Clan's longhouse. He didn't seem wild or dangerous back then. Quiet, wary, aggressive in a defensive way. *Cornered.* But not submissive, not humbled or defeated. He should have been looking this way, but for some reason, he had not. Instead, his eyes blazed with anger, and his lips told her he wanted Yeentso dead. Even though it would mean his own death as well. What temper! And what pride. But what courage, too. Such an honorable way to face one's own deeds.

Frowning, she took her gaze away from the sky. If forced to die, he would do so with honor. He would not shame himself by begging for mercy, not him. He would go proudly, and his eyes would sparkle, and his back would be straight, unyielding.

Aware of her burning cheeks, she knelt to pull the weeds from the nearest pile in the earth. The next moon they'd be gathering the first crop of the sweet early maize, preparing it for the Green Corn ceremony, the second most important ceremony of the whole cycle of seasons. There would be solemn rituals, bountiful feasts, merry festivities and sacred and social dances, lasting from dawn to dusk, for many, many dawns. Oh, how she loved this particular ceremony! *Would he still be alive by that time? Would he be allowed to participate in the social activities? Would he be there, watching her dancing?*

"I wish it were already past midday." Tindee's voice jerked Seketa back from her thoughts, tossing her into the sweat-soaked reality of the heat and the buzzing insects. "I'm so tired!"

Seketa sighed. "I know. The sun is moving slower for me today, too."

"Why would it move slower for you, sister? You did nothing last night. We waited for you behind the tobacco plots, but you never came."

"Oh, well…" Seketa frowned, feeling her cheeks beginning to glow anew. "I didn't feel like smoking. I was tired."

Tindee's laughter rolled between the stacks of maize, trilling prettily. "We did more than just smoking, you lazy lump of meat. I told you not to miss it, but you didn't listen."

"What did you do?"

"Why would I tell you?"

Seketa laughed. "Because you always tell me, whether I want to listen or not." She picked up her basket. "Also, if it was such a good pastime, maybe I'll come tonight."

"We won't be doing it tonight. We need to sleep, all of us. I'm telling you, it was way after midnight, when I came back, and I had to sneak past grandmother's compartment like a real forest mouse."

"They didn't hear you?"

"No. Not even my mother, who sleeps next to me." The girl eyed the ripening ears of maize wistfully, running her fingers along one such. "I wish it were good for eating already. I'm starving." She looked up, her eyes glittering, full of mischief. "My brother told me this morning that he saw me sneaking in, but he won't tell on me. Not him. I know too many things about him and that girl from the Wolf Clan's longhouse. Until he makes her his woman, he will not dare to anger me."

Wolf Clan!

"I wish I knew what they decided to do about yesterday's game."

Tindee's snort was loud, full of meaning. "Why would you worry about that? I don't care for Yeentso. He is rude and violent, and he is always looking at me as though he would want to do dirty things. And I don't care for the foreign boy, either. Another violent good-for-nothing. This town will be better off without both of them, come to think of it."

For some reason, Tindee's words hurt.

"This boy is not rude and not violent. He is nice, actually. And he didn't hit Yeentso for no reason. We couldn't see, but Yeentso was the one to attack him first." Uncomfortable under the widening gaze of her friend, Seketa frowned. "Yes, it was like that. I know it now."

"How do you know? Who told you?"

"The foreign boy."

Tindee's eyes grew to enormous proportions. "You talked to this boy? When?"

"Yesterday." She pulled at another bunch of weeds. "It was in the evening, for a short time."

"Why?"

"I don't know. I just met him, by mistake."

"And you stopped to talk to him? You? I don't believe it!"

"Why not?" Seketa clenched her teeth, furious with herself for confiding in her chatty friend. She knew perfectly well why not.

"You are the most unapproachable human being that the Right-Handed Twin has ever created," cried out Tindee, drawing quite a few glances from the surrounding women. Lowering her tone, she peered at Seketa, her eyes glittering with excitement. "You never bother to be nice to boys; you never talk to them unless you want to scold them for something. But suddenly, oh-so-very-proud Seketa goes to a boy and asks him to tell her what happened?" The suggestive smile upon the girl's lips made Seketa wish to strike her friend. "Did you take your time to comfort him, to make him feel better? Did you?"

"Oh, stop talking nonsense!" Now it was Seketa's turn to cry out, then moderate her voice. "I can't believe I told you. You are so silly!"

"I'm not silly, sister." Tindee's voice trembled with barely concealed satisfaction. "I can see this spark in your eyes, and your cheeks are now the color of my festive dress. The one with the purple girdle. Just the same color."

Against her will, Seketa brought her palms to cover her cheeks. "It's hot! The sun is making my skin burn."

"Of course, Seketa, of course."

"Will you leave me alone? I can't believe I told you any of it. I will never tell you a thing in my entire life, not one single thing!"

"Come on, sister. Calm down." Grabbing Seketa's hand,

Tindee pulled her back into the shadow of the corn leaves. "I won't tease you anymore, I promise. This boy will die soon anyway, so he won't make us argue again."

"He won't die. I saw Yeentso this morning, on my way out. He was sitting, eating porridge. Or maybe it was a soup. Dying people don't eat."

"Yes, I saw him too. I was so tired I could barely see, and I couldn't care less for the annoying man." Tindee's pretty face crinkled with laughter. "But they sent me to bring him fresh water from the outside, so I had to see him, even if against my will."

Seketa nodded. "See? So he is not dying, therefore that boy won't have to die either."

"Oh, that's what you think. But not what our Clan Mothers think."

She felt her heart sinking. "What do they want?"

"They will be talking to the Town Council again. I overheard them speaking of this not long ago."

"What will they be talking about?"

"Well, you know how it is. The offense was made. Even if Yeentso heals with no trouble, they want compensation. He is in the longhouse now, of no use to the community. Neither his wife nor her sister went into the fields this morning. Further damage to the Beaver Clan. And the old healer woman was late for the fields, because she took her time boiling herbs." Serious for a change, Tindee looked around, thrusting her arm out in an exaggerated manner, pointing toward the densely planted stakes of maize. "See how we have to work harder now, because less women are here to help us out? Our clan deserves to be compensated, does it not?"

Involuntarily, Seketa's eyes followed her friend's hand, watching the cracks in the dry earth. There were yet many plots in need of watering, many plants in need of tending. They would have to work until the sun would be well on its way to its resting place, until dusk, maybe. Tindee was right about that.

"Well, the death of this boy won't make our work any

easier," she said uneasily, raising her gaze to glance at the platform towering high above the field. Two women sat there alertly, staring at the horizon, each peering at her different direction. Once upon a time, Seketa knew, there were no watching platforms, and people would just go out and work the land. Or so said the elders, although such stories did not make sense. How could people walk about or work the fields with no one watching? How would they manage to flee back into the safety of the town's fences in the case of an enemy's attack with no one watching to warn them in time?

"No, but our clan should be compensated," Tindee's voice broke into her thoughts.

"With what?"

"They were talking about hides, maybe. Like ten pieces of good hides with no holes and no tears."

"Oh!"

"Yes, oh. It wouldn't be fair if people would be allowed to wound other people, taking them out of the normal daily life, rendering them useless for the community. It would make a bad precedence."

"Oh well, I do see their point. Our Clan Mothers are wise." Seketa shrugged. "Well, the Wolf Clan would have to pay us those hides, that's all."

"If they think it's fair, yes, they'll pay."

"If?" She peered at her friend, puzzled. "Why would they argue? It's not fair to leave us with no compensation."

"Well, no, of course not. But they may be angry with the annoying boy for forcing them into this. They may not take it kindly."

"What will they do to him? What did you hear?"

Tindee shrugged. "I heard they may let him take the responsibility. He has seen close to seventeen summers. He is of an age. Old enough to tell him 'go and get those things to pay up, wild boy. By whatever means you have.'"

"Do you mean to say they would send him to obtain those hides all by himself?" gasped Seketa, aghast. "It's the same as to kill him right away. No one hunts outside all alone, no one! Not even the best of our hunters and warriors. And certainly not boys with no training or skill."

Shrugging again, Tindee turned toward the nearby row of stakes. "Maybe they do want to get rid of him. He is a nuisance, doing not one single thing right, bringing nothing but trouble. They hoped for something better than this, when giving the enemy cub a chance." She looked back, flashing a fleeting smile, one of those nice, unguarded smiles of hers. "Get busy. The old healer and one of the elder women are watching us. I don't fancy hearing any more lecturing about the unworthiness of the young girls. Do you?"

Picking up her basket, Seketa rushed toward the other piles of earth, wishing to put some distance between herself and her gossipy friend, her heart beating fast.

Why should she care? she asked herself, angered. This boy was of no consequence to her. Who was he, if not just another member of the Wolf Clan? A troublesome member, at that. Last night was the first time she had spoken to him, although for some time she had been aware that he was watching her, quietly and covertly. She had noticed, of course. Their town was not that large, and he had participated in many ballgames, if in not as many hunting expeditions as the youths were required to participate. He was not trusted. Apparently, with a good reason. And yet...

She remembered the way his eyes glimmered, large, beautifully spaced, challenging and haunted at the same time. And he was not the only one to blame for what happened. He didn't lie to her, of that she was sure. There were many witnesses to relate the story. He would be caught in his lies if he tried.

She pulled at the weeds angrily, throwing them into her basket without looking. A wise person would keep away from this mess, and she was held to be a smart girl.

CHAPTER 6

The razor-sharp stone snapped with a smack, coming off the wooden handle with what looked like finality. Some of the strips clung to it, not letting it fall off the handle entirely, but the sap could not hold it in anymore. A serious damage demanding a thorough repair.

Two Rivers cursed. He'd known the axe was going to break, but he'd counted on it to hold on until the end of the day. And it would have, had he been more careful. However, the stubborn tree, although blackened from fire and wobbly, was not damaged enough, and so he had lost his patience and struck too hard. Time after time. And now his axe was gone and the tree was still standing, challenging him.

He listened to the pounding all around as the people worked on the few of the remaining trees, taking them down. The new field had been overdue for clearing. The women of the Turtle Clan demanded it to be ready by the Planting Moon, but now it was already near the first harvest. No maize would be planted here now, but another crop of squash and beans could definitely make use of the newly cleared ground.

"You should have let it burn for longer than you did," said the middle-aged man, one of the Beaver Clan's esteemed members who came to help. He brought his axe down carefully, making it slide alongside the thick trunk, deepening the cut.

"We were afraid the fire would get out of control," muttered Two Rivers, frowning direfully at his broken tool. "It was raging too fiercely for anyone's taste."

"Well, then you should have planned it more carefully from the beginning." The older man squinted against the glow of the afternoon sun. "As it is, this field may not be ready in time for planting even the squash."

Two Rivers grunted, then threw the remnants of his axe to the ground, enraged.

"It'll take you time to repair that." The young warrior that toiled around the nearby stump straightened up and wiped his brow, smearing it with lumps of fresh earth.

"I know that!"

"Throwing it all around won't help the matter. Did you know that, too?"

"No, I was sure I'd pick it back up as good as new." He kicked the wooden handle, making it roll toward the stump. "It helps, it helps a lot. It makes me feel better."

"Oh, then go on, by all means." The young man grinned widely, unabashed. "Want to take my axe for a while, to channel your anger into a more useful direction?"

"Well, actually, yes, I do." Strolling toward the offered tool, Two Rivers found it hard to suppress his own grin, his mood improving. Iraquas was a friend of quite a few summers. Much younger and not interested in politics and the tortuous ways of the various councils, Iraquas, nevertheless, had offered the kind of friendship Two Rivers needed most – a simple, loyal companionship, with light banter and no difficult dilemmas. The youth had been a promising warrior, destined to become one of the leaders in all probability, but so far, the glorious destination of his people did not bother him. And so were the strange far-fetched ideas of his older friend.

"Don't break it," said Iraquas, offering the axe. "I love this particular tool. It will cost you more than just a repair if something happens to it."

"I will cherish and revere this sacred tool of yours." Grinning, Two Rivers went back toward the thick trunk. "Oh, I do need to best this old forest giant. It's time it cleared the path for the younger saplings, anyway."

Making himself comfortable upon a half-burned stump, Iraquas picked a greenish staple and began nibbling on it.

"You will not best it today, this much I promise you. It looks wobbly, but mark my words, it still has a lot of spirit under its bark."

"Like I said, you should have burnt this patch of earth more thoroughly," repeated the older man, stopping his chopping to wipe his brow. "We won't make it in time. Not with the War Chief planning another raid for the beginning of the Plants Growing Moon."

"A worse mistake than not to burn this field up more thoroughly, if you ask me." Chopping at the same cut with equal intervals, Two Rivers was pleased to hear his voice even, not gasping or trembling with an effort. It was a difficult task, but he needed to best this tree before nightfall. "Why would we raid the Rock People villages? They are small and unimportant."

"Because they attacked us, maybe?" suggested Iraquas, immersed in his tasty treat.

"They did not attack us. They raided the settlement of the Deer People to the west. It happened almost a whole span of seasons ago. Since then, we went to war against the Deer as well. They are not our allies anymore. Still, we are eager to avenge this long forgotten raid on the people whom we consider our enemies now, too."

"It is not as simple as that, Two Rivers," said the older man, pausing to catch his breath. "You speak well, and you do have a gift of good thinking. But sometimes this clear thinking of yours is not enough. Sometimes the matters are more complicated and they include honor, certain old ways, a measure of cunning thinking. Sometimes a simple display of power is required, to make our enemies think twice and thrice before planning their raids into our forests. This way, we spare our women and children the unnecessary fright and the need to run back behind our town's defenses, harming their spirits and their efforts in the fields." The old, squinted eyes flickered kindly. "Sometimes simplifying is not the best course of thinking. You should listen to the people around you, and not to your heart only."

"Well spoken," said someone, and many men stopped their

work, pausing to nod appreciatively.

Two Rivers nodded too, impressed.

"I appreciate your kind advice, Honorable Elder." He paused, studying the wooden handle of his new tool. "I will try to follow it, although, sometimes I cannot but stop and wonder. Our people's plight would not give my spirit rest. Sometimes, we may need to pause and examine our ways. Sometimes, we may need to restore to less usual solutions."

The older man's gaze measured him, kind, slightly amused. "Listen to your heart, do not close your ears to its whispering. But do not forget to listen to your peers as well. And to your elders."

He could feel the eyes of the people upon him, wary, their disapproval barely concealed.

"I cherish your advice, Honorable Elder," he said with a certain difficulty. From the corner of his eye, he could see Iraquas frowning, attempting to hide a grin, most probably. "I'm grateful."

To argue with the older, highly respectable man would have been the height of bad manners. He pushed his resentment away, resuming his treatment of the old tree, instead.

"He silenced you quite neatly, that old man," said Iraquas as they proceeded down the trail, heading back to the town. The dusk was still far away, but they could see the late afternoon shadows spreading down the fields of the various clans, as the women were leaving in a colorful procession that pleased the eye.

Two Rivers shrugged. "He spoke well. His advice was good."

"Oh, how very reasonable of you. But I bet that under this calm 'thank you for your priceless advice' you were like the rapids of the Northern River, swirling and shooting white foam."

"Oh, please!" He grinned against his will. "Since when can you see through people? Or since when do you care?"

"I don't, but I want to see you losing this temper of yours. It's quite a sight, so they say."

"It is not." He squinted, trying to see against the fierce glow of the setting sun. A group that neared them seemed to be in a hurry.

Iraquas saw them too, and as the newcomers hastened their step their hands made their way to the knives tucked in the sheath of their loincloths, just in case. A group of men hurrying up and looking agitated bade usually no good news. Was a raiding party spotted in the town's proximity?

The men were closer now, their faces glittering with sweat, eyes sparkling.

"Glad to see you are on your way already." One of the men waved his hand, his smile wide. "We were sent to hurry all of you back."

"Why?"

"Good news! The War Chief received the formal agreement of the Clans Mothers to proceed with the raid into the Rock People's lands. We will leave in two dawns." The man's smile widened, while his companions nodded vigorously. "The War Dance will be held with the coming of the first star, so you all should wash yourselves and prepare."

Iraquas' whoop could be heard on the other side of the Northern River, of that Two Rivers was sure.

"A raid in two dawns," cried out the young man, slapping his thigh with such force the smacking sound echoed between the trees. "Oh, how can life get any better?"

The other men laughed, their elation matching.

"They are in a hurry to proceed with the War Dance, aren't they?" commented Two Rivers, trying to share their excitement. What was wrong with him? He was no coward. Why couldn't he help but to think about the futility of it all?

"Well, there is no need to postpone the ceremony. The warriors should get into the right mood. And maybe we will be able to start out even earlier, if the Clans' Councils would prepare our supplies in a hurry."

"Also, it would be wise to make this raid official, before our Clans Mothers should change their minds." Two Rivers found it hard to suppress his grin. "With those women, one never knows."

The grins of the others sparkled mischievously.

"Yes, that's true, of course. One could never be too careful with the leaders of the clans and their switching moods." Seeta, an impressive, wide-shouldered warrior, chuckled. "Women!"

"They would never dare to go back on their word," cried out Iraquas. "It would be just too much."

But the others laughed.

"You are young, Iraquas. You haven't seen much," said Seeta. "And you haven't taken a wife yet. Wait and see until you learn how their devious minds work. You will be amazed."

"So what?" protested the young man, his eyes flashing. "I know how our councils work, and I say that the Clans Mothers had better not try to change our plans!" He glanced at Two Rivers, still seething. "Can they do that? I mean, can they tell us not to go after they had agreed? Would our customs permit something like that?"

"Yes, they can." Two Rivers hid his grin, amused by his friend's naivety, but unwilling to humiliate him by showing his amusement. The open laughter of the others was more than enough. "It would be frowned upon. And yes, it might not be too lawful. But they can do that. After all, they are the ones expected to provide us with food and clothing for the journey."

"Oh, yes? And we are the ones expected to protect them, aren't we?"

"Yes, of course. That's why they don't use their right of veto too often."

"They are using it often enough," muttered one of the men. "But yes, Two Rivers is right. Our laws and ways are well-balanced."

"Not well enough," insisted Iraquas, kicking at a stone. "We should not be forced into asking their permission at all. We are men, and our leaders are chosen and know better. We should be allowed to do our work uninterrupted."

"Chosen by those same Mothers of the Clans. Didn't you

know even this?" Seeta's grin was challenging, openly amused. He enjoyed baiting the young man, taking pleasure in putting him in his place, and it made Two Rivers angry.

"He knows who is appointing whom," he said impatiently. "Don't start feeling too good with yourself just yet. You are not that well-versed in our laws, either. You are not the War Chief and not the council member."

"And you are neither of these, too," growled Seeta, coming a step closer, threatening. "And you will never be one of them. You will spend your life arguing, speaking of your nonsense, not listened to at all."

"That's what you think." Two Rivers didn't move, glaring at the darkening face of the man, knowing that no attack would come, not this time. Seeta was a good warrior and a brave man, but he was bluffing more often than not. "You just wait and see." He shrugged, turning back toward the trail. "Go and talk to the rest of our party. They were leaving the field too, but might have been lingering."

"Don't give us orders, foreigners' lover!" Seeta's voice trembled now, his rage spilling. "I wonder what you are doing, spending your time in respectable company. I would expect you to huddle here in the woods with the savage cub you were defending so eagerly yesterday, maybe enjoying him like the last of the captive women. You are good for nothing else, you coward!"

He heard it like a thunder behind his back, the words hanging in the air, lingering, filling his whole being with the black wave of hatred, so intense he could feel its bitter taste in his mouth. The world stopped, died for a heartbeat, the regular sounds gone, with nothing left but those words. They pierced him and made his heart freeze, filling his stomach with ice, the blackish, muddy ice of the springtime.

He didn't remember himself moving. One moment he was on the trail, stunned, breathless, staring in disbelief. A heartbeat later, his body was pressed against his slightly taller rival, pinning the broad man to the tree, slamming his back against it, his knife pressing at the exposed throat, his eyes seeing nothing but the hated face and the widely opened, gaping eyes.

"Take that back, you filthy lowlife!" he heard someone saying, and it took him a moment to realize that it was he who had been talking. "Take it back, or I swear I'll cut your filthy throat and feed your rotten flesh to the wolves."

The eyes staring at him did not blink, glazed. Through the wild pounding of his heart, he could hear the others coming back to life, rushing toward them.

He didn't struggle, when they pulled him off. He didn't press the knife, either. But as their arms drew him back, he made himself ready, seeing the eyes of his rival filling with life, a whole gamut of emotions chasing each other across the incredulous gaze – shock, fear, hatred, fury.

As the man threw himself forward, he ducked, pulling away from the clutching arms, avoiding the punch. His own fist shot forward, colliding with the man's belly. The groan of his opponent was music to his ears, but the powerful kick of the decorated moccasin surprised him, connecting with his side, sending rays of pain up his own stomach.

Fighting to catch his balance, he saw the formidable fist nearing his temple and tilted his head in time to avoid the worst of the blow, feeling the man's knuckles sliding along his cheekbone, instead. It made his head reel, but he paid it no attention, clenching his teeth and hurdling himself onto his rival, oblivious of reason, his senses screaming danger.

His fingers claws, he grabbed the man's throat as they wavered and lost their balance, collapsing onto the ground. Struggling against the hands that were pulling him off, he pressed hard, anxious to render his rival unconscious, afraid of the danger he presented, now more than before, because of the insult. The kicks of the man were vicious, but they grew fainter as the gurgling sounds filled his ears, until he could not resist the others' strength any longer, pulled to his feet by the force that was not his.

Breathing heavily, he stared at his victim, watching him

squirming, coughing, his mouth wide open, gulping the fresh air. He tried to shake the hands off, but their grip tightened, digging painfully into his flesh.

"Let me go," he growled. "I won't attack him again." He could feel their hesitation enveloping him like a heavy cloud. "I promise!"

They moved away, one by one, and he shook his head, trying to make it work. It was full of hazy mist, the wild pounding of his heart not making the thinking process easier. Two of his companions were kneeling, helping the assaulted man up.

He took his gaze away, then bent to pick up his knife. They tensed, and he hurried to put it back into its sheath, his hands numb and trembling.

"Let us forget this event," he heard one of their companions saying. "There were words that should not have been uttered, and deeds that should not have been done. Yet, no one was seriously hurt therefore I propose to forget what happened."

He could feel Iraquas nearing, standing by his side, ready to help. It reassured him.

"I'm prepared to forget this," he said, surprised to hear his own voice firm. His heart was still pumping, and his limbs trembled badly.

Seeta rose to his feet, reeling, trying not to lean on his friends' arms.

"I'm not sure I'll forget this that easily," he said, coughing again to clear his throat. "But I will try." The dark glance he shot at Two Rivers said he would not be forgetting any of this. "Let us go and do our duty."

The silence returned as their steps drew away, dying gradually, swallowed by the deepening dusk. He listened to the wind, feeling it blowing strongly, rustling in the treetops.

Against his will, he looked up, taking in the glowering sky, grayish and displeased. He should not have lost his temper this way. What he did was beneath the dignity of the man he thought himself to be. No better than the hotheaded cub from across the Great Sparkling Water.

"Well, I take back what I said earlier." Iraquas' voice broke into his thoughts, light and trembling with amusement.

"What?"

"About you losing your temper. I've seen it now, and I don't want to see it again. Not a pretty sight."

"Oh, shut up!"

The young man laughed, unabashed. "Will you be pressing your knife at my throat if I don't?" He shook his head. "What a sight! One moment you were walking away all dignity and pride. The next, you are slamming him against that tree, about to cut his throat. And no one saw you move, I swear. It was as though the Evil Twin gave you some of his power." The narrowed eyes stared at him, partly amused, partly wondering. "You were at least five, maybe six steps away from him, but no one saw you moving, let alone leaping, or snatching your knife. It was hair-raising, to watch this."

"Stop talking nonsense," said Two Rivers, unsettled. He didn't remember himself moving or pulling his knife out either. "You were busy fuming about the Councils and Mothers of the Clans. You didn't watch."

"Of course, I was watching. When he said you should have been busy lying with that stupid boy instead of wandering around with *decent* people, I was angered as well. It was as though he was accusing you of lying around with me. As though I would let anyone do anything like that to me."

He felt his fists clenching again, going rigid, his nails sinking into the flesh of his palms. "The filthy lump of rotten meat! I should have killed him after all."

But Iraquas just shrugged, unperturbed. "You take insults too easily, brother. So what if he thinks you would lie with the boy. There are men who are doing these things. Nothing wrong about that."

"Well, it may be good for those who like it, but I don't appreciate being accused of such lovemaking. I don't do this."

"I know you don't, man! Calm down. What a hothead you are. Let us go to the stream and make ourselves clean for the ceremony." The young man brought his palms up, beaming. "I can't wait for the evening. Oh, I missed those battle preparations. It's been too long since the last raid."

CHAPTER 7

The drums beat evenly, rolling around the square, stern and soft at the same time. *Calming.* In the light of the flickering fires, the faces of the dancers looked strange, their paint still immaculate, their eyes firm, concentrated, their movements strong, in perfect accord with the drumming.

Mesmerized against his will, Tekeni watched the singers beating their sticks, following the lead of the main drum. They were painted too, and their low voices filled the square with a strange tranquility. They were yet to work themselves and the dancers up.

The memories of the War Dance of his people, the first War Dance in which he had been allowed to participate, swayed him, making his stomach heave. He had been one of the dancers back then, painted and clad in a loincloth only, holding an axe instead of a club. Oh, how thrilled he had been back then, how afraid to do something wrong, to shame himself in front of his people. To shame his father, the War Chief! He was too young to participate in a raid, too young to dance around the pole, but his father trusted him and thought him worthy, and he knew he would die if required to in an attempt not to disappoint the great leader.

He clutched his palms until he could not feel them anymore, pushing the memories away. His biggest fear back then was to make a bad throw, to miss the pole, or to hurl his axe with not enough strength for it to stick into the hard wood. If he did it right, he knew, if his axe would cut into the pole and remain there, all would be well. He would not shame his father, and the raid he was to accompany would be a great success.

Little did he know!

He could feel the salty taste on his lips, where his teeth bit into his own flesh. His axe had stuck perfectly, and everyone was proud and satisfied; satisfied with him, the remaining son of the great warriors' leader, the boy of the prophecy.

He had never been told what the prophecy was, but he heard the rumors about it, rumors that implied that either he or his twin brother were to do something meaningful. Something great, maybe. People were always whispering, and looking at them strangely at times, stopping the conversations when they neared. The whole region, the surrounding towns and villages, were shocked when Tekeni's brother died. It was not the part of the prophecy, that much was obvious. He could see it in their wondering eyes, in the devastated face of his father, but all he cared about back then was his private loss. A mother and a brother gone in one lousy, cold, hungry winter. It was impossible to grasp.

The drums peaked along with the monotonous voices of the singers, and his senses clung to it, desperate to push the horrible memories away, his teeth clenched, palms clutched, muscles tight, trembling with the effort. Nothing went according to the stupid prophecy! Only a few moons later, his father was killed, and he was captured, the only surviving member of his immediate family, the insignificant fragment, important to no one, just a wild thing living among the enemies, destined to fulfill nothing. The prophecy was wrong!

His eyes picked out the tall figure of Two Rivers among the dancers, the man's bare chest well-muscled, although he was a relatively slender man. The axe he held looked simple, not a decorated affair many of the other warriors waved. Why?

The dancers were beating the earth with their feet, stomping violently, tiring themselves, working up their spirits. Won't they be too tired to throw their axes when their time comes? wondered Tekeni. By this point of the ceremony, his people were already required to demonstrate their skill.

Regretting not having watched any of the other War Dances

that were frequent enough in this town, he looked with curiosity, his heart beating fast. He had never come to watch before. He didn't want to see these people, *the enemies*, demonstrating their strength and virility. He wished they would lose, battle after battle.

But now it changed. Now he had a plan, a good plan he needed to start implementing; and so this evening, he forced himself to come, afraid that he might have not been allowed to do this. Was he not confined to his longhouse until the decision of the Town Council? Was Yeentso dead or alive?

No mourning sounds came out of the Beaver Clan's longhouse during the day, so the hated man must have still been alive. But battling the death, or recovering? The people he saw earlier did not look concerned, but, of course, no one bothered to inform him of the developments. If he had not been liked before, now he was openly hated.

He shivered, listening to the drums, watching the warriors stomping their feet faster and faster, their faces glistening with sweat, their paint beginning to run. Two Rivers would be away for half a moon or more, and with Yeentso recovering, he, Tekeni, would need to watch his step. With no protection from the impressive man, he might be in grave danger because as clear as the sun in the cloudless sky, vengeful Yeentso would not linger with his wish to bring retribution. Unless it took him a long time to recover. Tekeni tried to suppress his fear.

"They are invincible!" whispered people around him, enthralled, caught in the magic. He concentrated, sharing their feeling against his will, impressed by the magnificent show of strength and aggression. It didn't matter if they were going to throw their axes or not. Their power was proclaimed regardless.

The crowds pushed, and the chanting voices dimmed as the War Chief began addressing the warriors, half singing half speaking, retelling old battles and wars in a beautiful, monotonous voice.

Listening intently, Tekeni jumped as a hand tugged at his arm, startling him. Heart pounding, he whirled around, his eyes finding it difficult to adjust to the darkness behind his back. Although being on the edge of the crowd, he still could not see at first who it was, with the people pushing all over, trying to see better.

Then his stomach twisted, and the current of excitement rushed down his back, his senses telling him that the gentle palm belonged to *her*, the girl from the Beaver Clan, while his eyes took in the soft outline of her slender face, set in the frame of now-loose hair, one long, luxurious tendril fluttering across it, making her blink.

Come. The motion of her head was unmistakable as she slipped away, the warmth upon his arm, where her hand had touched his, lingering.

Heart beating fast, he made his way out of the crowd, following the decorated skirt, listening to the rustling of the colorful beads. People frowned but let them pass, until the square dissolved behind their backs and the shadows of the longhouses swallowed them, with only the drums following along with the sounds of the chanting.

She went on briskly, her paces long and determined, full of purpose and, as the first wave of excitement faded, he began to feel unsettled. Where were they going?

"I looked for you in the Wolf Clan longhouse, and you weren't there," she said, frowning, as they neared the tobacco plots beside the fence.

He tried to make sense of it. "Why would I be there?"

"You were confined to your longhouse until the decision of the Town Council," she stated, halting abruptly and turning to face him, the frown not sitting well with her exquisite, gentle features. "You were not allowed to wander about."

"I wasn't wandering," he said, still puzzled. "I was at the War Dance. Everyone came to watch this, even the small children. There is not one single human being in the longhouses now."

She acknowledged it with the nod, not thrown out of her composure.

"Yes, I know that. But I never saw you attending any of the

ceremonies. So why now, all of a sudden?"

"I don't know. Why shouldn't I? I want to be a warrior, like anybody else. I should start attending those." He peered at her, encouraged by a sudden thought. "Why were you watching me?"

She gasped, and her eyes sparkled furiously. "I did not watch you. I never did!"

"Then how do you know I was not attending the other ceremonies?"

Even in the darkness, he could see her cheeks taking a darker shade.

"I didn't watch you, and I couldn't care less if you attended any of the ceremonies or not." Breathing heavily, she looked as though about to stomp her foot, the fringes of her festive dress fluttering with the wind, as angry as she was. "Everyone knows you are not coming to our ceremonies. There is no need to watch you to know that."

He stared at her, taken aback. Her hair was fluttering too now, the wind challenging the wooden combs that held it in place. It made her look fiercer, but prettier, with her eyes of a doe and her graceful way of holding herself, like a long-legged forest creature. He searched for something to say, wishing he hadn't spoken in the first place, his confidence gone.

"Well, this is not what I wanted to talk to you about," she said finally, frowning.

He said nothing this time, not wishing to help her out. If she dragged him here to yell at him, she might have saved them both the futile encounter.

"Why are you staring at me like that?" Her eyebrows almost met each other across her high forehead as her frown deepened, the flicker of embarrassment passing through her eyes. "I wanted to help you out, but maybe I should not."

The urge to strangle her welled. "How?"

"Yesterday, I promised to tell you if Yeentso would die or not. Don't you remember even that? Are you simple in the head?"

"I remember all of it!" he stated, his frustration with her overwhelming the sudden surge of panic.

"Oh, good. At least you remember things." She drew another breath, obviously trying to calm down. "Well, I always keep my promises. So I came to tell you that he is much better now, and it doesn't look as though he will die. I saw him this morning, but I had no opportunity to come and tell you, because we had to work until it was almost dusk. And then, when I did have the opportunity to slip away, you were not in your longhouse but in the middle of the crowd. Half of the town must have seen us!"

The warm wave was back, welling in his chest, unwelcome now. She remembered, and she did keep her promise.

"Both halves of the town were busy watching the dance," he muttered. "No one paid us any attention."

She shrugged. "Well, maybe. Let us hope you are right." Her eyes sparkled again, but now there was an amusement in them, too obvious to miss. "It was because of you we had to work until the darkness."

He felt like laughing, but not in an amused way. "Me? How so?"

"Well, because you wounded Yeentso, his wife and another woman of our longhouse stayed home, to take care of him. So there were less of us in the field. More work for everyone."

"Oh."

"Yes, oh. And I wish you would promise me not to lose your temper again, not in this way." She shrugged. "Anyway, our Clan Mothers would not demand your death now. So it all worked out quite well."

"Will he get better soon?" he asked, ice piling in his stomach, despite the warmth her words brought.

"Yes, I think so. He was eating this morning, then he slept through the whole day. So his wife and sister told us." She hesitated. "He wasn't able to go out and watch the War Dance yet, and he won't join this impending raid, obviously. But he will not die, and this is what must concern you the most."

Her preaching tone made his anger overcome his uneasiness.

"I'm not concerned with his well being. I was just curious."

She tossed her head high. "Well, you should have been concerned. If you are smart, that is."

"I'm smart enough to know that he will not forget what happened. He will seek revenge the moment he can walk straight. And then it will be back to either him or me hurt. With one of us killed, most probably." He narrowed his eyes, pleased to see hers widening. "More chances it would be me this time, because he would not challenge me openly against the Town Council orders. He is a coward, so he would try to ambush me, instead, or make me attack him again, maybe."

She took a step back, aghast. "He wouldn't do that. It would be against our laws. Your clan will pay our clan, and everything will go back to normal."

He let his eyebrows climb high, satisfied with her open dismay. "Who is not being smart now?"

Her eyes flashed again. "Don't you dare to talk to me like that! You were the one to start this trouble, not me. You were not *smart* enough to avoid this mess. Yes, I know he attacked you first," she added when he began to protest. "But you could have controlled your temper better, instead of cracking his head open the moment you could."

They glared at each other, oblivious of the wind, the rolling of the drums reaching them, but barely, alone in the whole world as it seemed.

What did she want? raged his mind, his anger more intense because of the way she stood there, so near he could almost feel the warmth of her body, his eyes taking in its gentle curves, the way the colorful belt tied her festive dress, enhancing her slender waist, the way the long fringes fell against the bulging of her breasts.

He clenched his teeth, fighting the urge to run away, or maybe, to step closer.

"So, you looked for me to let me know about Yeentso," he said, doing his best to sound calm. *Speaking of controlling tempers.* "I'm grateful for that."

She peered at him suspiciously. "You are? You didn't act this way until now."

"Yes, of course, I am. You kept your promise."

"Yes." Her smile was surprising, flashing out without warning, wonderfully warm. It made his heart race. "And I hope you will be more, err, tractable from now on. With me, and with other people. Even with this annoying bastard Yeentso."

He could not hide his shock. "Annoying bastard? Did I hear you saying that?"

"Oh, well." She shrugged, smiling smugly, happy with the effect. "Yeentso is not the best liked person in our longhouse. I wish our grandmother had chosen another man for my cousin to take." The frown and the smile were fighting each other across her face. "What? Why are you staring at me?"

"I… I don't know. I guess I was just surprised. I didn't think…" Now it was his turn to shrug. Embarrassed, he looked away. "I didn't think people did not like him, too. I thought everyone hated me and no one else."

The frown won. "No one hates you! Oh well, some people may hate you, but certainly not everyone. You are just not very well liked." She pursed her lips and looked like a person of knowledge preaching to a crowd. "You are a foreigner, and not a friendly foreigner at that. You are violent, and you have a shocking temper. Yes, yes, I know, you were provoked yesterday." Her hands came up as though trying to stop him from interrupting her speech. "But it is not the first time you were involved in violence. In fact, you were more times in trouble than not. So people do have a hard time trying to sympathize with you. Were you as nice with them as you were with me last night, they would have liked you a great deal better. The other adopted people are getting along just fine."

"That's what you think," he said, annoyed by the way she was preaching to him. As though she had been his elder. But the opposite was true. She had hardly seen sixteen summers. Maybe even less. And she knew nothing about life. "People hate me because I came from across the Great Sparkling Water, the lands of the real enemy. You fight your neighbors from time to time, but you do so half-heartedly. You are playing war with your neighbors, just like this raid." He gestured toward the rolling drums. "They are going to fight some people who attacked other people, but those other people are your enemies too, although at the time of the attack they were not. To me, it seems that they just got bored and could not get the permission to cross the Great Lake, to fight the real enemy. So they are going to relieve their boredom in a sort of a small war. To play at war and to enjoy themselves."

She peered at him wide-eyed, all sorts of expressions chasing each other across her face.

"It is not so," she said with none of her usual self-assurance.

"Then how is it?"

"Oh, well, the Deer People were not always our enemies. They were our allies until, well, until this incident last summer. You see, those two young men of the Turtle Clan, they were found dead, and all signs pointed that the Deer People did this. You should remember this. You were already here by the last summer." She flopped her hands in the air. "Oh, why do I bother? You are not listening, because you think you know it all!"

He could not hold his laughter anymore. "I'm not listening because I heard all that and more. Yes, I was here the last summer. I know the story, and to me, it makes no sense. You and the Deer People are the same."

"No, we are not!"

"Of course you are. Same tongue, same customs, same lack of carvings upon your longhouses." He hesitated, remembering his conversation with Two Rivers. "Same amount of clans even. Same everything," he ended triumphantly, her uncertainty making him happier than he had been in summers.

She glared at him, her nostrils widening with every breath. "And the people from across the Great Lake? How are they different, if it is so?"

"Oh, no, my people are different. Across the Great Sparkling

Water it is nothing like here. We speak different tongues, and we have different customs. Everything over there is not like here at all."

"They are not your people anymore, remember?" Her eyebrows climbed high, making her look again unpleasantly preachy.

"Yes, I remember that." The familiar dull pain in his chest was back, and he took his gaze away, peering into the darkness.

"There is another reason I was looking for you," she said softly.

"What reason?" He kept staring into the blackness of the night, but his stomach twisted with anticipation.

"I wanted to warn you."

"To warn me? About what?"

His disappointment welled, and it angered him. Why should he expect something else from her? She was so pretty and upright, such a perfect member of their society, and what was he if not a wild foreigner, good for nothing but making trouble?

"Well, you see, even though Yeentso will live, your clan would have to compensate my clan for the injury, and the way it made some of our people not go to work, while taking care of him. But the thing is…" She hesitated, and he watched her long fingers toying with the fringes of her dress. "Well, your clan members are angry with you, and they may want you to find the means to pay up all by yourself, with no help or cooperation of theirs at all." Leaning closer, she looked up at him, eyes troubled, glittering in the darkness, taking his breath away. "My friend overheard them talking about it this morning, and then I overheard them too, later on."

He felt his stomach sinking, her troubled gaze sending shivers down his spine. "What will I be required to pay?"

"They were talking about a certain amount of hides." She dropped her eyes. "Five hides, maybe. Cleaned and tanned, and ready for use."

"Five hides?" He heard the air bursting out of his own lungs loudly, desperately. "It will take me more than a whole span of season of coming to every hunting expedition, when I'm not even invited to join every one of them. And, anyway, I will get no chance to shoot anything. They used us, youths, to carry things, mainly. To row and to pitch camps, and to make fires and cook, while the older hunters did the hunting. How can they expect me to get those five hides? And to prepare them too!"

"Yes, I know."

She brought her palms up in a helpless gesture, but it made him feel infinitely better. She was as frustrated, as disappointed. She knew he had no chance, but she did feel bad about it.

"I will help you to prepare them. I can do that." She went on, frowning. "You have no mother or sister to do that for you, so I'm sure they won't object. You just need to find someone, maybe. Someone that may be willing to go with you, to help you hunt. Five hides is not a terrible amount. It's five shot deer. Not an impossible feat. They were talking about ten initially, so I hear. But your clan's council brought it down to five."

He could barely hear her, the thundering of his heart distracting, interrupting his ability to listen. She said she would work his hides if he would get them. But what did this mean? He didn't dare to think about it.

"Would you believe this?" She grinned, apparently oblivious of his agitation. "Ten hides would pay for a new canoe full of weapons and what-not. Your Clan Mothers almost had a fit, so I hear. Their faces were the color of my festive dress, they say." She pointed at her girdle, adorned by a strip of purplish shells. "Of that color exactly."

Against his will, he laughed. "The Grandmother of our longhouse is a tough old hag. They were lucky she didn't turn the color of the storm cloud."

"Oh, well, our Grandmother is not a soft girl, either." She beamed at him, eyes sparkling. Another long tendril escaped the hold of the carved wooden comb, fluttering across her face, making her blink. She tossed her head to make it go back, but the silky thread persisted, dancing against her cheek, enhancing the softness of its angle.

He reached for it without thinking. All he wanted was to help her remove the obstacle, but the touch of her skin upon his fingertips made him shudder, sending rays of warmth down his spine. The feeling was so intense, it made his stomach shrink, as though he were sick, his heart coming to a halt.

One heartbeat, then another. She stared at him, evidently as startled, and the look in her eyes did not help, enhancing the sensation instead of making it go. Oh, but he had to do *something*.

With an effort, he pulled his hand back, the unruly tendril still there, still fluttering, annoying in its insistence.

"Your hair… it's in your face…" he mumbled, finding it difficult to utter even those words.

"Oh, well, yes."

She pushed it away with both hands, impatient and so obviously embarrassed he wanted to laugh. A nervous laughter. The strange sensation persisted. It was as though they had done something, something that changed everything between them. *But what?*

"I think we should go back to the ceremony," she said, taking her gaze away.

It broke the spell.

He clenched his teeth against his welling disappointment. "Yes, we should."

In the silvery darkness, he could see her profile as she turned, the high forehead, the soft line of the oval chin, the darker shade of the full lips. In the daylight one could see all of it and more, he thought, remembering watching her through the last span of seasons, the girl of the Beaver Clan, the pretty, confident, unapproachable thing. Her aloofness was renowned all over the town. Many boys, and even men, were watching her, but none dared to offer her a stroll by the river. They knew better than to hurt their pride in this way. Even through the social dances of the great ceremonies, she didn't bother to be nice while dancing. Moving with the breathtaking grace, she would dance for the sake of the movement, oblivious of the wistful stares.

He pressed his palms tight, the urge to touch her face, to run his fingers along the lines of the exquisite profile, this most beautiful creation of the Right-Handed Twin, overwhelming.

"I thank you for being so kind to me," he said gruffly. "I will never forget. One day, I will repay you your kindness."

She beamed at him, her smile again wide and free of shadows. "I'm glad I could be of help, even if only a little. I wish I could help you more. You are not what they say you are."

It was impossible to control his limbs once again. He needed to touch her, just one more time, only this once, only for a heartbeat. He felt his nails sinking into his palms, the pain refreshing him, putting his senses back in order.

"Come, let us go back," he heard her saying, the beads of her skirt murmuring with the sways of the tanned leather.

Without the magic of her eyes, and no unruly hair fluttering against the exquisite face, it was easier to follow her lead, his heart returning to beat in a reasonable manner.

CHAPTER 8

Stifling a sigh of relief, Two Rivers leaned against the nearby rock, too tired to try to make himself more comfortable. The sleepless nights were taking their toll, making his head dizzy, his body stiff and crying for a well-deserved rest.

He watched other warriors squatting all around, smoking the pipe when it was their turn to take the revered, beautifully carved object.

"We will leave in two dawns," the War Chief was saying. "A party of twenty men. Good, seasoned warriors; no youths this time."

The men listened in silence, their faces sealed, impartial, as though carved out of wood, glistening in the light of a small fire, elated by the dance, yet as exhausted, their power drained. The clatter of the rattles and the drumming poured in, with the square still full of activity, the town's dwellers refusing to disperse, dancing on, social dances now.

He took the offered pipe, pleased to see his hand firm, not trembling. After the War Dance it was always difficult to control one's limbs.

"Only clubs and bows. Ten light canoes," the deep voice went on, ringing eerily in the surrounding darkness. "The Clans' Council will give us food for ten days' journey, but we will be eating sparingly, to ensure our well being should the journey take us longer to complete."

Inhaling, Two Rivers watched the old leader, marveling at the composure and the calm dignity the noble face radiated. The man had been almost a legend, having fought for more summers than anyone could remember, the war trophies mounting in the compartment of his longhouse, the tales of his deeds going ahead of him. Earlier, in the middle of the ceremony, it had taken the old leader a long time to recount his battles. The custom dictated that the most veteran warrior would tell about his wars and victories in between the dances, and this particular tale was taking the longest.

Not that anyone complained. The man's ability to relate the old stories was wonderful, inspiring, breathtakingly real, taking his listeners to the places and times they had never seen.

"Who will be chosen to join, Honorable Leader?" asked one of the men quietly.

"You will know with sunrise." The War Chief took the offered pipe, inhaling deeply, savoring its contents. "Now go back, or go to rest. I will need most of you present here, full of power and in the highest of spirits in two dawns from now." The stern eyes softened, encircling his audience, traveling from face to face. "I will be proud to lead the warriors of your quality once again, before it will be my time to clear the path for the younger leaders to take."

Unsettled, Two Rivers watched the meditative eyes clouding, wandering unknown distances, the quick spasm crossing the old face, lingering but only for a heartbeat. He held his breath. Had the old leader seen a glimpse of the future? Had he seen something discouraging there?

Forcing his eyes off the saddening face, wishing to allow the man privacy one deserved at such a moment, he got to his feet along with the rest of the warriors, eager to go back to the festivities all of a sudden. The tiredness was still there, but his spirit now craved the merry clamor and the loud commotion of the joyful townsfolk.

He frowned. The ability to see the future was unsettling, every time he had witnessed it. It happened to people on occasions, with no pattern or logic, no special foods eaten and no special beverages consumed. And no matter how reluctant one might feel, what conscious efforts one might have made to avoid this happening, it would pounce on you without noticing, filling your mind's eye with all sort of visions of undecipherable meaning. There were nights he preferred not to sleep at all.

The clamor of the square burst upon him, welcome in its colorful confusion, in its jumble of smells and sounds. He drifted toward the largest fire, hungry and not bothering to conceal it. There was not much solemnity about the social part of the ceremonies.

"Let us grab some food," cried out one of the warriors. "One can't be expected to dive into this mess on an empty stomach."

"No, and we can't look at those with our bellies growling." Indicating the circle of the dancers, Two Rivers grinned, eyes lingering on the prancing girls. "All those swirling skirts."

The warriors laughed.

"You can look around all you like, still living in your clan's longhouse. When you move to this or that swirling skirt's compartment, you'll be more careful with your eyes."

"And the other parts, too."

"Oh, yes."

Receiving bowls of hot stew, with pieces of meat floating near the surface, they squatted upon the ground, inhaling the delicious aroma.

"But you are not in a hurry to move to another longhouse, brother, eh?" said the first warrior, gulping his meal.

"No, I'm not." Eating heartily, Two Rivers watched the tall girl from the Porcupine Clan laughing, her hair long and luxurious, bouncing prettily as she tossed her head, well aware of the gazes she drew.

"He will be enjoying his freedom until he grows very old. Then he will start looking in a hurry, if his most precious of weapons would be still strong enough by then."

"I won't live to be that old."

The girl's eyes brushed past him, lingering for a heartbeat. It made him wish to finish his meal.

"Aren't you afraid to talk like that, brother?" asked one of the younger warriors. "It is not wise to tempt the bad spirits of the Evil Twin."

"You are talking to Two Rivers," said someone. "He is not afraid of the spirits. He'll argue with them until they'll leave him alone, defeated." The man shrugged, his face sobering. "He has a prophecy to fulfill."

"Oh, please!" Suppressing a sudden wave of irritation, Two Rivers took his eyes off the dancers, meeting the gazes of his peers. "There is no prophecy, and there never was. Why would anyone pay attention to the nonsense dreams of a troubled young woman that happened more than thirty summers ago?"

"Dreams are not to be taken lightly, brother." One of the older warriors gazed at him sternly, reprimanding. "The woman who gave you your life was visited by strange dreams before she conceived. She knew no man, but she grew you in her belly, nevertheless. Her mother had testified to that matter."

He remembered his grandmother, her large, brown hands, always busy, pounding corn, or working the flour into beautifully smooth dough. She had had a booming voice, and she would scold the children of her longhouse and make them work; still, all the boys and the girls loved to play in her vicinity. It was calming to know she was around.

She never talked to him about the prophecy, but as he grew up he had heard more than he wanted to, having noticed that there was no father in his life, while in the lives of his playmates there usually had been such a person. All he had was a silent, haunted woman for a mother, a woman who had not really been there, sitting in her corner, sewing all day long. Other women went into the fields, cooked and gossiped, laughing with each other, complaining about their men, dancing through the ceremonies. But his mother had hardly talked at all, seldom leaving their compartment, looking at him with those clouded eyes, opening her mouth only occasionally, to tell him how he would do great things – save his people – when he grew up.

He pushed the memories away, desperate to suppress the familiar frustration.

"I won't presume to judge people's interpretation of their

visions," he said, shrugging. "But I have my doubts as to this particular dream. There might be a simpler explanation."

Like a girl lying with a man, then losing her sanity when he would not take the responsibility, he thought, clenching his teeth. His father must have been a terrible man.

"You are not young anymore, Two Rivers," said one of the elders, shaking his head. "You were reluctant to take your destined path for too long, going against our ways and traditions instead. The people were patient with you, but it's time you correct your ways and start walking the straight path."

The others were peering into their bowls, uncomfortable with such an open reprimand. Two Rivers was not a youth of no significance to be scolded so openly, and in front of many of his peers.

He tried to appear as calm as he could. "I appreciate your advice, Honorable Elder. I will try to follow it, of course, but I do not think I've been presumptuous or obtrusive. I appreciate our old ways, our customs and traditions, as much as anyone, more than some."

He watched Iraquas and the other young men diving into the melee, their faces shining, glistening with sweat, the exhaustion brought earlier by the War Dance forgotten. Why didn't he have enough sense to join them from the beginning?

"You were heard saying that this impending raid on the Rock People's villages is futile," pressed the elder, eyes squinting.

Two Rivers cursed inwardly, glancing at the surrounding faces, surprised, caught unprepared by the sudden interrogation.

"Yes, I do not think we should war on these people. They were not our enemies until the beginning of the cold moons." He shrugged, angered by their stony gazes. "We have enough enemies to war against."

"You doubt the decision of your War Chief and the leaders of the town, yet you participated in the War Dance."

"I will never attempt to avoid my duty, even if I doubt the advisability of the mission."

The elder man shook his head. "You are arrogant, son, and

your self-assurance knows no bounds. In small amounts, such confidence is good in a warrior and a future leader. One should always listen to one's heart. Yet, in your case, it's a trouble because you hear nothing but your own words. You respect neither your elders nor your peers' opinions. You put your own opinions before anyone else's." The man's frown deepened. "It will bring no good, neither to you nor to our community."

He fought the familiar frustration, making tremendous efforts to stay calm. There was nothing new in this lecture. He had heard it too often, coming from all sorts of sources.

"I do appreciate your advice," he repeated politely, anxious to escape. "I will try to correct my ways."

Or to avoid your company, he thought, enraged. He may have been guilty of listening to no one but himself, but so were many of the leaders, this particular elder, the member of the Town Council, included. No wonder the councils could never reach an agreement without verbal fights, or worse, he thought, standing the heavy gaze, trying to appear as humble as he could. One was not to argue with the elders, but to receive their reprimands with humility and gratitude.

Luckily, more people approached them, leaving the emptying pot of stew, and the angry elder's attention was taken away. Avoiding their gazes, Two Rivers got to his feet, as though intending to fill his plate, changing his direction and sneaking toward the dancing circle the moment his intention was not too obvious.

The annoying man, he thought, seething. To scold him in public and in such a manner, as though he had been a stubborn, petulant child. He stifled a curse. One thing was good about this impending raid. He would have an opportunity to leave the town and its confusing affairs. Half a moon with no preaching elders and disappointed leaders, what an alluring prospect!

"So, the old warriors managed to gather some of their strength back." Iraquas' round face beamed at him, glittering with sweat and smeared paint. "I thought you were going to sit there and talk for the whole night, oh-honorable-elderly man."

"Thought you the youngsters might need some backing up." Still upset, Two Rivers forced a smile, but refused to join the outer circle. "In a little while," he said, waving his friend away.

The observers such as himself were more numerous than the dancers at this stage of the night, but the girl from the Porcupine Clan was still dancing, her eyes flickering, resting on him, beckoning him in.

He watched her thoughtfully, enjoying the sight of her swaying hips, the polished shells of her colorful girdle reflecting the light of the nearby fire. She had been widowed for some moons, although he remembered catching her glances before it had happened. *Could be a good way of spending the night.*

Beside her, a cluster of Beaver Clan girls was giggling, gossiping as they danced, with only one of them dancing for real. Seketa, the prettiest girl, Iraquas' cousin, a serious little thing, with much aspirations and no silliness. However now, the girl's doe-like eyes were not concentrated on the dance like one would have expected. Instead, they rested on none other than the foreign boy, who didn't dare to join the dancers, but who had enough courage to stand on the edge of the crowd, devouring the girl with his gaze in his turn.

Two Rivers hid his grin. The young cub had to have guts to mingle among the townsfolk after what happened on the previous day. Not everyone would dare to do that, risking getting into trouble with the incensed Beaver Clan people, with the rest of the town disliking him more than ever.

He was about to grin at the youth, wishing to encourage him with at least one friendly face, but then he remembered his own violent encounter this afternoon, and it made him turn away without a greeting. Curse that damn Seeta into the realm of the Evil Twin and his minions, he thought.

"Don't you have enough strength to dance some more?" The voice of the Porcupine girl tore him from his reverie, making his heartbeat accelerate.

"Maybe," he said, eyeing her flushed, heart-shaped face. Her lips were as dark as her cheeks, full and well-defined. "With you,

I will dance for the whole night. In the inner or outer circle, or anywhere else."

She laughed softly. "Come."

The pull of her arm was firm, uncompromising, and he felt the people's curious gazes upon them, some friendly, some wondering, some sparkling with rage like the eyes of Turea, Yeentso's sister. This one was as beautiful as always, tall and imposing, her wonderful hair flowing, cheeks glowing, eyes dark; but the creases of her frown made her look older, and the pressed lips were downright ugly.

He took his gaze off her and dove into the outer circle of dancers, following the uncomplicated steps, surrounded by wonderful energy, his anger receding, giving way to familiar elation. The simple pleasure of rhythmic movement took off the edge of the frustration, and the pretty sight of the Porcupine girl's shapely hips made his thoughts flow into all sorts of peaceful channels. She retreated into the inner circle of the dancers, teasing, but he knew she meant more than that while coming to invite him to dance. He pondered if it was time to beckon her and ease his way out.

"What are you staring at?"

Outside the dancing circle, an argument was growing, and he could see the Beaver Clan beauty making her way out as well, her frown troubled. The foreign boy, he guessed. Who else?

"Nothing!"

Another youth stood in front of the wild cub now, scowling. "Stop staring at the girls. They are not for your filthy eyes."

The look the foreign boy gave his offender was fierce, blazing with so much hatred, the other youth took an involuntary step back. More people drifted toward them, and even the dancers began stealing glances.

"Go away," hissed the cub through his clenched teeth. "I will look at whomever I like."

"That's what you think!" growled another youth, coming closer.

Encouraged by unexpected reinforcement, the first youth

stepped closer, and the silence turned heavy, encompassing.

Two Rivers hesitated, unwilling to be a part of yet another trouble involving the wild cub. He could feel the Porcupine girl coming closer, halting beside him. Flying insults could give them a perfect cover to slip away, as no serious fighting would develop on the ceremony like that. Too many elders were present, leaders and other people, with Clans Mothers already shooting gazes in that direction.

"Leave him alone, Hainteroh!" The Beaver Clan girl's voice tore the silence, making them all jump. "Stop looking for trouble."

They all turned to stare, even the older people. Young girls were not expected to burst into arguments or fights. It was none of their business, even if they were the obvious cause of those.

The girl licked her lips. "No one tells you what girls you can look at or not, so don't do this to others," she went on, as forceful as before.

The foreign boy looked as tensed as an overstretched bowstring, but at her words, Two Rivers noticed, he relaxed visibly. How obvious! He hid his grin.

"Stop this argument and go back to dancing," said an elderly woman, one of the Turtle Clan's Mothers. She glared at the youths. "Do as you are told."

They began shifting reluctantly, and he could feel the touch of the Porcupine girl's palm as it brushed against his arm, leaving a pleasant sensation in its wake.

"You, go back to your longhouse," went on the woman, addressing the foreign boy this time. "You were not to wander the town until the councils decided on your punishment," she added harshly, squashing the blushing youth with her gaze.

He still seemed as though about to argue, and Two Rivers could not but admire the boy's spirit. To stand up to the Clans Mothers took more courage than some people could gather.

"I thought I was allowed to attend the ceremony," he muttered in the end, dropping his gaze.

"To attend – yes. To stir trouble – no!"

The other women nodded solemnly.

"He stirred no trouble, Honorable Mother," said the Beaver girl quietly.

The elderly woman seemed as though about to burst as her gaze flew at the girl, blazing.

"How dare you to argue with your elders?" she demanded.

The Beaver Clan girl's face took the color of the purple shells adorning her tiny waist.

"I'm not arguing," she said, her voice trembling but only a little. "I'm simply telling what happened. I saw it all. The Wolf Clan boy did not stir trouble. Hainteroh and his friend did."

Another courageous thing, thought Two Rivers, admiring the girl for not giving up.

"Yes, there was no trouble," said another elderly woman, obviously trying to lighten the atmosphere. "I saw it, too. The foreign boy did nothing wrong this time."

"Still, he should leave," insisted the first woman. "He brings trouble, even if he doesn't mean to do so." She frowned. "Tomorrow he will be informed of the punishment regarding his past crimes, and then he would have ample time to think the things over and to start correcting his ways."

"What will be the punishment?" asked one of the older warriors, curious.

"I heard he would be required to pay ten hides. Ten good, large, undamaged pieces."

The crowd gasped.

"Oh, stop spreading rumors," cried out the woman of the Wolf Clan. "Ten hides? What nonsense! Who would agree to such an outrageous price?" She looked around, enraged. "Five hides was the agreed price, and it is too high also, if you ask me!"

"Your clan can get this amount and more," laughed someone. "Wolf Clan is not the smallest clan of the town."

"So what? Does it mean we should clothe you all, you lazy, good-for-nothing hunters?" The woman flipped her hands in the air, advancing toward her offender.

The laughing man retreated a step. "I didn't say that," he muttered, rolling his eyes. "All I did was to state that you can manage, and that the boy is lucky no one died."

"He is not so lucky," said another Wolf Clan woman. "He will be required to get those hides all by himself, even if it takes him summers to do so."

"Oh!" The air hissed loudly, escaping many chests. To send the young boy to hunt the deer, skin it, tan it, and prepare the hides was an unnecessary toughness. He had neither experience, nor the skill to do a half of it.

Two Rivers felt his own anger rising. The boy had been formally adopted, through the customary ceremony. He was supposed to be a part of the family that requested him, enjoying the real family life. Instead, he had been an outcast, with no warmth or protection, and now, with even his own clan unwilling to help him out.

"Why won't the Wolf Clan take responsibility for its members?" he said loudly before able to stop himself. Again, his tongue proved impossible to control.

Now the glares of the Wolf Clan women were upon him, while the rest of the people kept silent, holding their breaths.

"We are a part of a clan because without it we are nothing." He saw their faces, flickering strangely in the flames of the raging fire. It made him shiver, but there was no way back now. He shrugged. "Clan gives us protection and means to survive. Is it not the whole purpose of the extended families? Is it not why we give our clan everything it requires in return, so the person would not need to battle the challenges of life all alone?" Encircling them with his gaze, he saw people drifting closer, listening, their curiosity obvious but mixed with the usual apprehension. They did not trust what he said, not entirely. "This boy was adopted officially, *officially*. He is a part of the Wolf Clan, living in their longhouse, doing his part, hunting with Wolf people, fishing with them, clearing its clan's fields. How can the Wolf Clan Council shake off its responsibility to him? All of a sudden, he is a foreigner and has nothing to do with this clan. How could that happen? Doesn't this decision to make him face the reasonable claim of the Beaver Clan's people alone violate the most basic of our laws? Is it not going against our ways, our customs, our traditions?"

"No, it is not," cried out one of the Turtle Clan Mothers. "There were quite a few instances. When a person's crimes are too high or too unfitting, he or she might be expected to deal with the consequences of their deeds all alone." The woman's eyes flashed. "It is not your place to criticize the decision of a clan council. Let alone of the clan you do not belong to."

He took a deep breath. "Yes, I know it is not my place to try to interrupt the decisions of a clan council, *any of the clans*. But I do believe a person can sound his opinion. I was not setting myself in judgment, but I cannot turn my face from the obvious injustice. The crime of this boy is not high, or unusual. He did not try to murder the man he injured. Indeed, he acted foolishly, without thinking. But he had been provoked. I was there, I saw it all. There was nothing unusual about their fight. It happens often, regretfully so." He remembered his own afternoon encounter. Had he cut Seeta's throat, he would be in as deep trouble as this boy now, worse so, because the provocation was not as unbearable. Seeta did not try to touch him at all, but merely said silly things, while Yeentso was grabbing this boy's throat, threatening to kill him. He shook his head to banish the unwelcome memory. "I thought the Town Council was making inquiries, to determine the seriousness of the event."

"The Town Council would have done this had the victim of the attack died," said one of the elders softly. "As it is, this problem went back to the Clans' Councils, to close the matter between them."

Two Rivers nodded, forcing his face into stillness. Yes, he should have thought of this. There was nothing to add, really. If the Wolf Clan Mothers were determined to discipline one of its members in this way, then that was that.

The elderly women glared at him, victorious, their eyes

sparkling. He returned their gazes, then glanced at the boy, who stood there all ears, eyes traveling from face to face, listening avidly. The wolf cub's path was turning more difficult from turn to turn, and with such temper and so much pride he wouldn't go far.

"Five hides is not such a great price," said someone. "If you think it's so cruel and unjust, you can go with the boy, help him hunt. A hunter of your skill and experience would be of a great help."

Incensed, Two Rivers shot a glance at the speaker, a man of his own clan, residing in the neighboring longhouse.

"I may do just that," he said coldly.

"Instead of going with our raiding party?"

He wanted to kill the man for trapping him this way.

"Maybe."

He didn't have to do that, neither to take care of the boy, nor to do so instead of joining the warriors. The hunting could wait, should he decide to help. There was no need to create a scandal by refusing to join the raid after participating in the War Dance, and after being indicated by the War Chief as to the chances of him being among the chosen. And yet…

"If you are going, be careful. Aside from all sort of enemies lurking, through the last two moons, the other bank of the Northern River was spotted by footprints of a huge bear. The grizzled brown bear, most clearly, and judging by the signs - an old, vicious creature."

"Yes, we saw those prints!" cried out several voices. "The creature seemed to make the First Springs and its tributaries its own."

They were still talking as the idea flashed through his mind, too beautiful to disregard it right away.

"How many hides would the fur of the huge brown bear be worth?"

They all turned to stare at him, wide-eyed.

"What are you thinking?" asked someone suspiciously.

"Well…"

He rushed it through his head hurriedly, trying to play for time. He might have been acting foolishly, entangling the boy in an even greater danger than before.

The youth's eyes bore at him, expectant, sparkling with apprehension that had nothing to do with doubt or fear. Encouraged, he looked up.

"If the boy was to slay the beast and bring its magnificent fur home, would his offering make it right with the Beaver Clan People?"

The silence was heavy, encompassing. He returned their incredulous gazes.

"A boy can't slay such a beast. Even a hunter of many summers cannot be sure to trap the huge, grizzled bear and return home in one piece," breathed someone.

"I'll help him track the beast," said Two Rivers, aware of his own heart beating faster at the prospect of the adventure. He turned to the boy, narrowing his eyes. "What do you say? Are you up to the challenge?"

The boy did not hesitate, not even for a heartbeat.

"Yes," he said loudly, voice trembling, but only a little. "I want to do that."

"What do you say?" He watched them, amused by the various expressions crossing their faces.

"Well, it's a challenge," said one of the older warriors. He turned to the boy. "Are you sure you want to do this? Your chances of coming back from such an encounter are slim. Two Rivers will help you track the beast, will explain to you what to do, but he will not be hunting it together with you. It will be your challenge. Do you understand that?"

The boy licked his lips, then nodded, apparently unable to speak. His eyes, huge and glittering, clung to the man's face, so wide open they looked round.

Two Rivers began to regret the idea. From the corner of his eye, he saw the pretty Beaver girl stifling a cry, pressing her palms to her mouth.

"It may have to wait until I come back from the raid to the

lands of the Rock People," he said, trying to gain time. Maybe he'd find the way out of it by the time he came back. There was no need to worry but for the nearest future. In a moon from now, many things may have changed.

"Also, you can't decide on any of that without the formal agreement of the Wolf and Beaver's Clan councils," declared one of the women, her hands on her hips.

"Of course!"

"The bear may leave the area by then," said someone, disappointed.

"Not likely."

Involuntarily, he glanced at the boy again, meeting the firm gaze of the dark eyes, seeing none of the previous uncertainty.

"I would rather do it as soon as we can." The boy's voice did not tremble anymore, ringing clearly in the flickering darkness.

He tried to suppress his grin, proud of the young cub against his will.

"Well, we'll see what we can do."

In the corner of his eye, he saw the Porcupine girl gone, dancing again in the inner circle, her back turned to him. Oh well, he thought, shrugging.

CHAPTER 9

The footprint was huge and so wide he could put both his palms into the mud congregating in the main cavity if he pressed them tightly against each other, and still there would be some space left. What gigantic creature would walk on these feet, and why upright? No regular bear, surely. Unless he was an *uki*, or a flinty giant, one of the Evil Twin's creations that were reported to roam the land since the times immemorial.

Shivering, Tekeni rose to his feet, his gaze glued to the smaller cavities left by the sharpest of claws, of that he was sure.

"Seems like your friend did not leave the area after all," said Two Rivers, measuring the print in his turn. "An impressive creature."

Tekeni just nodded, not trusting his voice to sound firm enough.

"He has been around recently but not very recently, if all we have are those prints and nothing else." The older man got to his feet. "Two dawns, I would say. Or worse." He shrugged. "Well, let us hope we'll manage to tempt him back."

"To tempt him?"

"Yes, of course." The squinting eyes measured him, flickering with challenge. "Let us hear how you would do that."

"I… well…" Tekeni frowned, trying to think. "We need meat. If he thinks he can get something to eat, he would come."

"Yes, a promise of a good meal would make it worth of his trouble. But…" The man looked around, frowning. "This is not a good place to ambush such a fast moving creature of much age and experience. Judging by the size of these prints, your challenge has both qualities and more, so we will need to outsmart him, if we want you to come back with its magnificent pelt and the claws, won't we?" His frown deepening, Two Rivers looked around once again.

"What's wrong with this place?" asked Tekeni, mainly to prolong the conversation. Everything that kept them from proceeding seemed like a good thing to do now. "I can hide here in the woods or behind this cluster of rocks and shoot him when he comes."

Two Rivers licked his finger and brought it up in a showy manner.

"The wind," he said, raising his eyebrows. "Coming the way it's coming now, it will give your presence away before the beast will as much as glance at our offering. We don't want it feasting on you instead, do we?"

His stomach tightened so painfully, he almost shut his eyes, feeling his cheeks beginning to burn. However, the older man's laughter rang lightly, encouraging.

"Don't feel bad. You are learning, and you are asking good questions. That's why I explain it all and ask for your opinions. Not to ridicule you, but to make you learn. If I do it all by myself, you will not learn half of it."

He turned to study the print once again, and Tekeni appreciated the gesture, knowing that the man was allowing him to calm down in privacy, to think it all over.

"What we would need is a more open space," Two Rivers went on, as though talking to himself. "At least fifty or so paces from the woods. This way you will be able to see and shoot with nothing to obscure your vision. Like this clearing with the spring we left not long ago."

"But the clearing has no rocks, no cliffs. Where will I hide?"

Fearing to hear that he would have no hiding place at all, Tekeni took a deep breath, preparing for the worst. This man had been so good to him since the trouble with Yeentso, helpful, supportive, kind. Yet, it was he who suggested that he, Tekeni, should go hunting the giant grizzled bear instead of five deer. So maybe all he wanted was to see the show, the spectacular death of the stupid youth torn to pieces by the bloodthirsty monster. Could he really trust the man the rest of the town distrusted so openly?

He bit his lips. At the time, it seemed like an appropriate solution, a beautiful alternative. Yet, most of the people thought differently, with Seketa being plainly terrified, shooting furious glances at the man through the whole discussion of details that interrupted the dancing. She clearly did not trust Two Rivers, or his judgment, and there were many who shared her doubts. Too many people were killed or injured by the fierce, bad-tempered grizzled bears, too many to count. And there were only a handful who owed the magnificent furs to soften their bunks and the beautiful necklaces of giant claws to adorn their chests, all of them grown-up, experienced hunters and warriors. No youth had boasted such possession.

The thought of Seketa brought the familiar wave of warmth. What was she doing now? It had been five dawns since they had left the town, crossing the Northern River and wandering its western banks, seeking the creature. Five dawns of peace and quiet. They had been very careful, making sure to leave no marks, to listen intently, and not only because of the bear. The warriors' parties may be lurking, on their way to this or that raid. Two lone hunters would be an easy target, maintained Two Rivers, as they hid their canoe in a small inlet. Armed with bows and knives only, they could offer no decent resistance. There was a reason why the hunting was done in large, well-armed groups.

"We return to our camp and hope to find something worth shooting at on our way." Two Rivers was on his feet again, looking resolute.

"A bait?"

"Yes, a bait. We will offer your creature a good meal, served prettily and with a great reverence. He won't be able to refuse."

"Will we drag it all the way to the clearing?" asked Tekeni, unable to even fake laughter, the memory of the giant prints clouding his mind, making it fuzzy, paralyzed with fear. Oh,

Mighty Spirits!

"Yes, we will drag it to the clearing, and we will build a small, unobtrusive fence. And we will make an offering to the spirits to make the wind stay the way it was for long enough."

Tekeni blinked. "A fence?"

"Yes, a fence." His companion's face lit with an amused smile. "Unless you plan to face your projected adversary with no cover at all."

"Oh, yes, I understand." Embarrassed, Tekeni busied himself with inspecting his bow. "I need to make sure it's in a good shape," he muttered.

"Yes, you will have to make sure of that. A torn bowstring would see you dead very quickly." Climbing the trail with the practiced skill of a good hunter, Two Rivers turned his head, grinning. "I know how you feel, but I do believe you can do it. I wouldn't bother to drag you into this enterprise if I did not, would I?"

"It can be quite a sight, they say," muttered Tekeni, picking his step between the slippery rocks adorning the bank.

"What?"

"The bear tearing someone apart." He studied the muddy ground, seeing the trails left by multitudes of smaller creatures.

"Oh, yes, of course. I've seen this, too. That hunter did make it, though. He was a resourceful man, played it dead for the mighty bear to get over his initial rage, then used his knife when the creature paid less attention. By the time we had come within a shooting range he was still alive." The man kicked a stone, grinning at the memory. "Bleeding mightily, I must admit, but living to sport quite a few impressive scars."

"Who was it? Do I know this man?" asked Tekeni, forgetting his own plight for a moment.

"No, you don't. He was killed by the enemies a few summers later. It was before you were captured."

For some time, they proceeded in silence, the light atmosphere gone again. On what side of the Great Sparkling Water was this man killed? wondered Tekeni. Must be on the other, *his*, side, judging by his companion's suddenly hostile silence. He pressed his lips tight.

"When you will be behind the fence, waiting for the bear to come, you will be scared out of your senses," said Two Rivers, when they emerged from the woods and stood upon a high bank, facing the river. "It's nothing to be ashamed of. Everyone would feel that, whether they would admit it later or not. The trick is not to lose your presence of mind. If you start to think of the ways to get away, you succumb to panic, and you are done for." A glance shot at Tekeni was piercing but kind. "Concentrate on your mission. Remember what you came to do. Think about that and nothing else. Realize that there will be no way back. You came to kill the creature, and this is your only way out. Put all your thoughts into the first shot and think of nothing else. This way, you have a chance. The first shot is most likely to seal your fate. Or at least, spare you a lot of pain and running around."

"Did you do this?" asked Tekeni, feeling his lips dry and quivering. Trying to appear as calm as he could, he kicked a stone and watched it rolling down the cliff.

"Yes, I did. It was also a sort of a challenge, an attempt to prove my worth. But I wasn't as young as you are. I'd been to a few raids by then, so I was sure I could manage." A chuckle. "That confidence melted away by the time I was half way through the waiting."

"And then what happened?"

"I shot it, and I still don't remember how. I was too terrified to pay attention. But at some point, when the beast was roaring and charging toward me and I was sure I was done for, I noticed that it had been roaring strangely, in a sort of a gurgle because of all this blood gushing through its mouth. At this point, I realized that I was safe, safe to jump around and shoot all the rest of my arrows until it was dead. It was an incredible feeling, well worth the anguished waiting and the fear."

"So you do have a magnificent fur adorning your bunk?" asked Tekeni, breathless.

"Yes, of course."

"And the claws?"

The man shrugged. "I do have a double row of those, but I don't wear them. Something to do with a certain dream and my guiding spirit."

"Oh."

He watched the river raging far below. *Would he ever cross it again? Would he live to see more than a few more dawns, until they managed to shoot something to lure the bear?*

"If you manage to do that and live, you will take a great step toward the acceptance of the town." The man seemed to be also immersed in studying the opposite bank. "Five hides are just a payment. Not a step into bettering your life. While a fur of a huge brown bear is a statement. A statement of a proud person who would not be put in his place. They keep saying that you are in the wrong, because you don't follow the rules, but let me tell you something. You are not in the wrong, because this is who you are. You cannot change. You are not a person to just blend into the background. You are standing out, and this is what angers many people. Your origins are only a part of the problem. Had you been humble and quiet, anxious to belong, you would have blended nicely, accepted like any other average person, local or not."

A mirthless grin stretched the man's lips, but his eyes still wandered the distant shores.

"You are not that sort of a person, and people like Yeentso or those youths who tried to pick a fight with you on the day of the ceremony, and many, many others, even your Clan Mothers, are sensing that, and oh, Mighty Spirits, it angers them greatly. They are desperate to put you in your place, by all means they have." The measuring gaze turned to Tekeni, resting upon him, reflecting half amused appreciation. "Well, take this advice from me, boy. If you can't blend, don't try. Stand out and be yourself. They wanted you to get them five hides, counting on you exhausting yourself by trying to comply with the request, remaining poor for some summers, paying your debts instead of gathering possessions? A sure way to put you in your place. A good solution. Well, they won't get this! Instead, you are going out and bringing them the magnificent fur of the huge grizzled bear. A payment worthy of your crime. You almost killed a man, a man older and stronger than you, and you go and kill a bear, another worthy adversary, to pay for this crime. People will hate you all the same, but they will be afraid of you now, too, because you will not be a foreign cub of no significance anymore. After this, many would pause to think before crossing your path. Those youths from the ceremony, and the cowards like Yeentso." The piercing gaze bore at him, full of meaning. "You will not be loved and cherished, but you will be respected. And admired, too, if you will go on proving yourself the way you feel fit, and not the way they want you to do it."

Shaking his head, the older man turned back toward the river, kicking a stone in his turn.

"You have potential. And your path will be different, more difficult to walk, but you should walk it proudly, with no misgivings, because this is what you are." The smile was back, with a twinkle creeping into the dark gaze. "And it will make it easier to get the prettiest girl as well. Now, this Beaver Clan girl is not a coward like Yeentso or those boys who are coveting her. She is smart and courageous, and she had evidently been sensing the same qualities in you, arriving to her own conclusions. Some women are good at that, you know? They can smell it in the man, can see who would make a good father to their children." Laughing, he raised his hands as Tekeni tried to protest. "Don't turn all red on me, protesting your innocence. I heard what she said, admonishing this other youth, and you've been evidently watching her while she danced. That youth was incensed for a reason."

"Many are watching her," muttered Tekeni, his throat dry, lips having difficulty forming the words.

"Oh, yes, she is a pretty little thing and very upright. I would advise you to keep away from trouble, because she will bring you trouble. But this would go against my previous advice.

Don't try to blend into the background. Kill the grizzled bear, court the prettiest girl, fight for her if you have to. You can't pretend to be an average person because this is not what you are."

Tekeni's head reeled, and he welcomed the wind as it tore at them, strengthening with the sun rushing toward its resting place.

"You are like this, right?" he said quietly, watching the deepening shadows. "You are not blending. But..." He bit his lower lip, compelled to say it, but afraid all the same. "You are not happy. You are standing out, and you are following your truth, but... Is it worth it?"

The amused smile was back, stretching the man's lips, filling the prominent eyes with a spark of appreciation. "Oh, this is a difficult question to answer. But yes, it has its price, not to be just an average person." A shrug. "Is it worth it? Maybe yes, maybe not. Depends on what you want out of life. You are still very young, and you have time to think, to sort yourself out. I don't think you will be like me, but who knows." Another shrug, a widening grin. "I'm a mess, boy. Much worse than you are. You had a happy life and happy family back with your people. I can tell. Your troubles began with your captivity. But mine? Oh, mine began before I was born."

"How so?" Wide-eyed, Tekeni peered at the man beside him, taking in the proud profile, the strong cheekbones, the high brow, the long, eagle-like nose. Good hunter, good warrior, a prominent man everyone talked about, and yet a strange person that not many liked or trusted.

"Oh, it's difficult to tell. There was a prophecy, a dream of a girl who conceived without having a man in her life. The Turtle Clan accepted it, but she kept insisting, her dreams getting more powerful, until people started to believe her. The child was supposed to belong to the Great Spirits, conceived miraculously. They say the Grandmother of the Clan tried to get rid of the baby when it was born. She was not successful. She came back, awed, refusing to tell anyone about what happened."

The mirthless grin was back. "Try to grow up surrounded by such an air of mystery and stay sane. With everyone looking at you, awed and suspicious, expecting you to do what? To perform a miracle? Not the childhood I would wish on anyone. And it doesn't get any better." The man's eyes left the darkening bank, traveling downwards, following the strong current below their feet. "I wish I didn't have to return every time I leave. I wish I could start anew, in a place where no one had heard a thing about me."

Mesmerized by the toneless voice, Tekeni shivered. "What did the prophecy say?" It seemed that the man was relating someone else's story.

"Nothing that you, or anyone else, would care to hear or understand."

"It must be important if they are still expecting something from you."

"They are expecting from me nothing but to fit, to do as I'm told, to be the part of the herd, going after our leaders, asking no questions. They want me to swallow their lies and thank them humbly, time after time. That's all that is expected from me. Nothing to do with prophecies."

"They want that from everyone."

"Yes, they do."

"What's wrong with that?"

"Nothing, except that our leaders don't know what they are doing, rushing from one thing to another, warring on everyone, eager to take offense and make more enemies. They are behaving no better than youths of your age, grabbing their knives, or their playing sticks, at every opportunity." The fleeting smile was amused again, gone before noticed. "They are as mindless as a forest deer, and they can't see beyond the tips of their noses."

"The leaders of the town?"

"Of the whole nation!" Two Rivers flopped his arms in the air, exhaling loudly. "And the Rock People are no better. And the others too." He glanced at Tekeni, his grin back in place.

"But don't feel too good with yourself just yet, because I'm certain your people are no better. You said they war on each other, don't they?"

"They don't war on each other, no clan against clan, or town against town. But if by 'my people' you mean all the people from the other side of the Great Sparkling Water, then yes, of course, they war against other nations."

"Stupidly at that!"

Tekeni felt the air escaping his lungs. "Not stupidly. They war against the enemies, against the people who want to destroy their towns and their fields and their way of life."

"What's different about their way of life?"

"Oh, well, there are differences." He clenched his teeth, enraged by the cold amusement the man's grin radiated. "There are! We are the People of the Flint, but our neighbors, the People of the Standing Stone, are such an annoying nation. It's like having a bunch of cheeky squirrels by one's side, always there, trying to steal, ready to bite. And then, there are the Onondaga, the People of the Hills, such violent, arrogant people!"

"And they are different from your Flint People how?"

"I don't know. But they are, they are different. And they are evil, too."

"You don't know how, but they are different and evil." The glance shot at Tekeni was openly derisive, the lifted eyebrows making him wish to break something. "It seems to me that you are ready to be a part of the herd, treading as mindlessly as the next person, repeating what is said to you, asking no questions." Turning away, the man shrugged. "Good for you."

Struggling to keep calm, Tekeni pressed his lips. "But why do you think you know better than our leaders, Mothers of the Clans, or the elders? How do you know the enemies are not evil, not different?" The silence of his companion made him feel stupid. "Yes, well, maybe there is not much difference. Like you said, I should know better. But still, other nations are sending raiding parties to our towns, our villages. Should we do nothing? Let them burn our homes, kill our men, and take women and children?"

"We are doing that, too." The man picked a stone, weighed it on his palm, then sent it flying down the cliff in a perfect arch. "When you lived in your town of those Flint People, you feared our raiding parties. Now if your Flint People came here, firing fire-arrows into your longhouse, will you sit by, or will you join the defenders of your current place of living?"

"I'll join the defenders, I suppose," muttered Tekeni, not sure what he would actually do in such a situation. It would be wonderful to hear the tongue of his people outside the town's fence.

"And there you have it. We offend them, they offend us. They attack, we retaliate. Or the other way around. We war and war for summers, for longer than anyone could remember, and we have less and less people and less food to sustain a normal way of living." Another stone went flying, following the first in the same impressive half circle. "And there are many of us. Four nations on our side of the Great Lake, and how many on yours?"

Tekeni hesitated. "Five."

The man acknowledged it with the nod. "Everyone warring against everyone, with no order and no rules. As though we are nothing but mindless creatures, with no ability to think or to speak our minds. Where do you think it will lead?"

"I don't know." Tekeni frowned, sensing where the man's questions were heading but unable to fight the urge to argue. "In the end, someone will win, I suppose."

"In what way?"

"The others will perish, or they will be too weak to send any more raiding parties."

"More chances that all our nations will perish. And not at the hand of each other. The starvation and the diseases will do the work."

He remembered Little Falls and the horrible winter three summers ago. The cold was terrible, and there was not enough firewood to warm the longhouses, and not enough food to fill people's bellies. The warriors were busy warring the whole summer, with no time to hunt enough meat to stock for the winter, or to catch enough fish. And the women and children were afraid of the raids which, indeed, kept coming, and so not enough firewood was gathered, and hardly an adequate amount of corn stored.

He clenched his fists tight, fighting the familiar wave of dread and desperation. The illness spread like a wind, making people cough and burn with fever and gasp for air. The oldest dwellers of longhouses and the youngest were the first to succumb, dying quietly, with no power left in their bodies even to cry out. Others battled the bad spirits, drinking potions that the healers prepared, inhaling the sacred smoke. Some took longer to recover than the others. Some died despite the potions and the prayers. Tekeni's mother and brother among them. She had been heavy with child, her inner powers insisting on the attempt to sustain her unborn baby, failing to save them both.

As for his twin brother? He felt the salty taste in his mouth, where his teeth bit into his lower lip. He had always been the stronger of the two, as though having sucked the power belonging to his brother while still in their mother's belly. He overheard one of the elders saying that once, talking to others, unaware that he, Tekeni, was around and listening. They said that if the miraculous pair, the twin sons of the War Chief, were destined to fulfill the prophecy, the other twin would have to find the way to regain the strength taken by his brother.

With a desperate effort, he pushed the memories away, back into the dark corners of his soul, concentrating on the river and the calming presence of the strange man beside him.

"The disease spreads more readily when people are hungry," the man was saying, his eyes again on the darkness of the opposite bank, wandering unknown places. "And the hunger comes with the neglected fields, when the women are spending more time watching for invaders and running back into the town upon every real or false alarm. Also, when the men are busy warring, instead of hunting and fishing. Then many people are dying through the cold winter moons."

"Yes, I know that." He had a hard time recognizing his own voice. "But what can you do? How can you change it?"

A meaningless question, just to take his mind off the memory of the dim, smoke-filled corridor with the dying fires, the groans of his mother filling his ears, the stench of the blood and some other discharges penetrating his nostrils with every breath, smoke stinging his eyes, coughing too, fighting the nausea, dizzy, but not dying, not like his brother.

"Me? Well, alone, I cannot do much." Apparently oblivious of his young companion's agitation, Two Rivers shook his head. "But if the people were prepared to listen, to help, to cooperate, then we might manage to do something."

"How?"

"Call the meeting of the nations and talk about all this."

"What?" Forgetting his own plight, Tekeni peered at the man, astounded. "You mean to talk to them? To talk to the enemy?"

"Yes, to talk to those people who are not so different from us and who may prove not as evil as we think they are." Two River's hearty laughter shook the air, as he turned around, openly amused. "You should see yourself now, boy. Eyes as round as two plates and the mouth to match, round and gasping. Have you seen a ghost? A forest giant?"

"I..." He tried to collect his thoughts, embarrassed. "I don't think they would want to talk."

"Well, until we try we would never know, would we?" Another bout of hearty laughter. "Well, wolf cub, let us go back to our camp, to rest and prepare our plans for tomorrow. We don't have all the time in the world. Two, three dawns and I want us to sail back. This restful journey is a welcome diversion, but all good things must come to an end." Turning around, he began descending the trail, still chuckling, enjoying himself.

He must be insane, thought Tekeni, following, his thoughts in a jumble. To talk to the enemy, any enemy? What a thought!

CHAPTER 10

A gust of wind pounced out of nowhere, scattering the carefully tucked pile of husks, sending them rustling all over the place. Stifling a curse, Seketa tried to push them back together without getting up, the tip of her moccasin proving not as effective as her hands would have been.

"I told you we should have put them in a basket," said one of the girls, frowning at the mess.

"Then do it," Tindee's eyes flashed as she tossed her head high. "Why are you staring at it? Pick up the husks and put them in a basket. You can use mine, if you want to." She narrowed her eyes. "Don't wait for anyone else to do it. It won't happen."

"Why me?" muttered the girl angrily, yet as another glare flashed, she dropped onto her knees, collecting the wet leaves.

"We are almost done here," said Seketa, picking the last of the maize. She wiped her brow, then glanced at the sun. "I hope they are not planning to grind them today."

"Trust them to make us grind corn until Father Sun goes to rest behind the western field." Tindee held her half-naked cob at arm's length, frowning at it. "I'm so tired, I can barely see."

Seketa grinned against her will. "What's new about that?"

"Oh, nothing, nothing. Except that you missed a lot of good time while sleeping snugly between your blankets."

"Like what?"

"Like good time, sister." Stressing her last word, Tindee looked up, eyes flickering. "You seem to think that life is about work and ceremonies and nothing else. But you are wrong, you know? There is more to it than being the best behaved person in the whole town. You will turn into one of the Clan Mothers if you are not careful."

"And what is wrong with that?" Now it was Seketa's turn to frown. "What's wrong with being a Clan Mother? Yes, I want to be in the Clan Council when my time comes. I want to influence things. I want to be involved. Why wouldn't I?"

"You want to tell people what to do, that's what you want." Tindee's laughter rang prettily as she ignored the glances of two youths who went by. Pushing her hair away with a self-conscious gesture, she stretched. "I wish we could just nibble on this maize ear, instead of grinding its seeds all day long. They should make us grind the second harvest of the white corn, not this one. The sweet green corn is a waste to make into flour."

"We still want to eat cakes and buns on the Green Corn Ceremony," said one of the girls. "You can't just nibble on raw maize through the days of the festivities."

"Yes, I can," insisted Tindee. "If it means no grinding corn for the next few days, I'm prepared to go hungry."

"With so many of our men going out to raid the enemy lands instead of hunting, you may go hungry for quite a long time," muttered one of the older women, sighing.

Hunting! Seketa's heart missed a beat, caught unprepared. For the past few days, she let no thought of adventures outside the town enter her mind, whether those of the warriors who had left five dawns ago, or those who went on wild hunting challenges. Every time she remembered the night of the War Dance, her stomach would twist, constricting violently, making her wish to lean against something. To track a huge brown bear, to come against it face to face, a monster who was not afraid of the hunters, making their hunting grounds into his territory? Oh Mighty Spirits, but a handful of seasoned men would dare to try such a feat. Even less would come back to tell their story. None of them youths of no experience!

She clenched her teeth tight. It was impossible, unachievable, a plain waste of a life. He may have been just a wild, foreign boy, but he had been a member of their town, now a Wyandot man, formally adopted. Unruly, short-tempered, but a good person too, with his shoulders nicely broad and his eyes large and sparkling. Not silly and not boring like the other boys. Proud, strange, fascinating, with even his accent pleasing the ear, and his fingers soft, hesitant, brushing against her cheek, confident and afraid at the same time.

She shivered, then frowned against her rising anger. Why, why did Two Rivers have to be there on that fateful evening, seemingly helpful but not really. The fur of the killer-bear was worth more than five hides, more than ten hides even, but it was not worth this boy's life, curse the damn man into the realm of the Evil Twin.

"Stop dreaming, sister." Tindee's voice broke into her thoughts, welcomed against her bubbling anger. "It looks as though you've been sleeping not so well, after all."

"I'm not, I did not," protested Seketa, feeling ridiculously guilty. "I slept well."

"Of course." Her friend's eyes sparkled suggestively. "You haven't been thinking about stupid boys trying to hunt grizzled bears, have you?"

As the other girls began to giggle, Seketa gasped, her anger splashing now with force that startled her more than it did her companions.

"And what if I have? Does any of this concern you?" She glared at them, meeting their surprised gazes. "And he is not stupid, just so you know. He was offered a challenge, and he accepted it, like a great hunter and warrior should. He will come back, carrying the magnificent pelt and the claws, you just wait and see. And then you will be the ones feeling stupid, for doubting him and for saying bad things about him!" She sprang to her feet, snatching the heavy basket. "We are done here, aren't we? We are doing nothing but gossiping now."

The silence behind her back hung as she stormed off, trying to walk proudly, with her back straight, despite the heavy basket. How dared they, those fat, stupid rodents! Sitting there so idly, laughing and saying silly things, accusing him of stupidity, when he had been so incredibly brave? What did they understand?

Slowing her step, she dove into the shadow of the nearest longhouse, pausing to catch her breath. The fires beside the high wall were almost extinguished, but the dark embers still radiated heat, not helping one to feel cooler. With cooking usually done in the mornings, those fires were of no use through the hot summer afternoons.

These days more than ever, she reflected. With the fruits of the first harvest picked, the women of the town were now too busy preparing for the second most important ceremony in all four seasons – the Green Corn celebration. Shelling maize ears and grinding corn into flour was only a part of the frantic activity.

Nearing the facade of the building, she paused again, putting her basket down and eyeing the glaring print it left on her palm. The stupid thing was really too heavy. Trying to improve her grip on the woven handle, she didn't pay attention to the muffled voices until they penetrated her mind, making her concentrate. Low and halting, they made her feel strange, as though she had been eavesdropping.

"They won't be back until the moon turns into a sliver. Ten dawns or more, I would say."

The man's voice made Seketa wince as she recognized it, the well familiar voice of her cousin's husband. He was healing well, she knew, feeling better, much better than he chose to present to the people of the town. There was no need to keep to his bunk in the longhouse anymore, still he didn't go out, preferring to be pampered and fussed about, was Seketa's private conclusion.

"Not ten dawns surely." The woman's voice cut him sharply, impatient. "They received food for less than this period of time."

"And what does it tell you, sister?" Yeentso's laughter rang hollowly, full of contempt.

"It tells me that they have food for ten days only!" said the woman angrily.

"Oh you women think that you can control us so easily, eh?" Another outburst of derisive laughter made Seketa as angry as the woman sounded. "Well, they will use your food carefully, keeping the bag with the sweetened maize flour to the very end. They will eat it sparingly and will have no trouble staying away for whatever period they would feel fit. You women are too full of yourself. You think you can control us all the time. But it is not so."

There were a few heartbeats of furious silence.

"I will bring this matter up on the next gathering of the Clans Councils," said the woman in the end, voice shaking with rage. "I wonder what the Mothers of the Clans would say about this possibility taken into consideration before the raiding parties set off."

"They know. Of course, they know. They are not as simple as you are." The man laughed again. "But let us not argue about this. If the raiding party comes late it will serve your goals well, will it not, sister? What are you up to?"

Soundlessly, Seketa placed her basket upon the ground, wondering why she kept listening. It was not the decent thing to do, and she could not explain her lingering here if questioned, eavesdropping on the people of her longhouse. Scowling, she stared at the basket, massaging her palm. She had every right to stop and rest. The damn thing was really too heavy.

"Ten dawns, you say," repeated the woman more calmly. "Well, it can be enough. Maybe."

"Enough for what?"

Her voice filled with venom again. "Enough to make the disgusting troublemaker wish he had never been born."

Seketa caught her breath.

"The boy?" asked Yeentso, seemingly as surprised. "Why would you hate him?"

"Not the boy!" cried out the woman. "Why would I care for the filthy cub? He is your problem, not mine."

"He is." The growling tone in the man's voice made Seketa

shiver in the warm afternoon breeze.

"And he is growing stronger as we speak. He'll give you more trouble as the time comes." The woman paused. "If he comes back having killed the beast, he will gain much admiration. He won't be an insignificant cub anymore."

"He won't kill the bear!"

"With Two Rivers' help, who knows?" The woman's voice rang contemplatively, and Seketa could imagine the well-defined eyebrows climbing high above the coldly sparkling eyes.

She knew the woman well, a prominent member of the Porcupine Clan's longhouse, a future part of this clan's council for certain, always asked to organize sacred ceremonies and games, having been oh-so-very efficient and sharp-minded, married to a prominent man, and Yeentso's only sister. A beautiful woman, remembered Seketa, but a cold, unfriendly one. If you were sent to help her, you knew there would be no friendly treatment. And there was some sort of a scandal connected to her and no other than the notorious Two Rivers. Another brilliant mind bent on no good. She frowned.

"And this is the man you are after, sister, aren't you?" Yeentso's voice brought her back from her reverie.

"I'm not after anyone," said the woman sharply. "But yes, I would love to see this man disgraced. He brings nothing but discord to our town. We would be better off without him." More silence. "I spoke to my husband's uncle in the Town Council."

"And?"

"He is prepared to bring the matter up before his peers."

"What matter?"

"Of Two Rivers' cowardice and his way of avoiding doing his duty."

"Oh, the raid."

"Yes, the raid. He was among the chosen. He participated in the War Dance." The woman's voice shook. "His excuse not to come along was laughable. The bear hunting, I ask you? Chaperoning a stupid boy of no significance? Does he think this town's people have no eyes to see and no minds to speak?"

"The War Chief agreed. He gave the man his blessing to do so. He even praised him for his willingness to help the filthy cub."

"Oh, please!" Her voice peaked again. "I was there. I saw it all. Two Rivers was the one to suggest it in the first place, and he put it in the way the stupid boy could not have refused without losing his face forever. He tricked them all. The War Chief, of all people, should have seen through him, but he did not. He always liked the man." She paused again. "But it is not so with the Town Council, or with the leading people of some clans. Two Rivers is nothing but a nuisance, and the councils know it. He'll bring our settlement, our whole nation, no good."

A gust of wind made Seketa shiver, cold upon her sweaty neck. She began lifting her basket.

"What changed? What is different now? How is it all connected to the raiding party this man did not join?"

"The War Chief," she said simply. "He will not be here to throw his weight behind the man when the Town Council would discuss his inadequate behavior. Many of the prominent men, warriors, mostly his friends, are not here to back him up. It would be easy to provoke him into saying stupid things, doing stupid deeds."

Yeentso's sudden laughter made Seketa jump. "Oh, sister, you have a devious mind. Remind me not to cross your path or leave you angry for longer than a dawn or so."

The heavy basket cutting into her palms, Seketa began easing away, anxious to put as much distance between her and the place she was not supposed to be at.

Some people were horrible, just horrible, she thought, making her way toward the second longhouse belonging to her clan. Two Rivers was a strange man, annoying in his disrespectful attitude toward the old ways. Still, he did not deserve to be made to wish he had never been born, not by a filthy manipulation, because of something that he did on an impulse. Whether the projected hunting was a good or a bad idea, he was there, helping the Wolf Clan boy, making sure he succeeded without getting killed, of that she was sure.

Oh, benevolent spirits, oh, the Right-Handed Twin, please let him succeed, she whispered, shutting her eyes. *Please, let nothing bad happen to him.*

CHAPTER 11

Two Rivers felt the need to take a deep breath, his stomach heavy, twisting uneasily. The torn carcass below their feet seemed to dominate the clearing, glaring at them with its missing lower parts and the ravaged stomach. Whoever had enjoyed this meal through the night must have been a real monster.

He glanced at the youth beside him.

"Our friend seemed to find our offering worthy of his time," he said, mostly because he felt that something needed to be said. Something light, non-committal.

The boy nodded, his lips pressed, eyes glued to the half-eaten carcass, face lacking in color. Taking in the tense shoulders and the lifelessly hanging hands, Two Rivers frowned, fighting the wave of compassion. He wasn't sure he would switch places with this youth if offered. It was one thing to think about the upcoming feat, to dominate the fear and get ready to face the monster, but quite another to watch the actual deeds of the giant beast. How could a normal forest creature eat so much in one night, tearing so viciously at the flesh of a mature deer? But maybe he was an *uki*, after all, a wandering giant, not belonging to the forest at all but to the wicked creations of the Evil Twin.

"He is quite a large creature," he said, compelled to keep talking. "But his size doesn't matter. One good shot will take the monster down like a silly squirrel."

"Yes," muttered the boy, not moving and not taking his eyes off the clearing.

Two Rivers sighed. "You don't have to do this, if you don't want to. No one will know if we found that bear or not."

The unanimated figure came to life at once. "You will know, and I will know." The youth turned sharply, eyes haunted but flashing, the colorless lips steady, not quivering. "I will go down now, and I will wait for him to come back. He will come, won't he?"

"Yes, he will. Somewhere around early afternoon, I assume. He would be hungry again, and he would want to finish his meal."

"But I should be down there now, shouldn't I? In case he comes earlier."

"Yes, now it's time to hide behind your fence."

This time, Two Rivers suppressed his sigh, not wishing to weaken the youth's resolve. The boy was destined to go through it all while waiting down there. From the bottomless fear, through the urge to crawl away, to the resolution to die bravely, he would feel it all, wavering between elation and desperation, wishing for the ordeal to be over, one way or another.

He remembered his own trial too well, although close to ten summers had passed since it had been his time to crouch behind the pitifully small, low fence.

"Don't lie behind the fence the whole day. Stretch your limbs from time to time. You can sit or even walk a little. Don't get your muscles cramped by doing absolutely nothing. You will need your body alert, your instincts sharp. If you get sleepy you are done for." He reached for the youth's bow. "Let me check this thing again."

"It's good. I checked it three times through the night. And the arrows, too. They are all in good shape." The youth looked up resolutely, his eyebrows meeting each other across the handsome, well-defined face. "You did so many good things for me. I'm grateful. I will never forget." His frown deepened. "I should go."

Curiously touched, Two Rivers did not try to suppress his smile. "I'll be waiting for you here, and may the benevolent spirits and the Right-Handed Twin himself watch over you, enjoying your bravery."

He watched the youth's back disappearing down the invisible trail, appreciating the lightness of his step. Oh, the cub was a brave little thing; and proud, oh yes. It would be a terrible waste if he was destined to die on the clearing this afternoon.

Shielding his eyes against the rising sun, he watched the opposite hill and the sharp cliff protruding out of the brilliant green. A much better vantage point, he reflected. And much closer, too. Not a bad distance for an arrow to make its way toward the clearing.

He glanced at the torn carcass, squinting to see the fence better. They had built it on the previous day, after shooting a deer and dragging it all the way to this place, careless of the blood and the splattered meat, anxious to make their trail as attractive as possible.

Placing their bait in the middle of the clearing, they then checked the wind, and praying it would not change in the course of the next day, they began working on the fence, placing it at about twenty paces away from the carcass.

Twenty paces was a good range for a lethal shot. Any farther and the arrow might miss, deflected by the wind, not to stick deeply enough to reach the beast's vital organs. A good strategy that the boy appreciated with no argument, agreeing that his hiding place should be located in a closer proximity, taking away his chance of escaping in the case of a bad shot.

Not mentioning it at all, they worked on the twisted pine branches in silence, constructing the meager shelter. Five paces long and half a human's height, it offered some cover, but no protection.

"Remember that brown bears cannot see well," repeated Two Rivers several times. "Don't make sharp movements, and the beast might not notice you even if you stood at your full height. Rise slowly, aim carefully, then shoot. After that, be ready to run really fast, preferably shooting as you go."

He remembered the boy nodding thoughtfully, braiding the twigs, fastening them to each other, immersed in what he had been doing. If he was sick with fear, he did not show it, although Two Rivers' experienced eyes could discern the signs, the tension in the stiff shoulders, the slightly trembling palms, the overly concentrated gaze.

He shook the memory off, watching the clearing, still vacant, washed by the strengthening sunlight, with no noticeable activity of humans or animals alike. The boy should have reached the place by now, but there was no sight of him, and Two Rivers was ready to bet the best of his birds' traps against the claim that the boy was descending the path exaggeratedly slow, prolonging his walk as much as he could.

Again, his eyes drifted to the opposite hill. To reach it and make himself comfortable upon the protruding cliff would take time. He would have to make a considerable detour, to circumvent the clearing and the adjusting trails. The smell of a human might spoil it all, might cause the bear they had made such tremendous efforts to lure, turn suspicious, might make it more aggressive or frighten it away.

He measured the sun, then shrugged and got to his feet. The trip would give him something to do, and it would also put him within a shooting range, just in case. Of course, one was never to interrupt this sort of a challenge. The boy had to face his fate and best it, or perish while trying. He had to do it all by himself. And yet…

He shrugged. This hunt was his idea, and the boy was truly too young for such a trial. He could shoot quite well, of that he was sure now, letting the boy hunt the deer on the day before. Still, there was a glaring difference between hunting and being hunted, and in the case of a surprised, possibly wounded and blinded with rage giant, the hunter could turn into the hunted in a matter of a heartbeat. And then it would be the real test for the youth who had seen no battles and no real hunting trips. If he panicked, he would be done for, and even if not, his chances were painfully slim.

Making his way along the trees lining the side of the opposite hill, careful to make no sounds, Two Rivers grinned, enjoying the walk and the calm morning chirps. There would be no harm in being able to help should the matters take a turn for the worse. The boy deserved that for all the bravery he had shown so far. And also…

He frowned, unwilling to remember the dream. Last night it had been bad again, with the old vision returning, more vivid than ever, so real he could remember its smells and its sounds, the roaring of the invisible waterfalls, the rustling of the trees, the voices of the people, and the peculiar accent of their speech. He had dreamed about that place before, but with fewer details, with no sounds and no smells.

There must have been the growling of the falls somewhere out of sight, for he had always known that the dream was happening a short walk from a very large river and its lethal rapids, but he never remembered actually hearing it, while this time it had been distinctive, ominously near, promising danger. He would be required to jump into these falls, he knew. It was some sort of a test, to prove something, to make himself heard.

Yet, what kind of a test could that be? he had wondered, as he lay on his back in the grayish predawn mist, soaked with sweat, although in this time of the night, it was actually chilly enough to make one use his blanket. No one could jump into this sort of rapids and come out alive. Not in this place. So it must have been a way to kill a person, a prisoner – *had he been captured?* – instead of the customary gauntlet along the carpet of glowing embers. Those foreigners must have had different ways. And they were foreigners, oh yes, easy to tell by the sound of their words, understandable but barely, just a strange blabbering to him.

He pushed the memory away, his sense of well-being disappearing. The accursed dream had always been there, returning every now and then, disturbing in the way it repeated itself, presented in more and more detail, gaining power with the passing of time. *As though the time to do that was nearing.* He had been successful in his efforts to dismiss it, but never for good, never entirely. And oh Mighty Spirits, but this night it hit him with such vividness, such realness, leaving him breathless, shamefully afraid. He had been there, on that foreign shore. *He had been there!* Surrounded by locals, some hostile, some doubtful, some just curious. It happened in the previous times too, but back then, no familiar person was among the crowd. While now…

He shivered, suddenly cold in the warm morning breeze. This time it was different, because this time the boy was there as well. Somewhere there, invisible but present, and he had known what to do. Lying by the embers of their small, long extinguished fire, surrounded by the cold predawn mist, wavering between the sleep and the reality, he remembered how his heart began beating calmer because of that knowledge. The boy knew what to do. And he was not afraid. He knew this place and those people, having some ridiculously easy solution that made the test of the falls possible.

He shook his head, pushing the dream away, measuring the sun. It was already high. He needed to hurry.

Climbing the opposite hill, eager to reach the cliff now, he wiped his brow. From this vantage point, the part of the clearing was clearly visible, the carcass of the deer they had shot muffled, covered with clouds of buzzing flies.

He could see the boy crouching behind the fence, clutching to his bow and the quiver of arrows, not daring to move. Stupid! At this stage, the hunter should be relaxed, should sit and even walk a little, be alert and ready, careful but not overly so, not in this part of the waiting. Crouching for half a day would do the youth no good, he knew. His muscles would be cramped, and his senses sleepy.

He took out his own bow and made himself comfortable upon the wide tier, enjoying the breeze, rechecking its direction. The wind hadn't changed and he nodded, satisfied. The bear would not smell the boy, while his own arrows, if proved necessary, would be assisted by the wind and not hindered by it. A closer proximity would work better, but he still could make a good shot even from such a distance. And a good shot it would have to be. If the youth did not manage, he, Two Rivers, would have no more than a few heartbeats to take the bear down before it was too late for the boy.

The heat grew as the sun reached its zenith and began rolling down toward the opposite hill. Drifting in dreamless reality, Two Rivers glanced toward the distant river. But for a good swim, he thought, wiping his brow, aware of the sweat rolling down his back. Contemplating whether to take his shirt off, he wished for the breeze to return. What a heat!

He wiped his brow once again, then froze, startled. The air stood motionless, still, accumulating the heat. Nothing swayed the top of the trees below his feet. *There was no breeze anymore!*

He caught his breath, peering at the fence, seeing the figure of the boy curled behind it, a small, insignificant spot, foreign to the realm of the wild, both of them not belonging there.

He calculated fast. With no wind, the bear might smell the boy, yet it was not a likely possibility, not with the strong odor of the rotting meat dominating the air. The wind was of some help, but it was not critical. The boy would manage if he kept to his senses. A significant *if*.

He heard the flopping of wings as a flock of birds took off, rising above the tree tops to his left. Eyes narrow, he watched the green foliage swaying with no rhythmic monotony. Something was progressing down the hill, shoving its way, pushing the bushes and the saplings away. Something determined and forceful, sure of itself and mighty enough to create all this clamor.

He clutched his bow tightly, tearing an arrow from its quiver. There was no need to see the actual progress of the beast. There could be no doubt about who it was. The bear was coming to relieve his hunger, and it was coming from the wrong direction.

Tekeni's nostrils caught the unpleasant smell before he heard the snapping of the breaking bushes.

Heart coming to a halt, he turned slowly, like in a dream. The world around him seemed to freeze as he watched the trees some fifty paces away from him. They didn't move, a part of the turned-to-stone world, but something was coming from that direction, threading carelessly, breaking branches on its way. Something fierce, forceful, monstrously huge!

He peered at the greenish foliage, unable to get enough air but acutely aware of his surroundings, of the birds which seemed to stop chirping, and of the small creatures scampering away, disappearing into their comfortably small hideaways. The air was motionless, grayish in color, lacking its usual vitality.

One heartbeat, then another, then ten more. He counted them, unable to move. His limbs seemed to freeze, paralyzed, too heavy to lift, and his head was clear of thoughts, any thoughts. He felt neither fear, nor anxiety, nor any other feeling, for that matter. His mind went blank. Clear, vacant, impossible to gather enough concentration to think. But what was there to think about? The bear was coming from the opposite hill, with him, Tekeni, hiding on the *wrong* side of the fence.

The nasty smell grew, as did the sound of the breaking bushes, now joined by a heavy breathing. Only a real monster would breathe so loudly, to be heard from such distance. But of course! Only a real monster could devour half a deer in one night.

Sweat trickled down his forehead, accumulating in his eyebrows, threatening to penetrate his eyes. But for a gust of a fresh breeze! Oh all the small and great *ukis*, even the elements were against him, making the wind blow steadily for three days, then taking it away at the height of his trial. Were the Great Spirits angry with him for attempting the impossible?

He drew the bow closer to his chest. There was no point in crouching behind the fence anymore, being on the wrong side of it; still, he sat there, the effort of changing position too great, requiring more strength than he could muster at the moment.

The smell grew, and then he saw it, the brownish spot in the lake of green, not in front of him but to his left, a mass of wet, muddy fur sparkling with drops of water. Raising its massive head, the creature sniffed the air, presenting the wideness of its side.

He knew he should do something, maybe get up and shoot before it charged toward him. The moment the bear would see him, he knew, he would be covering the distance in two, three powerful leaps, leaving its victim with not enough time to gasp, let alone stretch his bow, aim, and shoot.

Painfully slow, moving like in a dream, he got to his feet, feeling them trembling, holding him but barely, the fence behind his back reassuring, promising support.

His hands shook badly as they groped after the first arrow, his fingers cumbersome, having almost no feeling in them. The creature paid him no attention, not noticing anything alarming, probably, but it was sniffing the air, looking in his direction.

He raised his bow, feeling it moving painfully slow, spending hundreds of heartbeats on every movement as it seemed. To straighten his hands – another eternity. To adjust the arrow – more of the countless time.

The bear was coming, skipping lightly on its four paws. He could not get enough air. The bow was dancing in his hands, making it impossible to aim. There was no point in trying to pull at the tight string at all. He would only manage to get the arrow leap into the air.

The stench was overwhelming now, something wet and rotten. He thought of the foul breath of the creature upon his face, when it would be busy sinking its teeth into him. It made him wish to vomit.

Like in a dream, he watched the drops flying off the bouncing fur, the dry patches of it jumping softly with every skip. The bear was so close now he could see the pointed nose, the round ears, the small eyes darting, strangely thoughtful. It went past his fence, hardly twenty paces away, paying it no attention. He tried to comprehend it. Why wasn't the monster charging?

And then it dawned upon him. The fence was there last night

when the bear came to discover the dead deer. It was a familiar thing by now. Bears did not see well, said Two Rivers, and the man knew what he was talking about. He seemed to know everything.

Don't make any sharp movements and he may not notice you at all.

The words rang in his ears, accumulating power as he watched the gigantic creature slowing its step, sniffing the air once again. The carcass, he realized. The bear was looking for its unfinished meal.

A low growl, and the giant resumed his walk, hastening his step. Clenching his teeth against the trembling, Tekeni raised his hands, still painfully slow, but steadier now, his fingers beginning to feel again. It was as though someone else were doing all this, with him watching from the side, not knowing what this person would do next.

The bowstring hissed beside his ear, exaggeratedly loud. How come the creature was not startled by it as well?

He watched the arrow sticking into the wide side, burying deeply into the grizzled fur, and then the ethereal feeling was gone. The world came back to life with a deafening roar. It crushed down his stomach, freezing his insides with so much dread his heart came to a total halt.

More roars came, thundering in his ears, intensifying, as the bear turned around, already on its back paws, enormous, a real giant, blocking the sky.

For a heartbeat, it hesitated, wavering, its grunts making strange gurgling sounds. Another hiss of a bowstring interrupted this, before the bear charged, getting back on his four legs. Did he shoot again? He did not remember himself doing it, yet his quiver was lighter now, with only two arrows left.

Darting aside, Tekeni felt his hands tearing the third arrow, before the quiver fell to the ground, impossible to reach again. It was the third arrow, but he did not remember himself shooting the second one. Yet, two sticks now protruded from the monstrous side. Another hiss and a new feathered shaft was fluttering in the beast's eye.

His own heart thundering in his ears, Tekeni jumped over the low fence, desperate to find some sort of protection. How stupid! A powerful paw swept the woven branches away as though it were a heap of leaves.

With the foul breath upon him, mixed with the repulsive aroma of fresh blood and some other discharges, he half crawled, half rolled away, disregarding the tearing pain in his upper arm, where one set of claws brushed against it, clutching the knife in his sweaty palms – *how did it get there in the first place?* – seeing nothing but the mess of the wet fur and the giant limbs.

The agility of the beast was frightening, but as it turned to charge again, blind with rage and bleeding, it wavered and fought to keep its balance, giving Tekeni a much needed heartbeat of respite.

Scrambling to his feet, he darted out of the monster's sight, the realization dawning, giving his limbs power. The beast was wounded, wounded badly. It was bleeding and wavering, still full of fighting spirit but weakening rapidly.

He whooped with joy, forgetting his fear and the necessity to keep quiet. Bettering his grip on the knife, he leapt toward the wide back, plunging the sharpened flint in, not aiming anywhere in particular. The beast was dying! He was killing it, despite the plan going wrong, despite the fear, despite the misgivings. He was killing it all alone, with a few arrows and his knife. Ecstatic, oblivious of his safety anymore, he clung to his dagger, feeling it slipping away, stuck deeply in the mess of the wet pelt, reluctant to let go.

It was a mistake. A desperate growl pierced his ears, and the foul breath was again upon him before the powerful paw sent him flying amidst a searing pain. He crashed to the ground, but kept enough presence of mind to jump onto his feet despite the pain. The bear was charging again, but it did so slowly, shakily, and this time, he found no difficulty in dashing out of its path.

Clutching to his arm, feeling it slippery, pulsating with pain, he watched the bear struggling to get back to its feet, still angry, still revengeful. The blood was flowing in between the bared fangs, making the gaping mouth look grotesque and evil, the sounds bursting through it strange, adding to the eerie sensation. Another eternity and the monstrous head flopped forward, crashing into the earth.

It was a ridiculous sight. Head reeling, legs trembling, hardly able to support him, he found it impossible to stifle a giggle. It was really too funny, the way the powerful creature just lay there, hiding its face as though ashamed of the failure, having lost to an insignificant creature, a mere boy.

The thought made the laughter burst out unrestrained. It made his stomach hurt, and he clutched onto it, trying not to lose his own balance. Still, soon he was on his knees, gasping for breath, the laughter impossible to control, making his eyes water. He hadn't laughed so hard for summers, since that time when he and his brother were running away from the angry bees after an unsuccessful attempt to get to the honey.

In the end, he just sat there panting, watching the fallen giant, unable to get up. The laughter did take the last of his strength away, but it made him feel better, relaxed, purified, indifferent to the pain in his arm and the side of his chest where the monstrous claws left deep, gaping lines.

He would have to take care of those, he knew, before the wounds began to rot. And he would have to skin the bear quickly, before it would begin to rot, too. If he sat here for days on end, unable to move, they would both rot. The thought brought the hysterical laughter back.

"I have to do something about the two of us, eh, Elder Brother?" he said, addressing the bear, his breath coming in gasps, tears of mirth rolling down his cheeks. "We won't stay here feeding coyotes and wolves, will we?"

Yet, for the life of him, he could not get up, and it spoiled his mood, made him curse. But then he remembered Two Rivers.

"Forget it," he said to the bear. "Just forget it. Two Rivers will be here soon, and he will take care of the two of us."

CHAPTER 12

The darkness was thickening rapidly as Two Rivers swam back toward the shore. Climbing the slippery path, he sighed, tired but perfectly satisfied, in peace with the world for a change.

What a day, he thought, shaking the water off, wishing to have a dry cloth to wipe himself. With no friendly warmth of the sun, the wind was piercingly cold, cutting through his skin.

He should have washed earlier, he knew, but skinning the bear was not an easy task. It had taken him the whole afternoon and the main part of the evening, with the boy being of no help at all.

Ridiculously chatty, unable to concentrate, the cuts upon his chest bleeding and his hands trembling, the youth sliced the pelt itself twice, until Two Rivers told him to be off. There was no need to ruin the beautiful fur, and the boy's wounds needed to be cleaned, some of them deep enough, inflamed already, glaring with its dirty, reddish mess.

He had told the boy to go down the shore and soak in the river for all eternity, until he called him back. Then he resumed his work, anxious to scrape the fat lining the inside of the pelt as much as he could before the darkness fell.

Even though immersed and in a hurry, he yet found it difficult to suppress his grin. So much bravery and fierceness in one young cub, he thought, shaking his head. To gather one's senses and actually make the first shot took more courage than many men could muster. But to fight the beast, to shoot it again and again, to dart around it, and then actually attack it with one's knife, why, this kind of a deed was as rare as a fresh ear of maize in the dead of winter.

He shook his head again, remembering himself watching the fight with his own mouth gaping, the bowstring and the ready arrow forgotten in his frozen hands. It was incredible, a privilege to see, the fierce cub against the old giant, a rising life against the setting one, no hunting at all but the animal-like fight of two cornered, bloodthirsty creatures. It was as though one of the spirits has gotten into the boy, taking the traces of humanness out, filling him with a vicious, dangerous energy belonging to the forest. A breathtaking sight, told and retold by many storytellers, but nothing like the real thing, he knew now, nothing at all.

It was already dark when he came back, still wet and frozen, the armload of firewood he had gathered on his way scratching his limbs. The boy was dozing off beside the stretched pelt, exhausted beyond words.

Two Rivers sighed. As tired as he had been, he knew his duties were far from being over. A fire had to be made, to keep them warm and protected at night, and a meal organized. He was famished, and the boy obviously needed to maintain his living forces as well. Even if not seriously, the cub had been wounded, and the sprout of energy gushing inside his blood after facing such a violent encounter and coming out of it alive would be wearing off by now, leaving the boy empty and spent.

Luckily, their bait was not far away, still in a fair condition. Slicing the delicate meat padding the deer's ribs, Two Rivers grinned again. It was very considerate of the bear to eat only one half of the offering, not touching the other side of the carcass at all.

As he had expected, the smell of the roasted meat brought the boy back to life. Paces unsteady, shoulders hunched guiltily, he neared the fire, the earlier frantic spark gone from the thinned, drawn face. Even in the poor illumination of their small fire, the youth's paleness was as obvious as his exhaustion.

"Help yourself," said Two Rivers, motioning at the fire. "The meat is almost ready."

"I'm sorry that I was of no help," muttered the boy, not

moving toward the indicated place. "I was useless."

He didn't try to conceal his laughter. "Oh, you were useful, wolf cub. This pelt is magnificent, the largest pelt I have ever seen. The holes you made in it notwithstanding."

"Oh, well, yes…" The boy shivered, hunching his shoulders against the new gust of wind. "I'm sorry I was so useless in skinning it."

"I didn't mean these holes. I meant the holes made by your knife while the creature was still alive, still full of the fighting spirit." He studied the piece of meat, frowning at its blackish crispiness. The lack of freshness demanded that the meat should be roasted this way. "Sit down and eat this," he said, thrusting the stick into the boy's hands. "Get busy and make yourself useful by talking less nonsense."

He picked another stick, taking his time to choose the best among the pieces of meat.

"No one would expect you to be helpful after such a feat. I was surprised you managed to stay around at all. Believe me on that. Many old, seasoned hunters would not have been able to do half of what you've done, trying to help me skin your bear." He met the dark eyes, peering at him anxiously, wide open and expectant. "Understand this. When we built our fence, we were counting on you shooting the beast, taking it down from a relatively safe distance. We were counting on you *hunting* it! But what you did was quite a different thing. You faced your adversary. You challenged it to a duel, a face-to-face battle. I haven't seen it happening in my entire life. I saw people fighting predators, a bear or a mountain lion, but they did so when cornered, having no other choice. While you just stood up to it and fought it, having all opportunities to try to crawl away, or just to wait quietly, hoping it would finish its meal and go without noticing you. It could have happened, you know? You could have waited, but you chose not to."

He fought the temptation to sink his teeth into the new roasted piece, placing it upon a clean-looking leaf, instead.

"It was quite a sight to watch from where I stood. I had a

good vantage point, having switched our place for a better one. I was playing with an idea of helping you, should you find yourself in a desperate situation, but obviously you needed no help from me." He shook his head. "You could have shot your bear when it appeared, still at a respectable distance. I saw you standing up, clenching your bow. But you did not. You waited for it to come close, to face you. Why would you do that?"

The boy's smile was small and surprisingly shy. "I was too afraid to shoot earlier."

"Then what changed?"

"I remembered you saying that they don't see well. At some point, I realized it was hurrying toward the deer, not toward me. Then I knew I might have a chance."

"Everyone knows about brown bears and their inability to see well."

"Yes, of course. But I forgot." The boy hesitated. "I was too afraid to remember."

"I see."

With the third piece of meat ready, he allowed himself to sit back and eat it, before returning to more cooking, resigned to the necessity of roasting all the meat he had cut. The boy was evidently famished, and it was a good thing. He needed to restore his energy, in case his wounds were deeper, more dangerous than they assumed.

"The sight of these claws upon your chest is a good thing," he said, wishing more than anything to sit back and stuff his pipe with the ground tobacco he always made sure to bring along. "No one would be able to imply you shot your beast from a great distance or did so with my help."

The handsome face darkened. "Would they try to do that?"

"Of course. Those who have no courage of their own would always try to find the lack of it in others. Especially in people like you. You make them feel their cowardice more acutely, you know that?"

"I wish we didn't have to go back," muttered the boy, eyes fixed upon the glowing embers.

"No? And where would you have us go? Back to your people?"

Amused, he watched his companion's face closing abruptly, the large eyes dropping to study the damp earth.

"No, of course not. I didn't mean it that way." The youth swallowed, frowning painfully. "I just wish people would stop looking at me, eager to find more evidence of me doing everything wrong."

He acknowledged it with a nod. "Like I told you before, it'll take time to make them trust you. But you made a giant step toward your goal. Everyone will respect you for what you did. No one will dismiss you as a wild cub anymore. I predict you would be invited to join many hunting parties, and it won't be long before our War Chief decides to let you join the War Dance. He is an exceptional man, and his eyes are not clouded with prejudice."

In his mind, he could see the noble, wrinkled face of the old leader, the deeply set, narrow eyes, eyes that could blaze with rage and passion, or sometimes just mild amusement and calm patience, the penetrating eyes that seemed to be able to see through people. A perfect leader.

He shivered, remembering the unsettling sensation on the night of the War Dance, when the man talked about their responsibilities and the impending raid, until his eyes suddenly clouded and he had said that maybe it was the time to clear the path for the younger leaders to follow.

His worry mounting, he remembered the last conversation with the man, after the night of the War Dance, the day before the warriors were destined to leave. He was not required to explain his decision. The man just grinned lightly and told him to go with his heart. Just like that. No questions asked, no explanations required, no reproaches sounded. Nothing but the deep, penetrating gaze that seemed to look straight into his soul, accepting and even slightly amused by what he had seen there. Did the man understand any of it? he wondered, not sure he himself could understand his own decisions.

Please, don't let him die, he thought, suddenly cold, shivering, the bad feeling back, making his stomach turn. *Oh, benevolent spirits, oh Right-Handed Twin, please keep him safe for as long as you can.*

"I wish I could tell you how grateful I am." The boy's low voice brought him back into the chilliness of the night on the other side of the Northern River. "You have done so much for me. I will never be able to repay. Never!"

He fought his smile from showing, grateful too, because the boy's words made the strange sensation go away.

"Don't think too much about any of it. I did nothing I didn't want to do, and you repaid me already with this impressive battle not many would be privileged to see through their entire lives."

CHAPTER 13

The War Chief was dead!

Standing at the edge of the chanting crowd, murmuring the customary address of the condoling song, Seketa tried to concentrate on the words she had been repeating.

Wipe away the tears,
cleanse your throat so you may speak and hear,
restore the heart to its right place,
remove the clouds from the sun in the sky.

The words made sense. There was a danger in the deep grief, danger of losing one's mind. There was also a need to release the dead spirit, to placate it and to let it go, so it wouldn't come back to harm the living. The ancient ceremony was wise.

Still, the grief persisted, refusing to leave the distraught townsfolk. The War Chief was expected to see more seasons to come. Having survived many summers of warfare and daring deeds, the fearless leader was not expected to meet his end on a simple raid in the lands of the small neighboring nation. *This* did not make any sense.

She remembered the man's face, brown and wrinkled, looking at the world with the calm, reserved dignity, with not a drop of malice or pretense. The man was liked and admired greatly. Why did his time to depart to the Sky World come so soon?

She looked up, trying to see the platform tied to the lower branches of the pine tree, but the surrounding people blocked her view. The body would be left there for ten dawns, for the people to mourn, before it would be removed to its final resting place deep in the woods; and the new War Chief would be elected by the War Council.

Who?

She suppressed a shrug. Did it matter? There was no one like the old war leader, no one. Everyone knew it, but what could they do about it?

She tried to concentrate, but her thoughts refused to organize into a proper flow. It had been too hectic, too upsetting through the past half a moon. Since the incident at the ball game, she'd known no peace, she realized. As though it had been her fault, as though she had been the one to do the unspeakable, she and not the wild boy.

The fluttering sensation in her stomach was back, and she let her gaze wander, trying to catch a sight of him somewhere in this crowd. He would be here, surely. Since coming back, bringing the magnificent fur, he had been vindicated of charges against him, restored once again to be a full member of the society.

She tried to suppress a smile, remembering how he had come up, heading for *her* longhouse, proud and alone, struggling under the largest fur she had ever seen, offering it proudly to the Mothers of her Clan, his eyes reserved, his lips pressed, the cuts upon his chest glaring, telling the story without a word being uttered. Not a wild boy anymore, but a man, a hunter, a fierce warrior who had challenged the forest giant and came back wearing a necklace made out of the terrible claws.

Oh, how proud she had been while watching him, the only person to believe in him, the only one to state that he would be back through those ten dawns that he was gone.

She knew he would be seeking her with his gaze, but when it happened, she had found it necessary to lean against the wall, her stomach fluttering, limbs going numb, the intensity of his gaze sending unsettling waves down her spine. Oh no, he did not forget her while fighting the beast. He might have grown and changed, but he would still be watching her when she danced.

The chanting died away, and she shivered, listening to the

murmuring of the people and the speeches of the town's elders, her cheeks burning as though caught doing something wrong. On that day, two dawns ago, she had been planning to find him in the evening, to take him away and ask all about this hunt, wishing to be alone with him, but afraid of it too, protected by darkness, seeing nothing but his eyes and the outline of his face but feeling him as intensely as on the evening of the War Dance. He would tell her all about his battle with the beast, she knew, and maybe, maybe he would gather enough courage to touch her face again.

However then, on the same afternoon, the warriors came back, carrying along their dead leader, their wounded struggling to get out of the canoes, Iraquas, her favorite cousin, among those carried home because he could not walk, the wound upon his backside stitched but bleeding, brownish red and glaring.

She remembered watching the pale grayish face, seeing the beads of sweat and the bruises, her dread welling. Not Iraquas, not the fearless, cheerful, restless Iraquas, who had always made her laugh with his jokes and all sorts of mischievous deeds. Anyone but him! And yet…

She bit her lips, reluctant to remember the sense of acute disappointment that kept surfacing. Why had it had to happen on the day of *his* triumph, of all days? Why not later, just a day after, really. And then she knew that she had been a terrible person to think this kind of thoughts.

She sought him again, but the people of the Wolf Clan were too far away, on the other side of the mourning half circle, with the devastated Turtle Clan's members separating the mourners. The deceased leader belonged to the Turtle Clan. So instead, her eyes caught the sight of Two Rivers, standing a little apart, his face pale and haggard, lips murmuring the words along with the rest of the mourners, but his eyes sealed, unreadable, as dark as the lake on the moonless night.

She knew what troubled the man, what made his face turn into stone. He loved the War Chief, admiring the old leader greatly and making no secret of it. Out of all respectable people, the old leader was the only one capable of making the rebellious man listen. There were occasions, ceremonies and just evenings, when their quiet conversations would last deep into the nights.

She watched the well-defined, narrow face, with its high cheekbones and prominent nose, a handsome face, but alien somehow. There was something outlandish about this man, something different and strange, as though he didn't truly belong to his own people, as though, indeed, he had been sired by the Great Spirits themselves.

She had heard about the prophecy, of course; everyone had heard about it. His mother conceived miraculously, while being still untouched by a man. But what did it mean? Seketa didn't know. She was too young to mingle among the people of influence, and the occasional rumors did not awaken her interest enough to listen.

There was some unclear destination in this man's fate, but whether he was destined to help their people or to harm them, she didn't know. Judging by his behavior, it could very well be the latter, was her private conclusion, but now, watching the grief-stricken face, she felt something close to compassion. The man was not truly bad. He was just different, odd, argumentative, but he did help the Wolf Clan boy gain his status, and he did love the old War Chief. His grief was clearly a genuine one.

"Seketa!" A hand touched her shoulder, making her heart leap.

She whirled around, startled.

"What happened?" she breathed, peering at Tindee's frowning face, embarrassed by the glances shot at them. The head of the Town Council was speaking amidst the deep silence.

A wave of the slender palm was her answer as she watched Tindee's back disappearing toward the well-swept path, which was kept perfectly clean for the condolence ceremony as the custom dictated, with no thorns and no broken bushes.

She hesitated, then began easing away, trying to attract as little attention as she could. The Mothers of her Clan were listening, wholly immersed, grief-stricken and shattered, yet very little was likely to escape their watchful eyes, an improper behavior less than anything.

"Your glorious hero almost got himself into more trouble." Tindee was waiting behind the curve of the trail, her lips twisted in the typical challenging grin of hers, but her eyes were troubled, full of shadows.

Seketa gasped. "What? What happened?"

"You care, don't you?"

"No, I don't!" Involuntarily, she brought her palms to her cheeks, hoping that the burning sensation was not showing, the glittering eyes of her friend telling her that it was. "I do care, but not in the way you think."

"In what way, then, sister?"

"In a good way. He is a friend."

"A friend, eh?" The prettily round face beamed at her, satisfied. "Well, I'm here not because of this. I was sent to call for the medicine man of the Wolf Clan."

She felt her heart cascading down her belly. "Who got hurt? How badly?"

"Like you don't know!" The mischievous smile was gone, replaced by a troubled frown.

"No, I don't!" Seketa caught her friend's arm, when Tindee began turning away. "How should I know what happened? You make no sense."

But Tindee's eyes flashed at her, openly angry now. "Iraquas? Your cousin? Remember him? It seems like all you care about these day is the savage boy and no one else."

"Oh, Iraquas, yes, how is he?"

"Not good, Seketa, not good. If I was sent to interrupt the most important medicine man of the town on the saddest of the ceremonies, it has to be serious, no? But why should you care? Your soon-to-be warrior will be well, unless his own wounds rot, and it doesn't look like they would, judging by the way he keeps picking fights with people. So you can relax and not worry about anyone of your family."

She felt it like a blow in her stomach. "I do worry about my family, and I worry about Iraquas. I was sitting with him last night, until the moon began to fade. I kept giving him water, and I kept putting wet cloths over his forehead and chest, to make him cool. And we talked, too. He wanted to talk, and he didn't want to be left alone." She glared at her friend, enraged. "And you were asleep, very snug under your blanket. So don't tell me I'm not caring enough."

"Oh well." Tindee shrugged then turned around. "Come. Let us find the Honorable Healer."

"Did Iraquas' wound begin bleeding again?" asked Seketa, not pacified in the least, but following nevertheless. She needed to know what happened to the wild boy, what trouble he got himself into.

"Yes, it's full of smelly things coming out of it, and no one can wash the wound anymore because he is screaming with pain when they as much as try to touch it." The girl looked back, her eyes glittering with tears. "He won't live, Seketa. They all know he won't!"

"But maybe the healer…"

She felt her limbs heavy, numb with desperation. Another condolence ceremony, but this time a smaller, quieter affair. Iraquas was just a young warrior, not a prominent man, not yet. Not ever now. Just a promising youth, like the foreign boy, but not even with a glorious act of killing the brown bear.

"What happened to the Wolf Clan boy?" she asked quietly, catching up to keep close.

Tindee shrugged. "Oh, he's got into a near-fight with Hainteroh and some other boys."

"Why?"

"Because of you, sister. What do you think?"

"Me? Why me?" Grateful for the briskness of their walk and the way her friend kept staring ahead, Seketa felt her cheeks beginning to burn anew.

"I don't know. I wasn't near until they were shouting, threatening each other. But it was about you. The boys from the

Porcupine Clan did not like the way he keeps staring at you."

"It's not their stupid place to say anything about that!" cried out Seketa, forgetting to keep quiet. They were back near the edge of the crowd, and some people turned to look, startled. She cupped her mouth with her palms. "It's not their rotten business," she whispered, unable to keep entirely quiet.

"Well, they think it is." The mischievous spark was back, lightening Tindee's dark eyes. "And you are not helping, the way you are gazing at him whenever you see him these days."

"I'm not!"

"Hush, sister. Stop screaming. You are disturbing the solemn ceremony."

More glances were shot in their direction, openly reproachful now.

"What happened in the end?" whispered Seketa, grabbing her friend's arm. "Who stopped the fight? Tell me before we find the Honorable Healer."

Tindee's eyebrows climbed so high they almost met the fringes of her fluttering hair. "Your glorious hero grabbed the knife, and it made the Porcupine boys back away. The same knife that killed the grizzled bear. I heard people saying that. They say there are cuts in the pelt to prove it. So, it's only natural no one wishes to face that knife just now, not so near the killing. The savage boy lives up to his reputation."

Another suggestive glance and Tindee was gone, diving into the crowd, pushing her way politely, muttering apologies. Thoughtfully, Seketa followed, her heart beating fast. He was feared now, the Wolf Clan boy. Feared and appreciated, even if not better liked than before.

Did he really kill the huge grizzled bear with the knife? It didn't seem possible. No one she knew had done such a deed, although there were plenty of stories to this end, told and retold by the best of the storytellers; stories of bravery and wonderful deeds, stories that were to be told by the winter fire only.

And yet, this one was no story. This deed had actually happened, only two, three dawns ago, done by a mere youth of seventeen summers, a person not grown-up or experienced enough to do a half of it. Two Rivers was there, helping him with advice, of course. Yet, the Wolf Clan boy was the one to face the beast. Not the renowned hunter and warrior, but him, and him alone. The frightful cuts upon his chest and his right arm proved that he had done it all alone and, indeed, in impossibly close proximity.

She breathed deeply, trying to calm the wild pounding of her heart. Tonight she would find a way to talk to him, to ask him all about it, to have him all for herself.

Two Rivers wiped the sweat off his forehead, feeling it trickling down his back, soaking his shirt, unpleasantly sticky.

Nauseated by the smell, he forced himself to lean closer, holding the burning hand of his friend, trying to give it strength. The smell was heavy, revolting, the distinct smell of corruption and decay, not softened by the pleasant aroma of burning tobacco.

"What do you see, brother?" he asked, noting the eyes of the wounded clouding, his life forces evidently weakening, beginning to wander, maybe already observing one of the Sky Paths studded with stars.

The feverish gaze came back, concentrating. "Nothing," groaned Iraquas. "Nothing but pain."

He felt the knot in his throat tightening. "Forget the pain. It is meaningless now, nothing but the shadow of the earthly life. Concentrate. Watch for signs. Prepare for the journey." He pressed the dry burning palm. "I'm here, keeping a watch. My strength is yours, if you need it."

The anguished gaze bore into him, burning his skin. "I try. I see nothing."

It took him a heartbeat to compose himself, to make sure his own voice was firm, not trembling. The effort made the sweat break anew, the pain in his head merciless, pounding like a heavily weighted war club, his stomach twisting violently, fighting the nausea, his throat constricting.

He swallowed hard. It was not the time to let the grief out. His friend needed his strength, all of it. The dying man should be surrounded by tranquility, by nothing but dignified calm. He should accept his fate and prepare for his journey toward the Sky World with proper serenity and peace of mind; otherwise, his traveling would be long and difficult, fraught with ordeals. Restless souls could get stuck half way, taking a whole span of seasons to reach the Sky.

"Think of the Sky World," he said, when able to talk. "Don't let the earthly thoughts overtake you. Call for your ancestors. Nothing will interrupt you now. I'm here and watching."

He caressed the feverish palm, feeling it shriveled, unpleasant to touch, already bony and thin, the life seeping out rapidly, as though in a hurry now. He remembered these arms, strong and masculine, swift, wielding an axe, or a war club, or a spear, their instincts good, their strength natural. A perfect warrior, now to go away from his clan and his people.

It should have been me, he thought, clenching his teeth until they screeched. *It should have been me leaving, not him*. If only there were a way...

"I will be here, to make you strong, to help you prepare..." He looked up helplessly, seeking the faith-keeper of the Beaver Clan among the surrounding faces, blurred in the dim smoke-filled air. The faith-keepers and the medicine men knew how to prepare a person, how to make one accept one's fate, to depart with appropriate calm and dignity.

People squatted around the fire, crowding the corridor, muttering prayers, staring at him, their gazes stony, unreadable, disapproving somehow. He didn't dwell on this. He knew what he'd done wrong this time.

Pretty Seketa, Iraquas' cousin, caught his eyes before he turned back, a beautifully painted bowl trembling in the girl's gentle arms, threatening to splash the water it held. He motioned her with his head, and she rushed to hand her vessel over, her face stark and grayish, eyes overly concentrated, lips pressed tight. It wouldn't be long before this one would flee into the freshness of the night, he knew.

The head of the Beaver Clan came closer, accompanied by a faith-keeper of another clan and some women. Two Rivers moved to make a place for them, but the grip on his arm tightened.

"Stay." The hoarse voice of the dying man was impossible to recognize. Did it belong to Iraquas, to the strong, cheerful, vital youth full of jokes and mischief? "You... you make me ready... You see me off. Not them. Only you." The feverish eyes clung to him now, huge and glittering.

"Yes, I will see you off, brother." He leaned closer, taking hold of the burning shoulders. "You will reach the Sky World soon, with your journey light and pleasurable. Grandmother Moon will take some of your hair, and she will weave it into her mantle. She is watching us now, smiling, proud of you." He saw the anxiousness receding, making the feverish gaze soften, clouding like that of a child about to go to sleep. It was difficult to form the words now. "And then *Gadowaas* will admit you in. He will reach for one of the stars, the brightest star of them all, and he will take it and add it to his belt, for you to have a proper guidance while traveling across the sky." He swallowed. "The South Wind will be your aid, and your journey will be wonderful, an endless tranquility and comfort. The Sky Path that awaits you is wide and easy because your life had been worthy." The air stood still, suffocating. He paused in order to clear his throat. "And one day, we will meet again. You will wait for me in the Sky World." He suppressed a humorless grin, so utterly inappropriate here. "Something is telling me you will not have to wait long."

The half closed eyes did not open, but the grip upon his arm tightened.

"One day, yes... but not soon. It will not be soon. I know this." The pull on his arm was hardly tangible, yet the effort left the dying man exhausted, covered with sweat. Clenching his teeth against his desperation, Two Rivers leaned closer, suddenly anxious to hear. "You are destined to do great things… I know you are. I always knew… I waited for you to start. I wanted to be a part of it." The dry breath burned his face, coming in gasps. "I knew you would leave one day, and I wanted to come with you. But maybe I could still follow… follow as a spirit. I can postpone this journey… for ten dawns every spirit can, can't it?" The sweat-soaked face twisted, losing its calmness once again. "You have to leave. You are not safe here… not anymore. I heard people… on the raid… the War Chief was worried. And when we came back… people talking…" The burning eyes bore into him, desperate. "Promise you will leave. After the rites for me are over. Promise!"

He could not get enough air. Fighting for breath, he stared at the agitated eyes, aware of his own welling dread, of the imminent, looming disaster, knowing that he was failing in his duty to help his friend calm. *Why were they talking about him now? Why would he have to leave? And where?*

"Promise!" The feverish gaze gleamed in the smoky darkness, unnaturally bright now, sending waves of panic down his spine.

"Yes, I promise. I will leave, but not before you are safely on your way. Not before I fast and smoke the sacred pipe and dance the sacred dances to help you find the right path." At all costs he needed to channel his friend's thoughts back into the proper direction. If he died restless, he might not manage to find the proper way.

"People are angry with you now… I heard them talking… They blame you for this failure." The eyes were clouding, the effort of talking taking the last of the dying man's strength.

"They can't do me harm." He pressed the already-shriveled shoulders, wishing he could have given them his strength. "I wish I could go instead of you. You are a better warrior. A better man. But that's why the Great Spirits want you, maybe. Because of your kindness. Who knows? The Right-Handed

Twin might have something in store for you. Something wonderful, something that will make the lives of our clans, our towns, better." He watched Iraquas' face calming again, the anguished features smoothing under his gaze. Heart peaking, he went on. "Yes, I know it now. This is why he has summoned you. And so we have to make sure you reach the Sky World soon, not forcing the Right-Handed Twin to wait. He has a wonderful work for you, now I know this. And while you are doing it from the world of the Great Spirits, I'll try to do something here, and so we will work together. Like you wanted. Like we always did. We have always fought together, haven't we?"

The knot in his throat was again too tight to continue. No, not always. This time he had abandoned his friend and his people, taking a pleasurable journey, preferring to guide a boy of no significance, enjoying a magnificent show of a bear hunt, while his friend fought and got killed.

None of it would have happened if he had come.

The knowledge tore at his chest like the claws of a ferocious beast. None of it! The War Chief would still be alive, and Iraquas would be cracking his jokes around the fire at these very moments and not fighting for breath, going away in an agonizing pain. It was all his fault. People who said so were right. He did participate in the War Dance. But by refusing to join the raid on the next day, he might have attracted the bad spirits belonging to the Evil Twin. He had made them interested and involved.

"Do you think so?" The whisper reached him but barely, the eyes peering at him half closed, their eyelids grayish and heavy. "A work up there? To help… to help you along…?"

"Yes, I know it now. You will do wonderful things to make our people lives better." He had to control his voice, had to make it sound firm. Again, he thought about no one but himself and his sense of guilt. What sort of a person was he! "You will work with the Right-Handed Twin side by side. You will be one of his most trusted aides. Not *uki* but one of the Sky Spirits.

And I will look for you every night, among the brightest stars. Every time I need help, and also when I'm just lonely and have stopped believing in myself."

The colorless lips were smiling now. Just a hint of a smile, but he could see it, and it made him feel better. He watched the empty chest rising and falling, slowing its motion, not laboring for breath anymore.

"You will always be there, in the sky and among the trees, watching and helping every now and then. I know it now. And I'm not afraid anymore."

The chanting behind his back intensified. He felt the clouds of smoke reaching, overcoming the stench of the rotting flesh.

The palm around his arm lost its strength; still, he clutched it, feeling it growing stiffer, not burning his skin anymore. Or was it just his imagination? The face upon the folded blanket was calm, set now, a face of a stranger.

He watched it for a heartbeat, then another. The light was gone. What made this man alive, what made his friend himself, disappeared, taken by the Grandmother Moon, responsible for giving and taking life.

He straightened up with an effort, his limbs numb from crouching for so long. Trying not to sway, he rose to his feet. The people were chanting, passing the pipe, inhaling the sacred smoke, murmuring prayers.

"He began his traveling," he said hoarsely, finding it difficult to recognize his own voice. "May his spirit have a restful journey."

People nodded, while others came down the corridor, prepared to support the mourners. The women were wailing, more than a few, and others tried to comfort them. The men were singing more loudly, as though crying in their own way.

He could not join their singing, his mind numb, tired, wishing to be alone. The vision of his favorite cliff beckoned, and he turned around without thinking, blinking against the smoke.

"Here." Someone thrust a pipe into his hand. "Sit."

"I... I need to go out... for a short while," he murmured, studying the long, elaborately carved pipe as though he had never seen it before.

"Not now," said one of the men. "Sit here."

He stared at them, trying to slam his mind into working.

"Let him go!" It was quite a scream, coming from his right. "I want him to leave and never come back."

The woman sprang into his view, a middle-aged, good-looking woman. *Iraquas' mother.* He felt like taking a step back.

"Go away. Leave this longhouse and never come back." She advanced toward him, her fists clenched. "It's your fault! Yours and no one else's. Your fault my son died, and the War Chief! You made it happen."

He stared at her, the suffocating sensation back, making his thoughts run in panicked circles.

"You bring nothing but trouble to this town, these people." She stood before him, hardly reaching his shoulder but fierce and frightening in her mindless rage. "You are a harbinger of disaster, and now you killed my son."

"Stop it, woman," said one of the men stonily. "You are crazed with grief, and you don't know what you are talking about."

The woman whirled at her accuser, her hair long and loose, jumping fiercely.

"I know what I'm talking about. I'm not the only one thinking that. Don't pretend you didn't hear any of it before." Her voice peaked, then broke. "My son should be alive now, healthy and well. He is dead because of this man. He brought the wrath of the Evil Twin upon our warriors by not joining the raiding party after dancing the sacred War Dance. He is responsible."

The silence lasted for a heartbeat, then another.

"Stop talking nonsense," said another man quietly. "Let your son's spirit depart peacefully. He is still with us, and your screaming will disturb him, will make his journey difficult." He sighed. "Bring your suspicions or accusations before the councils if you must, but let it rest for now. Don't make it harder for your son."

The woman's face crumbled, breaking before his eyes. He watched the others coming closer, pulling her gently, supporting her as she swayed. He could not get enough air. Picking his way carefully upon the crowded floor, he began easing down the corridor, his whole being dedicated to the effort of getting out.

No one said a word, no one tried to stop him. The silence behind his back was deafening, thick, pregnant with feelings, as heavy as a rocky mountain.

Refusing to meet his eyes, people moved out of his way, but it was a blessing. He could not meet their gazes, either. Or face their words. He needed to be alone. It was as necessary as breathing itself. If he didn't get away from this crowd, he'd faint, he knew. Or lose his temper and do something stupid, something unforgivable, something dreadful that would give them an excuse to get rid of him in a lawful way.

CHAPTER 14

Lingering around the sacred fire, keeping at a respectable distance, Tekeni saw Two Rivers storming out of the entrance, heading down the path, oblivious of the stares.

People crowded the sheltered fire just outside the facade, passing the beautifully carved pipe, inhaling deeply, releasing the sacred smoke, murmuring prayers, ready to support the immediate family of the dying warrior. The faith-keepers of the other clans took care of the ceremony, from time to time enhancing their singing, tossing the clothes of the departing soul into the fire as an offering to the Great Spirits, to make the dying man's journey to the Sky World smoother.

A sensible thing to do, reflected Tekeni, mildly curious. His eyes followed the tall figure of Two Rivers, puzzled. The man was obviously angry, inappropriately so. Grief could come out in all manners, but such anger was unwarranted, even in a mourning person. What happened inside the longhouse of the Beaver Clan? Did the warrior die already? Was it a difficult death?

He shivered, knowing that to die of rotting wounds was the worst death possible, a sure way to test the man's strength and endurance, a torturous way likely to unman the strongest. And yet, the young Beaver Clan man was a great warrior. He would die with honor, one could be sure of that. It had to be something else that made Two Rivers that angry.

He hesitated. To follow the man and talk to him was a logical thing to do. They would have enough privacy, and hadn't he come here in order to find him in the first place?

His eyes drifted toward the sheltered entrance that was

spilling out more people. Oh yes, the warrior must have died already. He narrowed his eyes, trying to recognize Seketa's slender silhouette among the crowds. She had been inside the house, helping along, he assumed, but now she might be coming out.

Hesitating, he came closer, unwilling to draw attention, wary of the gazes. Since coming back, carrying the magnificent fur of the giant bear, his life had changed, definitely for the better. His own clan's people were now smiling at him, swelling with pride, prepared to talk to him like to any other person, and not only to admonish or give dark looks. The Clan Mother of their longhouse had actually fussed over his wounds, insisting to tie the heated leaves of some plant to his chest, to clean the wounds and to take away the pain. As though he complained of pain. He tried not to sneaker. Three dawns since receiving the cuts would make anyone either die of rot or forget all about it. Still, her concern made him feel good, as though this leading woman really cared about him, like a Mother of the Clan should.

So it had been pleasant around the Wolf Clan people. And around some others. But not around the Beaver Clan dwellings. The Mothers of that Clan received his offering, *his payment*, with their faces stony, not about to forgive him, not yet. Not ever, maybe. And Yeentso was already well, up and about, making no secret of his hatred, causing Tekeni to shiver at the intensity and the darkness of his furious glances. No, the Beaver Clan longhouse was not a place to hang around, not even as a part of the condoling crowd. And yet…

He strained his eyes, trying to see better. She would be coming out now, a part of the grieving family. Was the dead warrior her brother? He didn't know. But even if not, he would be one of her cousins, for sure, being too young to marry into the Beaver Clan, like Yeentso who lived in their longhouse but did not belong to that clan.

The thought of Yeentso made him glance around, but in the agitated crowd, it was difficult to see anyone. No, he wouldn't be able to find her. But maybe it was for the best. To bother a person in grief was the height of bad manners.

He began easing away, thinking of the steep rocks adorning the bay just outside the town's gates. Two Rivers would surely be perching there now, on the edge of the cliff, defying the winds, challenging them to cool off his anger. *What happened inside the Beaver Clan longhouse?*

Deep in thought, he didn't notice the men until he was almost upon them, a group of dark silhouettes huddled next to the mass of the double fence. His heart coming to a halt, he slunk toward the nearby plot of tobacco, not willing to be detected, not by this sort of a group. Whoever they were, those people were up to no good, that much was obvious, their hunched shoulders and bent together heads suggesting a clandestine meeting.

"Many people believe in that now, but not enough to do something," a voice he did not recognize reached him, ringing softly in the crispy coldness of the night.

Tekeni held his breath. In order to reach the opening in the fence and the path leading out of the town, he would have to pass them, too close for them not to pay him attention, unless opting for heading straight away through tobacco plots. Silently and as quiet as a forest cat on the hunt, he took a few steps forward.

"They may be enough. There are many who think it's his fault." Another voice tore the darkness. "Many believe that now."

"And still it won't be wise to try and bring this matter before the councils." The first man paused, evidently to shrug. "Neither Town nor Clans Councils would deal with an accusation founded in misgivings and fears. It may have been his fault, and it may not have been. He did participate in the War Dance, but the War Chief gave him permission not to come. He can plead that he had not been invited at all. Not many warriors were selected for this raid."

"The War Chief is dead, and no one knows what occurred

between him and Two Rivers on the day of the raid, when they talked for so long the people began to wonder." This voice Tekeni recognized as belonging to the man of the Turtle Clan, Two Rivers' clan. Biting his lower lip, he froze, listening.

"So what do we do?" asked the second man angrily. "Nothing, as always?"

"We can still try to persuade the councils to listen to us."

The silence prevailed, interrupted by the moaning of the wind outside the fence and the chirping of the night insects.

"Or we can wait for him to do something stupid. He will not make us wait for too long, not him." The Turtle man's voice softened. "He is not the person to keep his opinions to himself, and now, distraught by grief, he will be quite vulnerable, angered more easily than not."

More silence.

"He can be provoked into doing something stupid," said the first man thoughtfully. "Yes, it can happen."

"Stupid like what?"

"Stupid like something violent. A killing would be perfect, but just a fight may be enough."

A sound of a kicked stone startled Tekeni, making him dive deeper into the low plants. If discovered eavesdropping on these men, he would be done for, he knew, his heart pounding, mouth dry.

"Yes, it can work." The first man sighed. "And it should be done quickly, while the matters are still fresh."

"Tomorrow I'll talk to some people."

"Yes, do that."

The rustling of the bushes told Tekeni that they were drawing away, walking slowly, not in a hurry. He breathed with relief, enjoying the crispness of the cool air, with no smoke and no mourning chanting and wailing.

So those people wanted to make Two Rivers do something stupid, he thought, getting up and looking around carefully. To provoke him into something violent, and so get him in trouble with the entire town and every council possible. Not a very difficult task, judging by the way the man stormed off earlier in the night. He looked angry and frustrated, and now, hearing those people, Tekeni began to understand better. Losing one's friend was bad enough, but to be accused of being the cause of it? He shook his head. No, it was anything but pleasant for the strange man now.

Back upon the path leading out of the town, he smiled to himself. He had been looking for Two Rivers earlier, mainly to have a friendly company and yet another interesting talk, maybe. But now, oh now, he had more than this. A chance to repay some of his benefactor's kindness was too great to miss. His information would be of an interest to the formidable man.

The wind greeted him, as fierce as always, coming from the lake, shrilling angrily. Shivering with cold, he hunched his shoulders, wishing to have a long-sleeved shirt now. In the scant moonlight, the strip of a lower ground looked barren, uninviting, the distant cliffs towering dark and unfriendly. The elements seemed to be in a foul mood, matching the mood of the mourning town.

Listening to the wailing wind, he hesitated, his uneasiness growing. Was it safe to go out with the spirits being so angry? Evil *uki* would be out there now for sure, roaming, all sorts of unfriendly spirits of ferocious animals and poisonous plants.

He took another step, then halted, his hand slipping toward his knife, pulling it out of its sheath as though on its own accord. A crouching figure was huddling behind the last pole of the outer palisade. Heart beating fast, he peered at it, then sensed more than saw its pose, desolate and not threatening, its back toward him.

One more step, and his relief welled, along with his excitement. She was just sitting there, hugging her knees, her head tucked safely in the space her pulled up legs created, a perfect hiding place.

"Seketa!"

She shivered, but didn't turn around or look up.

"What happened?"

Before he knew it, he was beside her, kneeling awkwardly, trying to see her better through the thick darkness, his heart was making wild leaps inside his chest.

"Are you hurt? Who hurt you?"

But her sobbing intensified and he could do nothing but reach for her shoulders and try to contain their trembling.

"Tell me what happened!"

"Iraquas is dead," she whispered, sobbing, her breathing coming in gasps. "He was dying for so long. So horribly. With so much pain. I couldn't stay."

"Oh." He let his breath out, trying not to let his relief show. *She wasn't hurt!*

"It is so horrible. This death. He does not deserve it. Anyone but him. Anyone!" She looked up, facing him, her eyes huge and glittering, wide open, having a wild spark to them. "Not him. Anyone but him!"

"Yes, I know." He searched her face, checking for signs of her being struck after all, just in case. It was red and puffy, but unharmed. He sighed in relief. "I thought someone hurt you."

"It's worse!" she stated, suddenly angry. "I would let people hurt me, even kill me, if I could spare him all the pain."

"Don't say that," he said helplessly, then regretted his words as her gaze grew angrier, flashing out of the darkness.

"I can say whatever I like. He was my cousin, my favorite cousin. He was my friend." She glared at him, fighting the sobs. "He was not your friend or a person of your clan. You have no family, so you don't know how it is. You don't know how it feels to lose someone close, really close."

He felt it like a punch in his stomach. Clenching his teeth against the old, familiar pain, feeling it as though someone were squeezing his entrails with a stony fist, he stared back at her, unable to speak.

"What? Why are you staring at me like that?" she demanded, her eyebrows creating a single line beneath the clearness of her forehead. "Iraquas was not your friend or family."

"No, he was not," he said, finding it difficult to control his voice and not caring about it. "But I do know how it feels to lose someone close. Better than you!"

She gasped and the fringes of her dress jumped angrily as she drew a deep breath. "Better than me? You have no family, and you don't care about the people who adopted you." Her eyes sparkled fiercely. "And anyway, no one of the Wolf Clan died. It's the Turtle and Beaver Clan people who are mourning. But why would you care about them?"

"Oh, yes, I don't care!"

He jumped onto his feet, seeing her doing the same, while the wind tore at them, as angry as they were. Her hair fluttered across her face, obscuring it, but she made no movement to push it aside, her hands rigid along her body, her fists clenched.

"Iraquas was my most favorite cousin, and he was a great man, great hunter, great warrior," she breathed through her clenched teeth. "I loved him more than anyone!"

He said nothing, too enraged to speak.

"If they adopt someone to take his place and his name," she went on, almost screaming now. "I will not accept this person, no matter whom it would be. I will not recognize this adoption. He will not be my cousin, and I will never address this person by this name."

Oh, yes, that explained some things, he thought randomly, clenching his teeth against his own fury, forcing his limbs into stillness. No wonder many called him Wolf Clan boy, or just a wild boy, never addressing him by the name given to him upon his adoption. What was that name? He didn't remember. He hated that name too, not accepting it any more than those others did, always thinking about himself by his old name, *his people's name*, or the shorten version of it given to him by his own family. Tekeni – Two, one of the two, a twin brother.

"I will not accept his death," she was saying. "No matter what they say in the condolence ceremony."

"You have no choice," he said tiredly, sorry for finding her. He would have been better off sleeping snugly on his bunk in the Wolf Clan longhouse.

She glared at him from under her brow. "Yes, I do. One always has a choice, if one is prepared to take the consequences. Everyone has a choice."

"That's what you think now." He studied her in the fading moonlight, so slender and graceful, so beautiful, even with her face puffy and her hair messed. So naive. What did she know about life? "One does not always have choices, and you better not make your people angry by resisting your clan's will. You may not like the consequences."

She pursed her lips tight. "Oh, and you know all about resisting your clan's will, don't you?"

He shrugged, glancing back at the shelter the narrow corridor of poles provided. What were they doing here in the cold, arguing about stupid things?

She suppressed another sob. "You can't tell me what to do, as though you know better. You are of my age, and you are anything but the most esteemed member of the community."

She took a step forward and stood next to him, challenging, looking anything but the strict, always groomed and well-behaved girl she was. He stared at her, speechless.

"Why aren't you saying something?" she demanded, her voice beginning to tremble again. "Tell me more about how I should be behaving. You know all about the proper ways, don't you?"

He could almost feel her, so close she stood, and he clenched his fists tight against the urge to grab her shoulders. To shake her back into sanity, or maybe, to press her to his chest and take some of her pain away.

He watched her twisted face, remembering the words of the condoling song: *wipe away the tears, cleanse your throat so you may speak and hear, restore the heart to its right place, and remove the clouds from the sun in the sky.* Would it help to tell her any of this now?

"You should go back and join the ceremonies," he said tiredly. "They will know the right words to tell you."

"And you?" she asked, her voice breaking. "Can't you tell those words to me now?"

The knot tightening in his throat was difficult to swallow this time. "No, I can't. I don't know these words." He took a deep breath. "My father refused to listen when it was his time to grieve, so I didn't listen too."

She peered at him, wide-eyed. "You lost your mother," she whispered, making it a statement.

He shrugged, finding it safer to keep his teeth clenched.

"Oh!" She reached out, touching his face lightly. "I didn't know. I'm sorry."

Her fingers were like a soft breeze, brushing against his face, sending shivers down his spine.

"How old were you?"

"Fifteen, I saw fifteen summers." He heard his voice low but firm, and it pleased him.

"Fifteen summers?" She leaned back, studying his face, her eyes narrow and attentive. "But it was when you... when you came here. You were fifteen summers old, weren't you?"

He just shrugged, wishing to talk about anything but this.

"So it happened just before that." Another firm statement. She was coming to her conclusions fast. "And your father? What happened to him?"

"Forget it," he said, this time his voice wavering, dangerously close to breaking. "Nothing happened to anyone. I don't remember my previous life. It never happened."

But her palm was again sliding down his cheek, warm and dry, her fingers lingering, barely touching, but leaving their prints nevertheless. He could draw the lines where they passed, he knew.

"I'm sorry. I should never have said what I said before. But I do feel your sadness now. I can feel it so clearly, and I wish I could take this burden away." Her face shone at him, beautiful in a breathtaking way, ethereal, but also belonging to a human girl, its warmth tangible, within an arm's reach. She was no *uki*. The warmth of her body told him this.

His hands came up on their own accord, taking hold of her shoulders, pulling her closer, desperate to feel her warmth, that wonderful, kind, supporting glow that her whole being seemed to radiate, taking the edge of the desperation away, softening it, making it possible to deal with.

She did not resist but kept peering at him, almost the same height as he was, wide-eyed, clearly surprised. Mesmerized, he stared into her face, unable to take his eyes away. Her lips were slightly opened, as though expectant, and he knew that he had to taste them, no matter what.

It was like lightning in the middle of the storm, those fierce flashes of energy going through his body, setting it on fire. Her lips parted, soft and pleasant, pressing to his, making the fire so much worse, the storm impossible to control, his limbs weak, his body drained of power but invincible too, relishing the feel of her body against his, demanding to have more of her warmth.

Another heartbeat of this and she turned her face away, trying to break free from his embrace, but although knowing that he had to let her go, his arms went rigid around her, not responding to the feeble attempts of his mind to take control.

She pushed him away again, but just as he managed to unlock his arms, she leaned forward, and he felt her arms sneaking around him, hurting the cuts upon his chest, facing him again, eyes shining, their glow stronger now, the eyes of a Sky Woman.

"We shouldn't do it," she whispered, her breath brushing against his face. "It's not right."

He just nodded, unable to form words, feeling his mind going blank again. This time the kiss was even fiercer, the largest thunderstorm since the beginning of time, since the earth had been created by water animals and birds.

He stared at her, breathing heavily, seeing the uncertainty in her eyes, and the fear.

"I'm sorry," he whispered. "I know we should not."

Another impossible attempt to let her go. If only she would help. But instead, she leaned against him heavily, as though having no power left as well. If he took a step back, she might fall, he thought randomly.

The wind swirled around them, in a fiercer mood than before. He felt her shivering, and it gave him strength to pull them both into the protective screen behind the poles.

"The Master of the Winds is angry," she whispered, then giggled and nestled against his chest, seemingly comfortable under the protection of his arms, her fear and uncertainty gone. "He thinks it's wrong, too."

"Yes, I suppose." He tried to concentrate, her nearness disrupting his thoughts. It was not funny. He needed all his strength to just hold her, to keep his arms from wandering her body, and it made him angry, somehow.

As if sensing his tension, she hesitated, then slipped out of his arms, light and pliant, again in perfect control. Leaning against the opposite row of poles, she regarded him with a glittering glance.

"It was insane, wasn't it?"

He just nodded, his disappointment vast. To hold her close, even if not allowed to do more, was better than to have her standing on the other side of the corridor.

"We can't do this."

"I know."

"Are you angry?"

"No."

He could feel her searching gaze, peering at him through the darkness.

"Yes, you are." She took a step forward and was again close enough for him to see the outline of her delicate face. "There are things people are not supposed to do unless they are older and want to live together. I know some boys and girls are doing it anyway, but this is wrong, you see? This is silly and not appropriate. Don't you think?"

He shrugged. "I was not trying to get you into doing anything. It just happened."

"But you've been looking for me?" She was not smiling anymore, and her sincerity made him feel dirty, guilty of every crime possible, most of all of trying to seduce her.

"No, I wasn't! I was on my way out. I would never think that you, or anyone else, would be hiding here, of all places."

"I was not hiding here. I just wanted to be alone." She frowned. "And why would you go out at night? It doesn't make sense."

He said nothing, watching her, his heart still pounding.

"You are not telling me the truth."

"Yes, I am."

"Then tell me why?"

"I was looking for Two Rivers."

"Oh." All of a sudden, she looked disappointed, offended even. "At night? Outside? You are talking nonsense." Impatiently, she shook her head. "What do you want with this man, anyway?"

"I needed to tell him something." He clenched his teeth, hating the acute sensation of being guilty, as though caught doing something wrong. "He is a good man. He was kind to me. There is nothing wrong in seeking his company."

"He is not a good man. He is responsible for what happened to our warriors."

"What? He is not!"

"Of course he is. He participated in the War Dance, then did not join the raid. It brought the wrath of the Evil Twin and his minions upon our men. Those who were brave enough to join, that is."

He gasped at the wildness of her accusation. "He is a brave man. And he didn't join because he wanted to help me hunt the bear."

"Which he made you challenge in the first place," she stated, tossing her head to banish the tendrils fluttering across her face. "He made you risk your life in order to avoid going with our warriors. He used you. Can't you see it?"

He peered at her, aghast. "He didn't use me. He helped me! He helped me to gain respect of the people, to make them treat me differently. He said it would happen, and it did. Maybe not your clan, but the people of my clan are respecting me now."

"That is because you did a very brave thing. You killed the grizzled brown bear, and from a short distance, too. Of course they respect you now, as they ought. You proved your worth." She leaned closer and was facing him again, eyes frowning. "You did it and not him. He just made you take the challenge, and then he came along, to see what would happen. That's all he did. This man is strange, and he cares about no one but himself and his strange, perverted ideas."

"No, Seketa, no. You are wrong." He threw his arms in the air, as though trying to push away her accusations. "He is none of this. He guided me all the way, explaining and teaching me. He taught me so many things! And yes, his ideas are strange, but maybe he is right about them, too. When you talk to him, some of what he says makes sense."

"He made you go after that bear, a youth of seventeen summers," she said stubbornly, eyeing him from under her eyebrows. "It is unheard of. You could have been killed."

"But I wasn't, I wasn't killed. I killed the bear instead, and I would never have managed without him. It was such a huge monster, you should have seen it. Twice a man's height and so wide and old and angry. And stinking, too. Oh gods, it had such a foul smell." He took a deep breath, his stomach squeezing at the mere memory. "I would never have managed but for Two Rivers and the things he taught me while we were preparing the trap. He told me so much. And he believed in me, too. He knew I would manage, and I'm telling you, it gave me more strength."

She stared at him, wide-eyed. "How did it feel to face the monster? Weren't you afraid?"

"It was not that bad." For the life of him, he could not admit the deep, paralyzing fear he'd felt, its memory painfully fresh, squeezing his insides. "They don't see well, so I could dash here and there, and shoot at my leisure. Maybe if this bear were younger, more agile, I would need to work harder, but with this one, it was not much of a challenge."

Now even her mouth was opened and gaping. "Was it not

scary at all?"

"No, not really." He smiled smugly. "It's just the matter of a good shot and then some playing around. I probably should have gone on shooting it, but I thought it would be amusing to finish the fight face-to-face, to give the old giant an honorable death." He eyed her, feeling superior and very pleased with himself. "Two Rivers said it was quite a sight. He said he hadn't seen anything like that, ever. And not anyone he knew of."

Now he had taken it too far. Her eyes narrowed and her lips pursed, challenging.

"He did claw you," she said. "Quite tore at your chest."

Involuntarily, he brought his palm up, feeling the crusts. "Well, yes, of course. He was not a rabbit."

"So it was not such an easy fight," she stated, triumphant as though proving him wrong.

"Well, no. But it was not that difficult either." Angry with himself for letting his pride show, he shrugged. "There is no shame in bearing these marks. I did kill him face-to-face, and that's what matters."

She acknowledged it with a nod. "Yes, of course." Then her eyes lost their challenging glint. "I asked the Great Spirits to keep you safe. I made an offering when it was the third day of your journey."

"You did?" His stomach tightened so strongly, he found it difficult to breathe. "Why?"

Now it was her turn to shrug as she turned away, peering into the darkness of the corridor behind their backs.

He moved closer, desperate to feel her warmth. "What did you offer?"

"There was this bracelet," she whispered shyly, but he could hear a smile in her voice. "It was small, and I never wore it, anyway."

His heart was making strange leaps inside his chest, tossing itself against his ribs. "The Great Spirits liked it. They gave me great victory, and now I know why." Unable to keep his hands from doing this, he put them around her shoulders. "I wish I could let you know how grateful I am."

"It was not my offering," she said, and he could feel her shuddering under his touch. "It was your bravery and your determination."

"No. I was not brave. I lied before. I was too scared to shoot at it until it was very close."

She giggled. "I would think so. I don't know any hunter who would challenge the great grizzled bear face-to-face." Still chuckling, she turned back and faced him, so close again he could feel her breath upon his face. "But it doesn't matter. You went to hunt the forest giant, and you killed it in a close duel, like no other man of our town. You are brave, and you are strong and determined. Even if you do know what fear is." Her smile beamed at him through the darkness. "I'm glad I offered the bracelet. Next time, I'll offer something more precious. The first time you go in a battle I'll offer my most precious of possessions."

The knot in his throat was difficult to swallow. "Will you?" He swallowed again, hearing his voice coming out strange, low and distorted. "Will you be my woman when I've proved myself, when I'm good enough to ask your Clan Mothers?"

She seemed to stop breathing too, her eyes large and glimmering, sparkling strangely. Even the wind stopped shrieking, pausing, trying to hear better. The spirits, *uki* and the glorious night deities were listening, their curiosity great.

He counted his heartbeats, one, two, and then five more. She didn't move, didn't make an attempt to escape his arms. She just stood there, frozen like a stone. It was a strange feeling to hold her like that, her nearness sending waves of warmth alongside his body, her silence freezing his spirit.

He forced his arms off her shoulders. "You don't have to say 'yes.'"

She came to life all at once. "Can I say 'maybe'?" There was a challenge in her voice again, and it made him yet angrier.

"Maybe."

But now it was her turn to catch his arms, and he felt her

palms cold, brushing against his skin.

"You are such a spoiled baby," she said, laughing. "I can't give you the answer to that. Not right away. I need to think it over, do I not?" Then her laughter died as she peered at him closely, her serenity tangible in the brightening near dawn air. "But I'm pleased you asked. I can tell you that."

Unable to cope with the surge of relief that suddenly washed his entire body, he pulled her back into his embrace.

"Yes, it can be 'maybe,'" he whispered into her lips, not afraid anymore. "As long as it will become 'yes' when the time comes."

This time her lips felt different, warmer and sweeter, already familiar and not colored by misgivings.

"You will be mine," he whispered. "You just wait and see."

CHAPTER 15

The aroma that rose from the bubbling pot tickled Seketa's nostrils, making her stomach growl. Biting her lips, she watched the women using their sharpened sticks to pull steaming balls of corn out of the stew, to cool them for a while, before tossing them onto the bowls and plates extended from every direction.

Wiping the sweat off her brow, she turned her gaze away, disregarding the demands of her stomach. It didn't seem right to eat now, with Iraquas' body lying on its wooden platform, tied to the lower branches of the pine tree, like the War Chief's body on the other side of the town, near the cluster of the Turtle Clan's longhouses.

She had chanted and danced since early morning, and then listened to the customary words of the other clans' leaders, those who came to console the mourning people of the Beaver Clan.

Wipe away the tears,
cleanse your throat so you may speak and hear...

The words said nothing, not penetrating her mind. But the dancing helped, like always. The wonderful music and the rhythmic, monotonous movement helped her connect with the spirits, with her inner self, and now to mourn too, she discovered, as she felt herself drifting, reaching Iraquas' departing spirit.

It was still here, she knew, lingering, watching them, trying to participate, sad and reluctant to leave. She would close her eyes and address him quietly, by dancing and by her inner words, telling him how proud she was of him and how his journey would be a pleasant one, his stay in the Sky World wonderful and fulfilling. In nine days he would have to depart, she knew, allowed to linger for only ten dawns from the moment his body stopped breathing.

Leaning against the nearby tree, she watched the eating people and those who still crowded the boiling pots. So many of them! Oh, Iraquas was loved dearly. She smiled, satisfied. Her cousin was the best youth ever, and he would not be easily forgotten.

Tired beyond words and welcoming the respite in the ceremonies, she paused, hungry but refusing to eat. It was her own private sacrifice, an offering, of her hunger this time. Because she loved Iraquas dearly, and because last night she did not behave appropriately for a person in mourning.

She felt her face beginning to burn again. Oh, how could she? Laughing with this boy, allowing him to kiss her, and on such a night of all nights.

Her cheeks felt hot against her palms, as she tried to push the memories away. That first kiss, and then the last one, before it was too near dawn and they had to go back to her longhouse and the ceremonies. Oh Benevolent Spirits!

She almost shut her eyes in an attempt not to remember how his lips were soft and dry, hesitant in the beginning, but then firm and demanding, his hands powerful, strong, supportive and insistent at the same time, claiming their right to hold her. Oh, but it was a wonderful feeling, this sensation of yielding to his will, of letting go. Such a strange, unfamiliar thing. But she had wanted it from the first time she had noticed him, she realized, wanted to do just that, to melt into his arms and let him kiss her, or even worse. Oh, Mighty Spirits!

Involuntarily, she scanned the crowds. He had been there through the whole morning, she remembered, every time she would seek him with her glance. She needed him to be there, and he did not disappoint, standing among the consoling people, watching her, his eyes tired and ringed, but glittering, smiling, giving her strength. He could have gone to his longhouse to rest, but he stayed, and she appreciated that.

It would be good to be alone with him again, to feel more of his love. And maybe she should talk to her mother, let her know about his desire. He would make a good husband for her, such a brave youth, a future leader without a doubt, despite his wrong origins.

Yes, she thought, her heartbeat accelerating. She would talk to her mother, ask her to talk to the Grandmother of their longhouse, oh yes, at the first opportunity. He was good enough for her, better than many.

She frowned, searching the open space around Iraquas' tree. He was not among the people storming the pots with food, but maybe he had gone looking for Two Rivers. She had seen that man earlier, dancing solemnly or chanting, and then standing next to the platform, his face thinned and closed, eyes sealed, surrounded by dark rings, lips pressed tight, more alone that ever. Such a strange man.

Well, Two Rivers was still there, she discovered, like her, ignoring the food, enveloped in his desperation and loneliness, oblivious of the hostile glances. Many people were angry with him now, but he didn't seem to care, locked in his grief, indifferent. Iraquas was his friend, his only close friend, she knew, and how it must feel to be the cause of one's closest friend's death.

She shivered. Many blamed Two Rivers for the failure of the raid and the deaths. Well, the man must have been blaming himself as well, judging by the haggardness of his face and the stiffness of his shoulders, and the way his hands were folded lifelessly across his bared chest.

She studied him with some curiosity. Iraquas had been fond of this man. He had talked about him on the previous night, when she had brought her wounded cousin water and stayed to keep him company because he didn't want to be left alone.

Breathing heavily, fighting his pain and the fear, Iraquas talked rapidly, as though hurrying to tell her all about Two Rivers and what a great man he was. Apparently, he believed in the man the whole town had given up on. He didn't know how exactly, but his friend was destined to do great things.

Eyes glittering with fever, he had told her about Two Rivers' yet-unclear mission and how he wanted to be a part of it. If the man left, he would have left with him, he had said, and her eyes filled with tears against her will, remembering the broken whispering voice and the burning eyes of her beloved cousin. Oh, if only he could have stayed!

The tears were streaming now, impossible to control, so she turned her face away, desperate to hide her grief from the curious eyes. What did they know about her loss?

"Seketa."

His voice was coming from the other side of her tree. So that's why she didn't see him in the crowd. Staring stubbornly at the ground, she felt the warmth spreading, the familiar warmth that made her feel better.

"That bad?" Coming closer, he did not attempt to take her into his arms, not in front of everyone.

She just nodded.

"I'll bring you something to eat," he said after an awkward pause.

"No, no, I don't want to eat!" She looked up, blinking away the tears. "I will fast until it's his time to leave on his Sky Journey."

"You can't fast for ten dawns!" He eyed her warily, pale and tired-looking, but oh-so-very handsome with those large, luminous eyes of his set in the well-defined face. "You will be sick."

"So what?" But his concern made her feel better. "I won't die like him."

"You better not." He grinned all of a sudden and, caught unprepared, she could not fight her smile from showing.

"Can I be of any use to you all skinny and weak? Is that what you were worrying about?"

Now his eyes laughed openly. "Yes, you can. But I like you this way better." He measured her with his gaze. "With all the curves."

She felt her cheeks beginning to burn, acutely aware of the people around them, wishing them to disappear. "Oh well, Warrior. Bring yourself a plate of these corn balls and, maybe, I'll bite one of them."

His smile widened. "Yes, Honorable Beaver Clan Woman. You'll get your bite of a corn ball right away."

She watched him diving into the melee, swift and purposeful. A young wolf on a trail of prints, not a cub anymore but not a grown-up beast, either. Oh, but she remembered noticing it about him back in the storage room of his longhouse, when she had first spoken to him. He had moved like a forest predator. This is how he must have bested the bear, by being nimble and concentrated, by trusting his instincts. And by conquering his fear, of course. Oh, he would make a great hunter and a great warrior.

The struggle against her smile turned more difficult. It was inappropriate to smile now, not in the middle of her grief; still, her thoughts refused to return to sadness. She would most certainly speak to her mother this very evening. They would have to wait, of course, but not for too long. He'd already proven his worth, and maybe, after his first expedition with a raiding party…

"How are you, sister?" Tindee's palm brushed against her shoulders, pulling her into a light embrace.

"I'm good."

"You need to eat something. You've been dancing since dawn, and you never stopped for even a gulp of water."

She peered into her friend's usually mischievous eyes, now wide opened and full of concern.

"I will be good," she said, touched. "You've been doing all this, too. You do worry about his spirit as much as I do. You were fond of him no less than I was."

But Tindee shrugged, turning away abruptly. "I don't think of him now. He is dead. We can do nothing about it."

Unsettled, Seketa took a step back. "His spirit is still here. For nine more dawns, he will remain with us. And he needs help. He needs to be pacified. He cannot leave if he is angry."

"Oh, stop that, Seketa. Are you afraid of Iraquas' spirit? He was the finest boy that had ever lived. His spirit will be the last one to harm anyone, let alone his own family." Her friend's eyes flashed at her angrily, sparkling with unshed tears. "He, of all people. The best man our clan had. And what are you doing? Dancing yourself into exhaustion, trying to make him leave in peace. I wish he would stay, you know? Stay forever, to guard us and to laugh with us the way he always did." The tears were spilling now, running down the girl's cheeks, smearing the elaborate patterns painted for the ceremony. "Oh, forget it. You understand nothing!"

"Wait, Tindee, please!" Grabbing her friend's arm, Seketa struggled to not let it go. "Wait. You don't understand. I didn't mean it this way." She pulled strongly, making the girl turn back. "I know how you miss him. I miss him as much! I wish he could stay with us, even in the spirit." Peering at the stormy, tearful eyes, she forced herself into calmness she didn't feel. For her friend's sake. "But he can't, sister. He can't. He has to start his journey soon. He has no choice, and neither do we. We cannot cling to his memory and make him stay. We have to let him go, to help him step onto the right path. We can't think of ourselves now."

The gaze boring at her wavered, softening, filling with misery, then Tindee shook her head. "No, I do not accept it. I want him to stay, even if only as a spirit."

The rising voices caught their attention, and they turned toward the mats and the boiling pots, startled by the obvious anger in the loudly spoken words.

Heart twisting with worry, Seketa recognized Yeentso's voice, challenging and dripping with disdain.

"Go away. You have no business to eat the food of the Beaver Clan people."

She didn't need to hear the answer, knowing whom her cousin by marriage was addressing. Catching her breath, she took a step toward the growing circle of people who still crowded the boiling pots, but now it was Tindee's turn to grab her arm.

"Seketa, don't. It is not the time. Let them solve it by themselves."

"I'm allowed to be here no less than anyone else!" she heard the Wolf Clan boy stating, and her heart squeezed with pride.

"No, you aren't, you filthy foreigner."

She pulled her arm forcefully and rushed forward, her heart pounding. Yeentso was standing next to the sweating women, waiting for his bowl to be filled. Or re-filled, she presumed, as she eyed the hated face, taking in its smug, content expression. He had eaten already, heartily at that.

The Wolf Clan boy – *why did she still think about him in this way, what was his real name?* – stood a few paces away, half turned, balancing a bowl in his hand, as though he had just halted abruptly, his eyes blazing with fire, his free hand already on the hilt of his knife.

"Go away," repeated Yeentso, taking a step forward. "You are disturbing the mourning of the Beaver Clan people."

The youth did not take a step back, but he looked as though he might have. She held her breath, reading the uncertainty in his eyes. Clearly, Yeentso had seen it too, as he came closer, the half grin upon his face flickering, an unpleasant sight that made Seketa shiver with fear.

"Go peacefully," he said, voice ominously calm, but having a growling tone to it. "Don't make me throw you out of here by force."

All gazes were upon them, and the silence was heavy, encompassing. Even the birds stopped chirping.

She tried to understand what was happening, why no one interfered? He had every right to be here, like the other consoling people, from all the clans of the town. And yet, it seemed as though the crowd was agreeing with what Yeentso just said.

The man's grin stretched wider.

"These people deserve to mourn without the filthy, foreign

presence of the enemies who killed their loved ones. Don't you have any respect for the feelings of your new country-folk?"

They all peered at him now as he stood there, his lips pressed angrily, but his eyes widening, filling with doubt, dashing from face to face. Aghast, she followed his gaze too, seeing the accusation written clearly across their faces. So many of them, all of them against him!

"Oh, stop this nonsense!" A loud voice came from their right, startling people. They all turned to watch, even Yeentso and the boy, as Two Rivers pushed his way through the crowd.

Unable to breathe, but aware of the vastness of her relief, Seketa stared at the haggard face, set and as though carved out of lifeless wood, with no color applied to it, just a mask with empty eyes.

"Do you listen to yourself?" he said, addressing no one and not looking at anyone in particular. "So much nonsense in just a few phrases. How does it not make your heads ache?" He encircled them with his gaze, and now there was a flicker of emotion in the empty depths. "But what do you do? You are listening to it with nothing to say. Did you all lose your sense of right and wrong?"

They stared at him in silence, and she tried to sneak closer, to see what their faces held. Why didn't anyone say something? The man was talking a plain good sense.

"Because if this *Porcupine Clan man*," a light inclination of the head indicated the place where Yeentso still stood, as taken aback as the others, "seems to be chosen to represent the grieving Beaver Clan people, then I suppose all of us, those who do not belong to this family, should leave. Is this the desire of the Beaver Clan? To grieve alone? Is this *foreign to the Beaver Clan man* speaking your minds?"

A murmur went through the crowd, and Seketa breathed with relief. They were going to listen to reason. They did not lose their sense of right and wrong.

Then the trembling voice tore the silence, making her heart skip a beat. "Yes, I want you to leave. You, of all people. A person who is responsible for my son's death should not mar the solemnity of his rites with his guilty, unholy presence."

Iraquas' mother did not push her way into the circle of people, but they all knew who had spoken.

Her chest squeezing with compassion, Seketa watched Two Rivers take an involuntary step back, stifling a gasp as though he had just been punched in his stomach, his face turning yet paler, although it was anything but colored with life before.

"I may be responsible for his death," he said quietly, licking his lips. "But I do have a right to be the part of his rites, to make my contribution in an effort to lighten the journey ahead of him. I am allowed to do my duty to him."

Yeentso came back to life all at once. "No, you don't, you foreigners' lover. You forfeited your rights on the day you preferred to go away with the pretty boy instead of doing your duty by joining our warriors. They died because of you, our War Chief and the young man who called himself your friend. They died because you preferred to enjoy the favors of the foreign cub, away from this town, so no one would notice or interfere with your perverted activities, you coward!"

The air escaped loudly, coming out of many chests at once. Two Rivers seemed to freeze for a heartbeat, while his young companion's eyes grew to enormous proportion, dominating his face completely now, their glow so dark it cast the deep red of his wide cheekbones into a complete insignificance.

His right palm gripping the knife tightened until its knuckles went white, but it was his left arm that made a move. A bowl with the stew went flying, making its way in a perfect arch, to crush into Yeentso's head and send him reeling, crying out, the thick, scourging liquid running down his face, to soak into the decorated pureness of his shirt.

Still unsteady, but evidently blind with rage, Yeentso leaped toward his offender, who seemed to be ready, evading the initial attack, his knife out, limbs firm. Women were screaming now, and the men rushed toward the fighters, but Two Rivers was between them first, his hand grabbing Yeentso by the throat, its muscles tightening, lifting the large man off his feet with no visible effort, as though he had been just a child.

"Don't you ever call me that again," he growled, his voice unnatural, sending shivers down everyone's spine. Oblivious of the kicks and the punches of the assaulted man, he squeezed harder, now with both hands, making his victim gurgle and drool.

Numb and feeling as though in a dream – *no dream but a nightmare!* – Seketa stared at the purpling face of her cousin by marriage, terrified. It seemed to be swelling, twisted horribly, with its eyes rolling and its lips letting out the swollen tongue, a terrible sight.

People were upon them, yet it was the boy who reacted, grabbing Two Rivers' hand and pulling hard, making it waver, ruining the balance. In a heartbeat, Yeentso was on the ground, squirming and gulping the air, but Two Rivers paid him no attention, staring now at the youth, terrifying in his fury.

"How dare you?" he roared, but the Wolf Clan boy did not retreat.

"Please, listen to me," he said hurriedly, peering into the man's eyes as though trying to find the remnants of the sanity in there, as though trying to bring it back by the sheer power of his will. "You can't do it. You should not. They want you to harm someone, to fight or to kill. They need you to do it, to try you in the councils!"

Her heart coming to a halt, she watched them, unable to breathe. For a moment, it seemed that Two Rivers would strike the youth, with his knife maybe, killing him instead of Yeentso. Then the sanity flowed back into the anguished eyes.

"What... what are you saying?" he muttered, voice hardly audible now, but heard perfectly well in yet another heavy silence that fell.

The youth swallowed. "They want you to harm someone, to be able to try you in the councils." He swallowed again, obviously struggling not to drop his gaze. "I overheard them yesterday, talking behind the tobacco plots. I went out to warn you, but..." The intense gaze dropped eventually. "But I didn't... didn't find you."

"Who were they?" Two Rivers' voice was louder now, back in control, his eyes narrow, encircling the surrounding people, gaze heavy, pregnant with meaning.

"I don't know. I didn't see them well."

Yeentso was groaning on the ground, and women rushed to his side, sprinkling his face with water and trying to make him drink. The elders were next to them now, and the Clans Mothers.

"Say no more," said the Head of the Town Council, a stocky, middle-aged man with a wide scar crossing his face from cheek to cheek. "This is neither the time nor the place. I want you to leave, both of you. Go to your longhouses and wait for the Town Council to summon you for the questioning. Do not come here unless permitted by the Mothers of the Beaver Clan. Do you understand me?"

Shorter in stature and much less imposing, the stocky man possessed enough personal power to stare the taller Two Rivers down. It was not about the status, reflected Seketa, numb and unable to breathe properly. It was about the inner power. The Head of the Town Council had much of it, no less than formidable Two Rivers. As for the boy...

She glanced at his broad, handsome face, her stomach turning violently. His eyes were glued to the angry man, wary, apprehensive, but expectant too. He didn't bother to look at the surrounding people, the elders, or the head of the council. Even his rival, still groaning upon the ground, did not draw his attention. Eyes wide, he watched Two Rivers, waiting for the man's reaction. If the older man had decided to fight for his rights, she realized suddenly, to challenge the whole town, he would follow with no questions asked. What did he and Iraquas see in this man that the others did not?

She felt the tears so very close now, desperate not to let them flow. He was not allowed anywhere near her people's clan, not until the Town Council decided their fate. Oh, Mighty Spirits!

Clenching her palms tight, she watched Two Rivers nodding solemnly, talking at length, saying something, probably words full of dignity and pride.

She didn't listen, could not, even if she wanted to, her struggle against the tears and the pounding of her heart making her ears deaf. He would not be here, and just when she needed him most. Also, again, he was in trouble.

CHAPTER 16

The sun was lingering, stuck high above the distant trees. From his favorite cliff he could see it towering, glaring its disapproval.

Defeated, he lowered his gaze, to stare at the whitish foam the wind was creating upon the surface of the lake. They were all angry, the sun and the wind, and the deceptively bright sky with its pure, puffy clouds. Angry with whom? He knew the answer to that.

Narrowing his eyes, he tried to see through the mists of the eastern side of the lake, where the sky met the water and no land could be spotted. The vastness of the endless blue beckoned. What was to stop him from taking his canoe and sailing, just sailing, with no direction and no concern as to his destination? To drift with the wind and the current.

But not here. This lake was too small, too close to home, not like the Great Sparkling Water, only two days' sail away, holding the mystery. He had crossed it several times, always a part of raiding parties, always at the crossing point, to row for the entire day, switching places with his fellow warriors, wary and on guard, careful of surprises, never an enjoyable affair.

Oh, but what if he just sailed on, at the unfamiliar parts of the endless vastness, drifting toward the unknown? To his death probably, but what did it matter? His life was worth not much more than a broken piece of pottery by now. Directionless, colorless, fruitless, a mere existence, and now with no friends and no peers. The War Chief was dead, Iraquas was dead, both ending their lives untimely, because of him, because he thought about no one but himself. Himself and his strange, unacceptable ideas, seeing nothing but the general picture and so missing the wonderful details, like the trust of his friends.

He clenched his teeth until his jaw hurt, but the pain in his chest would not go away. How had it come to this? Just half a moon ago he had had it all, the status of a good hunter and a respected warrior, a man with memorable deeds to recall, enjoying the estimation of his townsfolk, the estimation colored by misgivings and wondering, but full of respect, nevertheless. How had it come to him turning into almost an outlaw, thrown away from his friend's funeral rites by the Head of the Town Council?

He looked up, seeking the answer in the clearness of the clouded sky, seeing nothing. Yes, he did not join the raid, choosing to accompany the boy on the bear hunting mission. At the time, it seemed like a good decision. The War Chief approved. They had talked about this and the other things deep into the night.

The pain was turning unbearable again. Why, why did this wise, outstanding man have to die? Him, of all people! Killed on a small, meaningless raid. Him and Iraquas, two great men, friends and sympathizers, taken away before their time, to leave him with nothing but agony and pain; and the open enmity of the town. No more friends, no more people to respect and admire, no one to talk to.

No one but the boy, the wild cub from across the Great Sparkling Water. He grinned grimly. What a spirit, matched by good instincts and a temper worthy of a fierce forest creature. Oh, this cub bore watching. Guided properly, the boy would make a great warrior, a leader perhaps. Quick, observant, with an admirable ability to learn; yes, an interesting type, if he survived to full adulthood. A great *if*.

Killing the bear had given the boy a serious edge, like he, Two Rivers, had predicted. Still, today they had shown that it was yet not enough, not with Yeentso lurking, seeking the opportunities to avenge himself.

Yeentso! He felt his rage coming back, crawling up his spine, making his stomach turn. Filthy, disgusting piece of excrement.

How dared he accuse him of cowardice; and of filthy things. He should have killed the lowlife. But the boy was right, too. People wanted him to do something stupid. They needed him to do so in order to get rid of him.

Recognizing the footsteps, he did not turn his head, but moved a little, making a room for the youth to sit. The silence prevailed, interrupted by the shrieking of the wind.

"I'm sorry you got in trouble on my account," said the boy finally, eyes firm upon the distant trees.

Two Rivers shrugged. "It has nothing to do with you. You give too much importance to yourself."

"No, I don't." The youth's voice held a grin now. "It was about me. At least in the beginning." Hands restless, fidgety, he pushed a stone down the cliff and watched it rolling, raising clouds of dust. "You could have just watched, saying nothing, like they all did."

"He was talking nonsense."

"But no one said a thing!"

Two Rivers sighed. "Yes. They were at a loss, or distraught, or afraid, or not caring enough." He watched the white foam upon the water, thinking of the spirits who must be living there, in the heart of this lake. "You do have a long way to go yet. It'll take you time to gain their trust, yet you are going into a right direction. But for Yeentso, you would be now somewhat further up the path."

"I will never manage to walk this path with Yeentso there, ready to stir trouble every time he sees me. He wants me dead. He won't settle for anything else." The youth's eyes clouded, staring into the misty distance. "So it'll be either him or me seeking the Sky Path to take not long from now. And whichever way it goes, the results would bode no good for me, anyway."

Glancing at the closed up, handsome face, Two Rivers shook his head. Oh, the cub had grown up through this past half a moon. Either that or he was wiser than he cared to display.

"You should have let me kill him." He shrugged lightly,

returning his gaze toward the bluish mass beneath their feet, not wishing to get into serious matters. "Who were those people you overheard last night?"

The youth tensed visibly. "There were three of them, but by the way they talked, it seems that there were more sympathizers with this plot. I couldn't see them. It was dark, and I had to hide behind the tobacco plots so they wouldn't see me." A frown twisted the fine features. "I think one of the men was from your clan, maybe even your longhouse. He has a deep voice and he talked strangely, swallowing words, difficult to understand."

"Anue, who else?" muttered Two Rivers, a tiny splash of anger coming back, then dying away. *What did it matter?*

"They said that many believe it to be your fault that this raid was a failure." The youth's voice dropped as though uncomfortable repeating the accusation. "But that it would not be enough to accuse you of something before the councils. So they said you needed to be provoked. Into a fight, or better yet – a killing."

He stared at the water, his head empty, devoid of thoughts. "Not a bad plan. Easily achieved, too."

"Yes, that's what they said."

"Well, they got that. A fight. If not the killing." He shook his head, trying to make the strange sensation of indifference go away. "So maybe now they can get what they wanted."

He could feel the youth's gaze leaping at him, consumed with curiosity. "What do they want?"

"I don't know. I think they would love to see me dead, but maybe a simple fight would not be enough to demand that." He grinned, meeting the wary gaze. "I should thank you, you know. You did the right thing by stopping me. I'm grateful."

The high cheekbones of his younger companion darkened. "I should have found you last night," he muttered. "I should have warned you in time."

He wanted to laugh. "Why didn't you?"

"I... I was looking for you, and then... then something

happened." The boy looked as though about to shrink into himself, hunching his shoulders, eyes glued to the step on the cliff they sat upon. "I couldn't go on looking for you. And then it was dawn already."

Now it was truly difficult to suppress his laughter. "I hope she was worthy of your time. The Beaver Clan beauty?"

The youth peered at him, aghast. "How did you know?"

"What else would keep a boy of your age that busy at night?"

"It was not like that at all!"

"No?"

"No, it was not. She is not that kind of a girl!"

"No, of course not. I remember her well. She was one of Iraquas' close cousins, the favorite one. Very prim, very upright, but he liked her all the same. She'll end up being one of the Clan Mothers, remember my words." He grinned. "The fact that she found you interesting says something about her. Not a narrow-minded woman, that one."

"No, she is not," muttered the boy, frowning. "But she promised. She'll talk to the Grandmother of her longhouse and the Mothers of her Clan when it's time."

Oh, the naivety of the youth. "They won't give you their permission, you know that, right?"

Now the boy turned as tense as an overstretched bowstring. "Not now, but maybe later. When I have proved my worth."

He felt the wave of compassion, not a very familiar feeling. "Yes, why not? With the passing of time, you will prove your worth. Of that I have no doubt."

He put his face into the wind, thinking of these two youths. So they were in love, craving each other's company, or maybe just lusting it. What was it like, to be in love at that age? He did not remember. Did he love a woman, ever? He could not answer that either. There were infatuations, brief cravings, strong desires, but a love in a sense of a wish to share one's life with a particular woman? He shrugged. Turea held his attention for longer than anyone, but she had been a challenge, an untamed beast, not a partner to live with.

"There was a legend." The boy's voice broke into his thoughts, lacking in emotion. "Back home, in Little Falls. They say there were two lovers. A warrior and a girl. She was to be given to another, so they decided to run away together. But he died in battle, so she took her small canoe and paddled toward the current and into the tallest of the falls, where the water gushes most strongly. They say her death song can still be heard on the nights when the moon is round and shining and the wind is right." The youth shrugged, and there was an obvious grin in his voice now. "It's silly. Why would she do this? And anyway, the falls are thundering like Heno when he is at his fiercest mood, so even if there was a song no one would hear it. No one but silly girls who were running there on every full moon, trying to listen. Stupid, isn't it?"

"Yes, stupid," he muttered without thinking, his mind going blank, registering the only words that mattered. "The thundering falls? Were there waterfalls near your people's town?"

"Yes, of course." The youth glanced at him, puzzled. "Our town is called Little Falls, but those falls are not little at all. They are not as high as some others, but they are wide and very, very powerful! You don't want to jump into those falls, believe me on that."

"Jump into the falls?" he repeated, ice filling his stomach, gripping it in its stony fist. The dream! The same dreadful, recurring dream, full of people talking a foreign-sounding tongue, expecting him to jump into the thundering falls in order to prove... what?

He tried to get a grip of his senses, fearing the vision, lest it gather power and take him now, even though he was wide awake and not alone.

"Are you well?" The youth was staring at him, perplexed.

"Yes, yes!" He clenched his fists until he could not feel them anymore, his nails sinking into his flesh. The pain refreshed him. "Tell me about your town." It came out curtly, like an order. He was hardly able to recognize his voice.

"Tell you what about it?" His companion's eyes were so wide opened they looked almost round.

"Tell me something in your tongue. I need to hear the sound of it."

"Why?"

"Just do it!"

"*She:kon. Skennenko:wa ken?*" It came out quietly, hesitantly.

"More. A longer phrase."

Now the youth seemed as though about to jump to his feet and run away. "It doesn't make any sense."

"It does. I'll explain later. But now I need you to tell me something longer. I need to hear the sound of it."

The next phrase was, indeed, long enough to feel the foreign tongue, to catch the words he thought he recognized. *The tongue from the dream.*

"You said something about filthy foreigners."

The youth blushed so profoundly he felt like chuckling for a moment. "I thought your people did not understand our tongue at all."

"Not much. It sounds foreign. But *okwe'ówe* is the same everywhere." He grinned. "Well, enough of your people's tongue, but tell me more about your town. How large it is? Does it have councils like us?"

"Well, yes, of course, it has councils." The youth shifted uneasily, frowning at the water below his feet. "The Town Council, and the Clans Councils. Like anywhere else." He glanced up from under his brow. "Why do you ask?"

"How large it is? Like our town?"

"No, it's larger. We have ten longhouses and those are longer. More than ten families each."

"An important town?"

"Yes, of course. My father was the War Chief of the whole area. Other villages were under Little Falls' protection."

The stony fist kept squeezing his stomach. It all fit, every little detail. But why? For what reason? Those people were his enemies. The most avowed enemies.

"Listen," he said, taking a deep breath. "I need to be alone now. I need to think. To think things over. I have to arrive at a decision." He met the troubled gaze and held it, forcing his impatience down. "But whatever it is, I promise to let you know before I do something about it. I'll explain it all to you, I promise."

For a heartbeat, the youth just stared, then the large eyes filled with comprehension.

"Yes." He nodded and began to get up.

"Come here just before sunset. I may need to talk in more privacy than our longhouses or the town's alleys provide."

The youth nodded again. "I'll come back," he said, disappearing back in the direction of the town's fence.

A wolf cub, reflected Two Rivers, but maybe not such a cub anymore. He glanced at the sky, seeking the still-invisible stars.

Why him? he asked the puffy clouds. *Why send this wild thing to come all the way from across the Great Lake in order to take a part in the unclear, tortuous game of spirits and prophecies?*

Think, he ordered himself. Start from the beginning. The prophecy, the wild dreams his mother was having when still carrying him inside her, conceived most mysteriously. What did it say? Nothing in particular, unless he was not told all of it. He was destined to be a great man, to save his people, *or some people*, and make their lives better. How?

He peered at the sky, but the clouds ran rapidly across the bright vastness, as though in a hurry to get away, indifferent to his dilemmas. And it was not that he didn't know what should have been done in order to better his people's circumstances, to save them, indeed, from a total destruction. The constant warfare was a horrible mistake. He had sensed it all along, with every fiber of his being, but it took him time to understand, to formulate it in his head. Too much time. He had seen more than thirty summers, and only now did he understand. And thanks to none other than the young cub.

He shook his head, grinning, remembering their journey, the days spent away from the town and its politics, away from the people he knew, traveling leisurely, tracking the bear, enjoying the rare sensation of peace and quiet; and of not being threatened. Around his country folk, he realized, he always felt alerted, on the defensive, ready to face their suspicious glances, ready to brush off their reprimands, their open critique, fight off their attacks.

However, with the boy it was different. The wild cub had more depth than he cared to display, and his life circumstances exposed him to more than a person twice his age should have seen. It made him more observant, less subjected to the convention, to the acceptable beliefs. To guide and teach him was a pleasure, but to air one's thoughts aloud with no need to be on guard was a true gift. What needed to be said was uttered, even if in the privacy of the woods with only one person to listen.

He peered at the distant shore, trying to keep his excitement at bay, for now he knew what should be done. The constant warfare would have to be stopped, any further warfare prevented. Councils of all towns and settlements should be called in order to unite the people eventually, to summon the councils of the other nations. To talk about the terms and to negotiate peace.

A difficult, seemingly impossible task, but one that needed to, at least, be attempted. With the cooperation of people and the help of the Right-Handed Twin, he may succeed in finding acceptable solutions to all sorts of problems that would undoubtedly arise. But then...

He clenched his teeth, determined to curb the bubbling excitement. His people, never willing to listen to him in the first place, were now less likely to trust anything he said. And then there was this dream. The test of the falls was the way to make the foreign people listen, he suddenly realized. It was the means to draw their attention, to convince them of his sincerity and maybe even the particular blessing of the Great Spirits. Them, the foreigners from across the Great Sparkling Water, the enemies of his people. If he managed the test of the falls, they would listen.

He took a deep breath, trying to calm the pounding of his heart. It was impossible, plain impossible, and yet the dream that had plagued him over the long summers, finally made itself clear, and through the wild cub, of all people. To take his canoe and sail for Little Falls, this large, influential town? What an absurd idea, and yet, with the boy, who would be only too happy to leave, it may work. It was worth a try. At home he had nothing now but hatred and mistrust.

A distant thundering growled, but the sky was still clear, the sun still stuck well away from the foamy water. He stared at it, willing it to move slower now. Whatever he decided, it would have to happen before the sunset.

CHAPTER 17

The growling of the distant thunder made Tekeni look up as he stood leaning against the fence, staring into the corridor between the two rows of palisade, pondering his possibilities.

To go back to the town seemed like a sensible idea. He was hungry and tired, and even though ordered to wait for the summons of the Town Council, not allowed as much as to look at the direction of the Beaver Clan people or their longhouses, he wasn't formally accused of any particular crime. He could go to his clan's longhouse and catch up on some sleep, couldn't he?

He measured the sun once again, undecided. It was still a long way until sunset, and he wasn't sure he wanted to come back as Two Rivers had told him to do. The man was too strange, too unsettling at times. One moment talking normally, like any other person, better than most, wise, perceptive, uncomfortably honest, slightly amused but never in an offensive way. Then all of sudden changed, staring at him, Tekeni, as though he had been an *uki*, asking him to do most unordinary things, plaguing him with questions and requests that made no sense.

Why would he wish to know anything about Little Falls or to hear the sound of its people's tongue? Was he thinking of organizing an invasion to the farthest of their enemies' lands, to make up for all the past wrongdoings? With the mysterious man, one never knew.

The drums rolled on, interrupting another thundering, announcing the renewal of the ceremonies. He thought about Seketa dancing, his stomach twisting. She was so gracious, so alluring, so beautiful, especially when dancing. Even this morning, when it had been nothing but very solemn ceremonial dances and she looked sad, pale and tired, lacking her usual enticing spark, even then, he could not tear his eyes off her, the memory of last night and their kisses making his knees tremble.

What did she think about what happened? The knot in his stomach kept tightening. Did she think him again to be just a wild boy who could not control his temper? Did she think he should have gone away quietly, with no fuss?

He ground his teeth. Yes, that's what she must have been thinking now, angry with him, disappointed most thoroughly. A hopeless hothead with no finesse, a wild boy, a savage.

He clenched his fists until his knuckles seemed to crack. Yes, he behaved most stupidly, throwing this bowl at Yeentso like an angry child. But it hit its target spot on the temple, making the disgusting man sway and almost fall. Had the bowl been a little heavier, made out of pottery and not wood, the damn lowlife might have lost his consciousness once again. He, Tekeni, could throw stones better than any other boy he had grown up with, using both his hands equally well.

The light footsteps made his heart leap with fright, and then with anticipation. Those did not belong to a man, and they were lonely, not accompanied by more rustling. Still, he took a step back, taking cover behind one of the poles, just in case.

"I knew you would be here!"

Not fooled by his semi-hidden location, she came closer, her face lovely, glistening with sweat, cheeks burning, chest rising and falling rapidly.

"Are you good?" he asked, coming out and eyeing her warily, looking for signs of her being angry.

"Yes, yes, I was in a hurry. I ran all the way. I hoped you were here and not in your longhouse." Her eyebrows climbed up suggestively, in mocking reproach. "Although the elders directed you most clearly to go to your longhouse and wait for their summons there."

"They just didn't want me to come anywhere near your clan's

people, that's all," he said, suppressing a smile, ridiculously relieved, but annoyed by it. He looked at her searchingly. "You agree with them, don't you? You think like the rest of them, that it was my fault again."

She returned his gaze. "Do you really care to hear what I think?"

No, I don't! he was about to toss back, but the sight of her exquisite face made the words stick. She came here, running all the way, looking for him, anxious to see him. Even if she had been angry with him, she was not aloof or indifferent. She cared for him, and her kisses were wonderful, making his heart race.

"Yes, I do want to hear what you think," he said, forcing his face into stillness.

Her smile was wonderful in its suddenness, like a sun peeking through the rainy clouds.

"Oh, if that is so, then I will tell you. This dirty son of a forest rat Yeentso proved once again how incredibly stupid he is, and how jealousy filled, and how afraid. Afraid of a youth who is already twice as strong, with more courage than he would ever dream to have. And the other people were stupid and afraid. And I was stupid and afraid, too. I should have said something. Maybe it would have brought people to their senses. Two Rivers was decent and courageous, but he always does it to people, now more than ever. No one wants to listen to him, so his intervention didn't help." Breathless, she paused, beaming at him, her eyes large and shining, happy with the effect. "I promise to be more courageous next time. I promise to interfere and to tell them what I think. To be on your side."

He stared at her, speechless. "Will you... will you do that?"

"Of course. I won't be so cowardly next time."

"You are not a coward. You interfered, back at the War Dance. Remember?" He grinned at the memory. "You made the Turtle Clan Mothers angry."

She giggled. "Oh, yes. I remember. It was scary."

"But you did it. For me." He shrugged, desperate to conceal his growing embarrassment. "Even Two Rivers commented on your courage. He said you are smart and courageous."

Her cheeks took yet a darker shade as she frowned, half amused, half put out. "Have you been gossiping about me?"

"No, of course not." He felt his own cheeks beginning to burn. "But Two Rivers said something like that once. He talks a lot, about many things."

"Oh, that he does," she laughed and then frowned again. "So where is he? I thought you two may be together now. You know, talking."

The way she dropped her gaze made him angry again. She surely didn't think…

"Yes, we talked for some time. But one can't talk until the sun comes down."

"So, he is out there, somewhere?" she asked, seemingly disappointed.

"Yes, he is always out there, on that cluster of rocks facing the lake. You can find him there if you want to."

She frowned at his tone. "Why would I want to look for him?"

Feeling ridiculous, but more furious with every passing moment, he kicked at a small stone, watching it rolling down the path. "I don't know. You asked where he was."

"I didn't ask where he was. I just asked if he is out there. And if you won't stop being angry for no reason, I will leave."

A silence prevailed, interrupted by another distant growling. A fresh gust of wind brought the smell of the nearing rain.

"I'm not angry," he said, glancing at the still glowing sun. "I just don't want you to think silly things."

"Like what?"

"Like, you know, the stupid things, like Yeentso said," he muttered, studying the remnants of the ornaments upon his worn-out moccasins.

"Oh, that! How silly you are. Of course, I didn't think he meant what he said. No one thinks that, not about Two Rivers, for sure. This man behaved loosely with more women than you can count. He has this reputation. He should have settled with a woman, any woman, long ago, but he has not. He prefers to behave like a decent man should not, to have his pleasure, and this is one more thing that will be held against him when he finally decides to take the right path." She peered at him, still preaching. "Also, there is nothing wrong with people who are inclined this way. They are useful to the community. They are half men, half women, and they are doing women's work, but with males' strength. It's useful." A sparkle crept into her eyes. "But you are not inclined this way, too. I know that now. You like girls. I found that out last night, didn't I?"

He tried to suppress his grin, still seething, but she came closer and stood next to him, eyes sparkling, challenging.

"Don't you?"

"Yes, I do." Unable to keep his hands from doing this, he reached for her, pulling her closer, marveling at the way her body tilted, nestling against his with such a natural, unashamed grace. "One girl, only one. The most beautiful of them all."

She murmured something and pressed closer, gazing at him, full of expectation, but when he tried to kiss her, she shifted her head out of his lips' reach.

"First, tell me something," she whispered, her breath brushing against his face. "Do you still want to move to my longhouse and be my man?"

His breath caught, he stared into the depths of her eyes, seeing the uncertainty and the expectation.

"Yes, I want that," he said, his throat dry.

"And what if you were made to wait a long time? Would you wait?"

"Yes."

She still peered at him, now openly troubled. "And if they say 'no,' what will you do then?"

"I..." He swallowed. "I'll go on proving myself until they see that I'm worthy. For as long as it takes."

That reassured her. Her gaze calmed, and she relaxed in his arms. "Do you promise?"

"Yes, I promise. You will be my woman and no one else.

And I will not give up until your Clan Mothers give us their permission." He looked at her searchingly. "Do you think they'll make trouble?"

She avoided his gaze, slipping out of his arms, instead.

"Come," she said, grabbing his wrist. "I don't want to talk about any of it here, where everyone can hear us."

He followed, puzzled, dragged as though by the sheer power of her will. The touch of her fingers burned his skin, although it was a light, delightful touch. Her palm was surprisingly soft for a girl working the land through the long summer moons, with the harvest time at its highest.

The wind tore at them, as always, while walking the ground exposed to the wrath of the lake and its elements. He enveloped her with one arm, sheltering.

"Where is this favorite spot of your friend?" she asked when they passed the cluster of higher cliffs. "I don't want him to run into us, either."

His stomach twisted with anticipation. "Up there, see this small trail? It's just a few heartbeats of climbing. But I know he will stay there until sunset, so we are safe wherever you want to go."

"Over there, in this grove. There is a nice little clearing I have in mind."

The light dimmed as they dove into a thick cluster of trees, feeling safer now. He tried to slow his step, but she pulled him on, unrelenting. *Where were they going?* His heart pounded, and he refused to think of the possibilities the privacy of the woods offered. She surely did not mean *that*.

"Here." Breathing heavily, she halted at the small clearing, extending her arm in a gesture of the hostess inviting the visitor in. "Is it not a pretty place?"

"Yes, it is."

He didn't spare a glance to their surroundings, knowing this clearing well enough. He had found it long ago, when first sneaking out of the town, on a foolishly desperate attempt to run away. He hadn't made it much farther than this same clearing, he remembered, just a scared, hungry boy of fifteen. He came back after darkness, to be scolded for his recklessness worthy only of savages from across the Great Lake. They thought he was just lost, wandering unfamiliar surroundings without permission. Him, who had never lost his way!

"I love this place," she was saying, apparently oblivious of his darkened mood. "I sneak here sometimes, when I want to be alone."

"Do you do this often?"

"No, of course not. How can I?" She smiled fleetingly but there was a tension in her face, and her eyes refused to meet his.

His stomach kept tightening. "Why are we here now?"

"I don't know. I just wanted to talk privately. Why do you ask so many questions?" Now her eyes met his, the frown sitting well with her lovely features, making her look even more attractive.

He found it difficult to make his mind work, the tranquility of the woods enveloping, whispering of its intimacy. His instincts urging him to pull her back into his arms, he hesitated, repulsed by her anger, despite the attraction. She was changing too fast, not always for the best.

She glared at him for a heartbeat, then turned away.

"I talked to the Grandmother of our longhouse," she said. "I should have waited, talked to my mother first, but just after the noon dances there was a good opportunity I couldn't miss."

"And?"

"And nothing. She said no, never, anyone but you." Her gaze bore at him, sparkling with challenge. "I tried to argue, but it only made her angry."

"I see." He bit his lower lip, feeling his stomach sinking, heavy with desperation.

"What are you going to do about it?" she demanded. "You made many fine promises back there by the fence."

Her chest rose and fell, making the fringes upon her dress flutter, seemingly as angry as she was. Fists clenched, lips pursed but trembling, she peered at him as though expecting him to do something, to make it all work despite her grandmother's refusal.

It set his nerves on edge, making him wish to grab her shoulders and shake her back into normality. She had no right to be angry with him about that. It was not something he did wrong, not this time.

"So?" She took a step forward, and he thought that she may try to strike him, seeing the fury, the helpless frustration pouring through her dark, glittering eyes.

"We'll think of something," he said, taken by compassion, forgetting his own disappointment. "Please, Seketa, stop being so angry. We'll find the way."

"Will we?" Her lips were still trembling, but at the sound of her name, the insane spark disappeared, bringing back the girl he hugged and promised to fight for earlier by the fence.

"Yes, we will." Now it felt only natural to draw her closer, feeling her warmth, and the pulses of her young body. "We'll insist, and we will not give up until they do. Like I promised."

He could feel her pressing against him, as though trying to hide inside his arms, making it difficult to keep his balance. His eyes caught her gaze, and what it held made his heart stop.

Knees suddenly weak, he sought her lips, and this time she didn't move away but pressed closer, her kisses as sweet as last night, but more ardent, more demanding, setting his body on fire, making his limbs tremble and out of control. He just *had* to feel her and not the soft leather of her dress, with all the beads and the fringes getting in his way.

"I don't think we should…" he mumbled when they slipped down, onto the welcoming softness of the grass, but she pressed her lips against his, wriggling to make herself comfortable.

"We made the promise," she whispered, and her eyes beamed at him. "And we will seal it in the only way that will make it real."

His breath caught, he stared at her for a heartbeat, taking in the beauty of her features, now ethereal, shining with an impossible light. Having difficulty forming words, he just stared, marveling at this gift that the Great Spirits had given him, the wonderful, thrilling, breathtaking gift worthy only of warriors and heroes.

"You will never regret this, never," he muttered, before giving way to the wonderful wave of warmth, of happiness, of the delightful pleasure with no misgivings, no fear, no pain, and no longing for home.

The time seemed to stop as they turned into one, one with the sky and the trees and the rustling wind, one with all the good *uki* who had surely inhabited this wonderful clearing, and most importantly – one with each other, their entwined bodies committed, belonging to one another forever.

The growling of the thunder grew in frequency, drawing closer, bringing along the scent of the nearing rain. He felt her stirring, raising on her elbow, his shoulder still numb from the weight of her head where it had lain earlier, leaving its print.

"It's Heno. He is giving us his blessing," she whispered, beaming at him, her hair falling over her shoulders, hiding the roundness of her breasts.

"Yes," he said dreamily, still floating, not wishing to come back to the real world. "He is not angry with us. He understands."

"Oh, yes, he does. Before he was allowed to marry his Rainbow Goddess he had to overcome many difficulties. So he always helps lovers in trouble."

"Did he?" He pulled her closer, enjoying the sight of her but wishing to feel her back inside his arms.

"Oh, yes. Don't you know this story?"

He shook his head, shutting his eyes in order to feel her better.

"What is your real name?" she whispered.

He didn't hesitate. "Tekeni."

"Tekeni," she purred, rolling the word around her tongue. "Tekeni." The touch of her fingers sent shivers down his spine as she slipped them along his chest, avoiding the crusted cuts, lingering around them. "The annoying old bear was very thorough. Promise not to challenge any more monsters from such close proximity."

"I promise," he said, laughing. "But I told you before. It was not of my choosing."

"I don't know. First, you bragged that it was all of your choosing, because it was too easy to kill the beast, so you wanted to challenge it properly. Then you said you were scared." She beamed at him, the tip of her tongue slipping out, sliding between her lips, teasing. "I don't know what to believe, so I choose to think that my man has no fear." Her eyes flickered. "And not much good sense, either."

He could not help but to double with laughter. "It was not like that at all. I have fear and I have sense. And I have the prettiest girl, too." He raised his head in his turn, eyeing her thoroughly, making her blush. "I don't know about the Rainbow Goddess, but my woman is as beautiful as the Sky Woman herself. And as courageous."

Her smile shone at him, wonderful in its open delight. "Do you think so?"

"Oh, yes, she is! Her eyes are shining like stars, and her body is beautiful and strong, fitting the brave woman who created our world and all that it has, even the Great Spirits. If this girl I love would have to create another world, she would do it easily, I know that."

"But she won't have to, will she?" She almost purred, her delight at his words too open to conceal. "You will not grow jealous as her divine husband did, throwing her through the hole in the sky and onto our earth?"

"No, of course not. He was stupid to do that. I'm sure he is regretting his deed until this very day, angry and alone in his Sky World."

"Yes, he must be feeling this way." She stretched and half closed her eyes. "You will not treat me badly. You will always trust me, won't you?"

"Yes, always."

The fresh gust of wind brought the first drops, and they looked up, but the sky was still clear if now grayish in coloring, with the sun diminishing, hurrying toward its resting place.

"We better make ourselves presentable." She sat up and looked at him, eyes glittering. "You look as though your bear just came back, and this time to chase you all over the place, rolling down the hills."

He regarded her with a glance, unable to suppress his laughter. "I can imagine that while looking at you. So very proper and prim, an impeccable member of the Beaver Clan, with all those leaves in her hair and the earth smeared all over her body."

"Oh, so that was the end of the pretty talk? Stars for eyes and all the beautiful colors, eh?" She narrowed her eyes and looked even funnier in her half amused indignation. "Maybe I should use some of my divine powers against you."

Chuckling, he tied his loincloth in place, slipping his girdle on, making sure the sheath with his knife was again within easy reach, as always, just in case.

She was smoothing her hair, trying to braid the wandering tendrils. He watched her picking up her trampled dress, shaking it to clean it of leaves and small insects, who seemed to be happy to find a home in its folds.

"It hurts?" he asked guiltily, seeing her face twisting when she got to her feet, remembering nothing but the divine pleasure. He should have been thinking about her too, should he not?

"No, not really." She smiled demurely, eyes gleaming with smug female superiority. "But they say the first time is never the best for the girl. I'm yet to enjoy our lovemaking better."

"Yes, I heard that too." He frowned. "I'm sorry about that. I didn't notice…" For the life of him, he could not take his gaze away, although he now really wanted to. "I'm sorry."

But she came closer, her smile wonderful, brushing his guilt away. "Of course not. You had done it just the way I wanted to. I loved the way you loved me. It was inspiring." Tilting her head, she regarded him with a measuring gaze. "I shall make a beautiful quill ornament for your moccasins, that inspired I feel. And, although I may have some difficulty working the fields tomorrow, I know our Green Corn Ceremony will be better, thanks to the inspiration you gave me."

He grinned in spite of himself. "I will give you more inspiration every time you will need one." Sobering, he pressed her closer when she tried to break free. "So what was your plan? What do we do with the Mothers of your Clan?"

"We just won't hide our feelings," she said, sobering in her turn. "We will go on with our lives, loving each other and not hiding it, until they give up. They can't go on refusing us for summers on end. Some time their resistance will crumble." Her smile turned smug, pleased with herself. "Until then, you will prove yourself more and more, and will be accepted and loved, and I will gain more influence in our clan because I won't be such a young girl anymore. You see? It'll work."

"It'll take summers to happen," he stated, his mood deteriorating, reminded of his troubles back at the town, mounting with every passing day.

"Maybe a few summers, maybe less." Smiling into his darkening face, she kissed him lightly, suggestively. "And in the meanwhile, we will love each other in the woods, every time one of us will need an inspiration. How about that?"

"It can work, yes."

He bent to pick up her prettily embroidered girdle, wishing to conceal his expression. Summers upon summers? It didn't seem like a very alluring prospect. In fact, the prospect of going back to the town now was not truly beckoning. Maybe he would better bring her back and then go to talk to Two Rivers as he promised. The sun must have already been nearing the trees on the other side of the lake, but if they hurried he may not be too late. The strange man would surely linger, remaining on his favorite spot for some time, for the entire night most likely.

Her gasp jerked him back from his reverie, making him straighten up so abruptly his head reeled. He didn't waste his time glancing at her. Instead, his eyes darted toward the place where his instincts told him there was a foreign presence, taking in the silhouettes, counting them before his mind could absorb this information, his senses screaming danger.

The men came closer, sure of themselves but wary, watching them like hunters do to their prey. Stomach filling with ice, he recognized Yeentso's tall, arrogant bearing before being able to see the man's face. Others, two more of them, were coming from among the trees, in a perfect arrangement of hunters closing on a trapped deer.

"Well, well," said Yeentso, slowing his pace, as though wishing to see them better, to take the whole picture in. "If I hadn't seen it with my own eyes!"

He laughed, and the other men joined them, three more voices and not two. There was another man coming from behind, realized Tekeni, his hand straying toward the sheath of his knife.

"It's not going to help you, wild boy. You realize that, don't you?" The tall man laughed again. "Better drop it now. Drop it!" The laughter died away, replaced by the curt order. "Yeandawa there behind you has an arrow pointed at you, so if you don't throw away that pitiful knife of yours in two more heartbeats, it's going to flutter in you. Or better yet, in the pretty back of your girl."

He could hear Seketa swallowing a gasp, but what made him release his grip and let the knife slip was the look in his rival's eyes. The man meant what he said.

"Good. So now we have the wild boy disarmed and as harmless as a newborn spawn of a forest rat." Yeentso didn't move, savoring the moment. "Then let us hear what do you think is going to happen now, pretty boy? Eh? Let us hear what you think."

He tried to make his mind work, his body frozen, turned into stone, the tickling in his palms and feet the only sensation making it alive. He was going to die, of that he had no doubt. And it wouldn't be an easy death, either. Would he manage to die in dignity, like a captured warrior, or would he scream and cry and beg for the final blow, shaming himself before these people? And before her!

The thought of her made his heart leap in fright, bringing him back to his senses. He needed to make her go away, somehow. These men would harm her too, especially the dirty Yeentso who now took his eyes off him and was staring at her with an unpleasantly strange, playful grin on his lips.

"So, as the boy seemed to lose his ability to speak, maybe you, pretty Seketa, will tell us what was happening here in the woods just now? Such a prim, upright girl of the Beaver Clan, have you been teaching the filthy foreigner good manners?"

The other men laughed again, but it was a forced laughter. He could feel that most clearly. Glancing at the man nearest to him, he saw him frowning, holding his bow, ill at ease.

"Come on, pretty girl, have you lost your tongue as well? You always have something to say, don't you? Running all over our longhouse, righteous and irreproachable, the model of behavior, always knowing what should be done and how. Unlike this friend of yours, that other girl, the one who is not above sneaking away for an occasional kiss with boys, and even men. What is her name?" He turned to his friends. "Have any of you enjoyed the kisses of that other girl? I bet you did."

One of the men chuckled. "Be sure of that. And she is good at it, too."

"And the other favors?" The smile of pure satisfaction was stretching the man's lips as he turned back at them. "Like the ones our Seketa was bestowing on the filthy cub. Have any of you enjoyed that?" The silence lasted for only a heartbeat as the question was clearly rhetorical. Why would anyone admit that? They were all married men. "So, today we learned that the appearances can misleading, and that our virtuous, impeccable

Seketa was the one doling out her favors with true generosity." Shaking his head in an exaggerated manner, the man turned to his friends again. "Who would have thought the haughty thing could turn out to be such a loose girl?"

With their tormenter's attention temporarily away, he leaned toward her, feeling her numb, frozen by his side.

"Run the moment we start fighting," he breathed, trying to will her back to life with the sheer power of his words. "Run like you have never run in your life."

She seemed to awaken all at once. "No!"

The short word echoed between the trees, startling them all. He wanted to scream with frustration.

"No?" Yeentso's attention was back on them. "Oh, so the honorable member of my wife's clan had found her tongue, and she is pleading that she has not been lying around with men, although caught all disheveled and hardly dressed, with none other than the filthy foreigner, spreading her legs—"

"It is not of your filthy interest!" she cried out, clenching her fists. "And if you will not let us go now, you will be in trouble because I'll tell our Clan Mothers everything that happened here, everything down to the last tiny detail. I'll tell them how you tracked him down, looking for him in the woods in order to kill him. I will tell it all, and I will be believed. You know I will be. They know me, and they know you. And they will believe me because you are a filthy liar and murderer and a lazy troublemaker, too. They don't need people like you in our clan. They will throw you out like the dirty piece of animal leavings you are!"

Fists clenched, she advanced toward Yeentso, trembling with rage, magnificent in her fury. The silence prevailed, interrupted by the growling of the nearing thunder.

His breath caught, Tekeni watched her, along with the rest of them, but when Yeentso took an involuntary step back, his full attention on the girl, he scanned the ground with a glance, spotting a pile of stones not far away from where he stood. Counting on the eyes of the others to be upon the furious girl, he took a small step toward his discovery, then another, his heart beating fast.

"If you don't let us go now," she screamed, shaking her fists. "I swear I will make you sorry, sorry that you had ever been born. Even if takes me my entire life to do that."

"Stop your blabbering, you dirty forest rat," roared Yeentso at last.

Leaping forward, he grabbed her by her shoulder, but she squirmed out of his grip, slapping his hand, sinking her nails into it in the process. He cried out and caught her again, more successfully this time.

"Don't you dare to touch me," she screamed, squirming and kicking wildly, but now, having her in a firmer hold, the man relaxed enough to enjoy the situation.

"Not so haughty anymore, are we?"

She kicked again, and as his palm clapped her face, trying to turn her head toward him, she sank her teeth into it, and the man howled, releasing his grip, if only partly.

Seeing his chance, Tekeni darted toward the pile of stones, picking one without looking, throwing it with not much of an aim, more careful not to hit her than to hurt him. Too small to do a real damage, the stone nevertheless brushed against the tall man's forehead, making him reel.

"Run," he screamed wildly, seeing her free for a moment, stumbling but holding on. "Run for the cliff."

He didn't dare to shout any more directions, as not to give them the idea of her possible destination, but he hoped she would understand. Two Rivers was not far away, certain to be still there, upon his favorite cliff. Barefoot, she had not much chances of reaching the town before they would catch her, but reaching Two Rivers might help. And also maybe, just maybe...

He had no time pondering his possibilities. Snatching another, heavier and better stone, he darted aside in time to avoid a smashing blow from behind.

A club swished beside his ear, and it made him shudder, his senses panicking, his fear sudden and paralyzing, the horrible memories of the only battle he had been a part of two summers ago surfacing all of a sudden, terribly vivid.

Turning around, he watched the man nearing, wielding his club again, but it was Yeentso's scream that brought him back to his senses.

"Yeandawa, get her, you stupid lump of meat. Don't let her get away."

The sounds and the smells came back in force, making his heart leap, his instincts deciding for him. From such a short distance his stone could not miss, crushing into his attacker's face heavily, making a smacking sound.

The man collapsed at once, like a cut down tree, to lie on the ground in a heap of limbs. Elated, Tekeni rushed to retrieve his fallen rival's club, forgetting about the rest of the attackers, until a blow from behind sent him head first into the sprawling man.

Disoriented for a moment, he still had enough presence of mind to roll away in time to avoid a vicious kick. His eyes caught the sight of Yeentso and another man towering above, and his knife lying in a tempting proximity.

He calculated frantically, scrambling to his feet, knowing that he had no chance, not with the two warriors' full attention upon him. Indeed, another blow sent him back onto the ground, gasping amidst a wild outburst of pain.

"Not so fast, wild boy," Yeentso was growling, his weight now upon him, pressing, interrupting his ability to breathe. He felt his head yanked backwards, then pushed into the mess of roots and stones, making the breathing into a yet more difficult affair.

The pain exploded prettily, like a colorful ball. He choked and fought to break free from the sticky earth, desperate to gulp the air for which the supply had been cut off so suddenly. The world swayed and the sounds receded, still he struggled on, terrified, absorbing kicks but caring only for the opportunity to breathe again.

Finally, the pressure lessened and he had been jerked around, to feel the clearness of the breeze and the rain in it, still not falling but already present in the air. It made him feel better.

Blinking to clear his vision, the taste of blood and fresh earth filling his mouth, making him gag, he felt a sharpness of a small stone against his palm, inviting, giving hope. His fingers locked around it as his ribs absorbed more kicks, his instincts urging him to strike out, but his mind whispering to wait for a better opportunity, to get the maximum effect of this last effort to do *something*.

He felt a drop of rain splashing, then another, and they paused, too.

"Finish him before the rain begins," said the other man thoughtfully. "We have to check on Yaree. The dirty whelp cracked his head quite open."

"He'll manage, and the rain won't begin for some time," said Yeentso. "The girl worries me, though. If Yeandawa lets her slip away, we are in trouble. She may be believed, although I doubt that. Not after my story will be heard."

"What will you tell?"

"That the dirty foreigner forced her, abused her for the whole afternoon, and now she is crazed with grief and doesn't know what she is talking about."

The chuckle of the other man was loud and surprisingly light. "A good one."

"But if Yeandawa kills her it'll be safer."

He wished he could rub the mud off his eyes, but to do so was to let them know he was still conscious, the effort of keeping still stretching his nerves, testing his willpower to its limits.

"Is the cub dead?"

The shadow fell across as the silhouette of one of them neared, leaning forward, studying him, probably. He heard the man's breathing, felt the hand grabbing his throat, pressing lightly, checking his heartbeat. Not Yeentso's hand. He suppressed his disappointment. But for a chance to hit the hated man before he died!

He took a deep breath, disregarding the pain in his ribs,

putting the remnants of his strength into bringing his arm up, crushing the stone it held into the man's face, feeling the sharp edges of his improvised weapon tearing the skin – such a pleasant feeling. The man gasped and disappeared out of his view, to clear the sight of the grayish sky once again.

"The filthy rat!" he screamed as Tekeni tried to make the best of it by rolling away before they came back to their senses.

It might have worked, had he been as agile as before, but with the obviously cracked ribs and the mud and blood blurring his vision, he was not fast enough. A vicious kick brought him back to his previous position, then he was jerked onto his feet.

"Hold his hands. Don't let him move!" yelled Yeentso. "The dirty cub is crazy, plain crazy."

He fought the grip that locked his elbows behind his back, kicking wildly, indeed, crazed with desperation. Oh, yes, he was crazy! Crazy to lose his guard in this way, to let himself get caught here in the woods, so stupidly, so carelessly, so foolishly unprepared. For this, he deserved to die. If only there was a way to make sure she had made it back to the town safely.

CHAPTER 18

The sun was about to disappear behind the trees of the opposite shore, and the growling of the thunder drew nearer, growing in frequency. There would be a storm soon, reflected Two Rivers, watching the rapidly graying sky. Nothing serious, just another pleasantly warm summer thunderstorm. Heno the Thunderer was a benevolent deity.

Still, to sit there, soaking in rain, was not the best of the prospects. He would have to return to the town soon, despite his resolution not to do so before reaching a decision.

To leave or not to leave?

The question kept circling in his head, examining all the possible angles, arriving at a dead end, always. To stay was fruitless, to leave was insane. The town of his childhood offered nothing but frustration, boredom, emptiness. But so did any settlement of his people. His reputation would go with him wherever he went. They all knew about the prophecy and about the strangeness and unacceptability of his ideas.

To leave it all behind by crossing the Great Lake, on the other hand, was tempting but plain insane. He had nothing to seek among the enemies of his people, nothing to ask, nothing to offer. Nothing but a spectacular death that they would be sure to inflict upon him. That might give them an interesting diversion for a day, but he would gain nothing but a painful end.

Even taking the boy along might not solve the problem. The promising youth was nothing but a child when he had left his people, with no influence and no weight. A son of a War Chief, admittedly, but still just a child. No one would probably remember him at all.

No. The attempt to cross the Great Lake was the worst idea of them all. And yet...

The scattered drops of rain sprinkled his face, waking him from his reverie. Time to go back, back to suspicious glances, hatred, and mistrust. He shrugged. The hatred was new, all the rest – not so much.

Hesitating upon the top of the trail, he watched the woods to his left, his instincts alerting him for no apparent reason. To scan the open patch of the land, all the way to the clusters of trees that began not far away from his vantage point, felt called for. As though unwilling to disappoint him, a figure sprang from behind them, progressing in a funny gait, seeming like running upon an uneven surface.

Puzzled, he watched her for another heartbeat, then rushed down the cliff, his heart beating fast. Something was amiss. Even from this distance, he could see that it was a woman and that she had been in some sort of a trouble, with her hair flowing wildly and her dress askew, but mostly because of the desperate way she ran. Were enemy warriors spotted in the proximity of their woods?

He hastened his step, but the girl must have been running really fast, as she was close by the time he reached the flat ground. Close enough to recognize her. The Beaver Clan beauty! His heart missed a beat.

"What happened?" he cried out, his incredulous gaze taking in the mess of her hair, the muddied, scratched face, the torn dress. Her feet were bare and bleeding. *Why would anyone run around the woods barefoot?*

"Please!" she gasped, swaying as though about to fall. "Please. You have to help him. You have to hurry. Please!"

He needed no explanation. "Where?"

"There, in the woods. The small clearing, next to the cliffs."

"Stay here!" he tossed, snatching his knife as he burst into a mad run in the direction she came from. She needed help, that much was obvious, but whatever happened back there in the woods, he knew the boy needed help more urgently.

Heart pounding, he thought about his club and his bow back in his longhouse. The knife would not be enough, so much he knew. But how many were they? And how far?

The man sprang into his view, bursting from behind the trees maybe ten, twenty paces away. Breathing heavily and not noticing Two Rivers at first, he scanned the cliffs, searching for the girl, probably.

He knew that one well, the stocky member of the Porcupine Clan, a quiet, unobtrusive type but not a very pleasant company either, with something shadowy lurking behind the smallness of his eyes.

His jaw dropping, the man stared at him for a heartbeat, appalled.

"Drop the damn bow," shouted Two Rivers, his rage bubbling, threatening to get out of control. The filthy lowlife was, indeed, chasing that girl. Did those people have no shame at all?

The man came back to life, bringing the bow up in one movement, shooting with not a heartbeat of hesitation. Astounded, Two Rivers ducked, more out of an instinct than as a thoughtful reaction, and the arrow swished by, scratching his ear, leaving a stinging sensation.

Heart racing insanely, he covered the distance with two powerful leaps, throwing himself at the man, careless of losing his own balance as long as there would be no range between him and the stretched bowstring. His knife made a fast work out of it, leaving the man gurgling, squirming on the muddy sand.

Breathing heavily, he sprang back to his feet, tearing the bow from the bleeding hands, snatching another arrow out of the fallen off quiver. There was no time to see if the man was dying or not. Back in the woods, the situation might have been bad. He might be too late already; still, he dashed into the dusk enveloping the trees, his ears pricked, trying to catch the sounds. There were too many clearings, small or large, to know which one he had been looking for.

Luckily, the voices reached him, carrying clearly, not very far away. Someone was talking, then came a muffled gasp, then more talking. He rushed on, more careful now of the noise he made. They might have been many, but the bow gave him a clear advantage.

By the time he reached the clearing, he already knew that there must have been no more than two, three people there, although only one voice was talking. Yeentso's. But of course!

Stifling a curse, his blood boiling, screaming for a kill, he covered the rest of the distance in a few leaps, careless of the noise now, bursting into the clearing, finding it difficult to see the silhouettes with the trees blocking the last of the light.

The kneeling figure caught his eyes, held behind by another man, struggling to break free. Good! The boy must have been still in high spirits, although covered with a mixture of mud and blood to the point of turning unrecognizable.

Eyes wide, they stared at him, all three of them, Yeentso' knife hesitating in the air, glittering darkly. He didn't waste his time on talking. As the man brought his arm up, whether to throw the knife at the intruder or to try to tell him something, Two Rivers shot, hardly aiming at all. From such a short distance he could not miss.

Not sparing another glance to the arrow fluttering in the wide chest, and the way it pushed its victim back with an admirable power, slamming the already sagging body against the tree, he leaped toward the other man, smashing his fist into the broad, astounded face, seeing it wavering but not falling, not disappearing from his view.

The man's knife was out in a heartbeat, as he released the boy's arms, but Two Rivers was faster, his other fist already sinking into the man's stomach, his own knife twisting, widening the wound to the maximum effect.

He didn't check on either of his victims again, but rushed toward the boy, who was still kneeling, now leaning on his arms, breathing heavily, evidently gathering his strength to get up.

"Don't!" he said, stopping the youth with his hands from getting any further. "Lie down. Let me see your wounds first."

"But we can't," mumbled the boy, struggling against the gentle push, his words muffled, unclear, coming with difficulty through the swollen, cut lips. One of his eyes was swollen too, badly at that, and the rest of his face was covered with so much mud and blood it turned unrecognizable.

Cursing, Two Rivers studied the cuts running down the high cheekbones and across them. He shouldn't have killed Yeentso that fast!

"Stop squirming like a worm," he tossed, annoyed. "Lie still, and let me see if you can be allowed to get up at all." The cuts looked superficial and not especially dangerous if washed and maybe stitched.

"Seketa... she needs help..." insisted the boy, resisting his touch as he leaned closer to study the bloodied chest and stomach.

"She is well. I saw her, and I talked to her, and she will probably be here shortly. Knowing this young lady, I bet she was running right after me, although I told her not to."

The cuts crossing the youth's chest did not seem deep as well, cutting the skin and some muscle, intended to inflict more pain than damage. What a filthy, stinking piece of excrement! He cursed, the desire to go and kick Yeentso's body overwhelming. A disgusting, loathsome, abominable beast. Even the captured warriors facing their difficult death were not tortured for the sake of inflicting pain. It was an old tradition, testing the man's strength and inner power, running the gauntlet but getting struck only once by each person. While this man had obviously enjoyed the process, hurting, but making sure his victim would not die fast, with his slimy friend helping readily. The dirty pieces of rotten meat!

"Well, it seems that you will live," he said curtly, still too angry to talk, but needing the distraction. His rage was again difficult to contain. "But we need to get you down to the lake shore, to wash all those cuts. So now go ahead, get up at long last, and see if you can walk."

Catching the youth across his shoulder, he helped him up, knowing that with all this desire to go and look for his girl in trouble, the young cub would probably not run around just yet. The bluish mess of the youth's ribs held his expectations in check as to the ability of his patient to get up at all.

"Thank you," muttered the boy, suppressing a groan, wavering and clutching to his supporter's arm. He turned his head, trying to face his rescuer through his unharmed eye. "I'm grateful. So very grateful. I will repay your kindness. As long as I live—"

"Later, wolf cub, later." He grinned, warmed by the boy's artless gratitude in spite of himself. "First, let us make sure you live long enough to be that grateful." Propelling the youth toward the path, he frowned. "We want to reach the shore before it gets dark, so lean on me and make your best to hurry."

The girl burst upon them as they negotiated their way out of the clearing, progressing more noisily than a hungry bear. Clumsy, still barefoot and limping, she rushed toward them, her face dirty, awash with fresh tears.

"Oh Mighty Spirits, I don't... I can't... I..." she sobbed, stumbling and almost falling on them.

The boy, who needed all of his concentration to walk, almost lost his balance trying to look at her and maybe to say something.

Taking more of the youth's weight, Two Rivers ground his teeth. "Stop it," he told her curtly. "Stop making this stupid noise. Come around and support him from the other side. Make yourself useful!"

It came out too sharply, but he didn't care. They needed to reach the lake before darkness, and it was difficult enough without her interception.

The girl pulled herself together with a surprising swiftness.

"Yes, yes," she breathed, placing her shoulder under the boy's other arm and falling into their step quite naturally. One moment a sobbing mess, the other an efficient female, the prim, upright girl that she was.

He tried to suppress his grin.

"Get your moccasins first. It'll make our progress easier."

Without a word she was gone, to be back in no more than a few heartbeats.

"Tell me what happened," he inquired, mainly to pass the time. Their progress was painfully slow, and he worried he would have no light to inspect the boy's wounds after the washing. The cub might need to see the healer, although he sincerely hoped they would be able to do without it. They were not going back to the town. Not if he could help it. The dilemma was over, and the solution was not of his choosing anymore, but surprisingly, it made him feel better, glad, relieved, even hopeful.

"We were in the woods," said the girl quietly. "Talking. And then they appeared."

"How many?"

"Four of them."

"Oh," he nodded. "So none got away."

She swallowed loudly and said nothing.

"And then what happened?"

Her hesitation was obvious. "Yeentso wanted to kill him, and he told us he would do this."

"Why didn't they let you go? I would think Yeentso was seeking no trouble with your clan. He should have let you go, then inform our boy of his plans."

Again, she said nothing, so obviously uncomfortable he felt like chuckling. For a simple talk, she would not need to take off her shoes and her girdle, nor would her hair be now full of grass and small leaves. Those two were loving each other there on the clearing, that much was obvious. Were they caught in the middle of the lovemaking? What a pleasure for the dirty Yeentso. That would make the lowlife feel safe to try and harm the girl as well. The despicable piece of rotten meat must have been pleasantly surprised.

"So you managed to kill one of the four, wolf cub," he said, wishing to change the subject. There was no need to embarrass them any further. "Not bad, I say."

"I would have… have killed more… if I had my knife or my bow," muttered the boy hotly, his words muffled but loud enough.

"I can understand the lack of your bow, but where was your knife?"

"They made him throw it away," cried out the girl. "They were afraid to get close to him while he was armed. Such cowardly, filthy lowlifes!"

"I see." As they came out of the woods, their progress became easier, not hindered by the uneven, slippery ground and the jumble of roots. "Let us hurry. I want to take care of his wounds before the last of the light is gone." He glanced at the girl. "So, how did you get away?"

"He threw a stone," she said proudly. "Hit Yeentso's head. Almost made him fall."

"It was a small stone," mumbled the boy, apologetic. "I got a bigger one later." Suppressing a groan, he bit his lips and stopped talking, obviously in pain.

"It did the work." Two Rivers shook his head, admiring them both. He knew the cub was a resourceful, courageous thing, yet his girl proved to be as good. She did her best under the circumstances, and her actions saved her lover a prolonged, painful death. Too bad they were not destined to be together.

Reaching the path that led toward the wide strip of the shore with various canoes concealed under the wooden tent, the girl hesitated, but said nothing until they reached the waterline.

"Why don't we take him straight away to the town?" she asked, frowning. "It's not a long way, and he needs to be treated by a healer."

"I'll tell you why if you don't think about it yourself by the time his wounds are washed and we are back on the shore," said Two Rivers, taking again most of the youth's weight. "Come. It's not long now, and you will be able to rest after we are done."

Leading his companion into the water, he glanced at the rough wooden construction not far away to their left. Luckily, in this time of the year, with the fishing season in its highest, some people were too lazy to drag their canoes all the way to the safety of the town's fence. They would have a chance to pick the best of the vessels.

He let the youth soak in the water for some time, trying to be as gentle as he could while washing the cuts. Still, by the time they came out, the boy was half conscious, exhausted from pain.

"Rest now," said Two Rivers, making his patient as comfortable as he could upon the sandy strip of the land.

With no mixture of mud and blood, the youth looked somewhat better, although pale and barely there, sprawling like a dead creature, the crusted marks from the bear's claws and the new cuts making a strange pattern upon his chest. His face looked bad, swollen and slashed and bluish with bruises, but this would heal, too. The cub was not going to die. That was the main thing.

The girl waited impatiently. "Will he be well?"

"Yes, he will." Glancing at her, he paused, taken by compassion. Another one looking bizarre, disheveled, and pale, the air of uncertainty surrounding her, atypical for this particular female. "You did a good thing. You saved him."

She peered at him with her troubled eyes huge and glittering. "You are going to leave, aren't you? You and him?"

"We have no choice."

"Why?" Her eyes were filling with tears, but her voice did not shake.

"Do you want us to go back and try to explain the deaths of four more people?"

"They were the ones to attack us!" she cried out, wringing her hands. "They were trying to kill us, and then I came to you asking for help. You had no choice but to kill these people. I'll tell it over and over, repeat it as long as I need to in order to make them listen. I'll talk to the Town's and the Clans Councils and all the influential people."

For her sake, he suppressed his grin. "They won't listen to you, not after what happened at the condolence ceremony this morning. We were told to keep away from the people of your clan, and from this same Yeentso in particular. We were told to stay in our longhouses and keep quiet. But what we did was just the opposite. We went out and killed Yeentso. And three more men, all of them good hunters and warriors, the best of the nation." He snorted, then shrugged. There was no point in getting angry because of that. "What do you think will happen to your pretty boy now? Will the Town Council pat him on his back and tell him to be more careful next time he wants to love his girl in the woods?" He shook his head as she tried to protest. "Yes, yes, I know. You two were just talking. But even this will not predispose them to listen to you more carefully. Good girls do not spend their time with boys all alone in the woods, especially not with the boys who are frowned upon. You give too much credit to your ability to orate and make them listen." He eyed her thoughtfully, feeling sorry for her. "He has no choice but to leave. To flee, if you want to name it for what it is. And if you care about him, you will help him to do so in any way you can."

She dropped her gaze, looking thin and forlorn, just a frail young girl that she was. "You've been thinking about leaving for some time, haven't you?"

Surprised by her perception, he hesitated. "Not for a very long time, but yes, I've been thinking about leaving."

"Where to?"

He eyed her with a growing interest. "To the lands of his people."

"Why?" Hugging her arms against the strengthening wind, she kept peering at the sand, her voice quiet and detached, as though someone else were asking the probing questions.

"I can't answer you that. This decision is based on many factors. It has something to do with certain dreams. And the prophecy." He shrugged lightly, grinning. "We have nowhere else to go, anyway."

"They say you did not believe in the prophecy," she pressed on, disregarding his attempt to lighten the conversation. "I heard you saying that, too. What changed?"

He spread his arms wide, defeated. "I don't know, Seketa. I truly don't know. But yes, something changed, and it has to do with your chosen mate. He is a part of it, I know it now. An important part, girl, and not just a tool. He'll grow into an outstanding man, both of us can see that, but there is more to it. Much more. He is a part of the change, but only with the passing of time we will know more, discover what his role in all this is."

"That's why you rushed to save him so readily. That's why you were prepared to kill your countryfolk in order to save him." It came out as a statement, an open accusation. "You are doing this for you, not for him."

He suppressed his irritation, seeing her scared but defiant, trembling with cold, or maybe with desperation. She loved him, this wild, savage cub, he realized, truly loved him.

"I will try to keep him from harm," he said quietly, wishing he knew what to say. "I will not use him in the way you are afraid I would. If he'll wish to go his own way when we reach his people's lands, I will let him go."

She watched him for a long while, her eyes huge and glittering, the unshed tears held back, not allowed to roll down her muddied cheeks. A few more heartbeats passed before she nodded and turned away.

"I will go back to the town now, and I will bring you things, food and clothes and your weapons. It may take me some time, to sneak around and gather those things. Will you wait until I come back?" She hesitated. "I want to say my farewells to him."

"Yes, I'll wait." Suddenly, he found his throat constricted. "You are a wise woman, wiser than your age warrants. And your courage has no bounds. He is lucky to have your love, even if you two were not destined to be together." He took a deep breath, feeling strange. "And who knows? He is not an ordinary person. Maybe he'll find a way to reach you, to make you his despite all the obstacles. I would bet on this particular stake, as impossible as it might look now. I would put many of my belongings against this wild bet."

Something crept into the depths of the bottomless eyes, something that made the desperate look go away.

"Do you feel it?" she asked in a small voice. "Do you see it in your mind's eye?"

He knew what she meant, and for a heartbeat, he hesitated. It seemed like a certain thing now, he was sure the boy would find the way. Or was it just wishful thinking, an attempt to make her feel better?

"I don't know," he told her frankly, unwilling to lie. "I think I can feel it, but I'm not certain. But then, when was I certain of anything concerning feelings or prophecies? I hope he will find you, that much I can promise you. I believe him capable of this sort of deeds."

Her smile shone at him out of the thickening darkness.

"Thank you," she said, turning around and beginning to ascend the path leading back to the town. "I do believe in your prophecy and your feelings and dreams."

"We will sail at midnight," he called after her. "If you don't manage to come back by then, I will tell him about this conversation and your trust and your confidence in his abilities. You are an outstanding woman. If I'll have a chance in helping him find you, I will help."

Alone at long last, he stared at the dark mass of the water, then shook his head and went to check on the boy, who by now drifted into an uneasy sleep, spread upon the sand, breathing heavily, jerking every now and then.

The cub will survive, he thought, examining the youth more closely. A few days of rest and the boy would be himself again, more useful than ever.

In the last of the dim illumination, he eyed the bluish mess of the youth's ribs and the way he jerked with every taken breath. Maybe half a moon, he thought, but he will be well, eventually.

The task of choosing the best canoe beckoned, and he

hurried toward the wooden tent, deep in thought. If the girl managed to gather a half of what she intended to bring, they would be off to a passable start. And she would manage, he knew. This woman was capable of many things, he believed now. If only they could have brought her along! The wildness of this thought made him chuckle.

CHAPTER 19

She watched the sun coming up from behind the trees adorning the inner side of the palisade, unstoppable and unwelcomed. Narrowing her eyes against the strengthening glow, she followed its progress, her mind numb.

Too tired to sleep, she had stayed near Iraquas' platform for the remainder of the night, doing nothing, not even praying but just sitting there and staring ahead, frozen, dead, turned to stone. The world as she knew it was gone, but as long as the night was there, sheltering, she could hide and rest and gather her strength.

The sunrise would put the end to it, she knew, wishing for it never to come. It would make her face people, talk to them, answer their questions. It would force her to pretend, to pretend that nothing happened, that nothing changed in her life, when everything had changed and would never be the same.

She shut her eyes, wishing the night to come back. *Please, not now, not yet. Just a few more heartbeats of peace and quiet in the merciful darkness, that same darkness that still saw them together. Just a little more time to prolong the night.*

Clenching her palms, she remembered how she had run back to the town, with this same darkness just beginning to descend, limping on her cut, hurting feet, in a frenzied hurry but trying to be careful, to draw as little attention as possible.

People were still chanting around Iraquas' platform, dancing and praying. The rolling of the drums told her that, but this time she gave no passing thought to her cousin and his departing spirit. She had been too busy for that.

Luckily, they all seemed to be busy as well, so no one noticed her sneaking into the storage room, lingering there for long enough to stuff a leather bag with all sorts of foods, dried meat and fish and berries, every piece of cornbread she could find, and then some more.

She was lucky enough to discover a pottery jar with the sweetened corn flour the warriors were taking while on the raids, to mix with some water when the need to eat quickly would arise. She tucked the whole jar into her bag, caring nothing for the Mothers of her Clan, who would be appalled to find so many items of precious food missing. There would be an outcry, and the search for the thief or thieves, but it would happen later, much later, when Tekeni and Two Rivers would be far away already, facing other dangers and threats.

The fear was back, clutching her chest in its freezing grip. To attempt the crossing of the Great Sparkling Water was an act of madness. Two Rivers was insane. He should have thought of a better solution. And yet…

She remembered going through his belongings, shivering with fear. To pillage her longhouse's storage room was one thing. She could always plead that she had been hungry, or sent by someone to bring the food to the mourning people, or just cry and demand to be left alone with her grief. She had every right to be in her own longhouse.

However, to sneak into one of the Turtle Clan's dwellings was a wholly different matter. She would have to explain what she had been doing in Two Rivers' family compartment, and there was no good explanation to that, not a single excuse.

So she went through his belongings in a hurry, tossing every item of clothing she found into her bag without looking, searching frantically for his bow and the quiver of arrows, finding a bird's trap in the process and, on the spur of an inspiration, tossing the intricate thing in as well. They would need to sustain themselves for quite a while, before reaching their dubious destination.

Relieved to be outside and inspired by the swiftness of her progress – it was still far enough from midnight – she eyed the deserted alleys of the town, then left her bag beside the tobacco plots and ran as fast as she could toward the Wolf Clan's longhouse. He needed to take his belongings too, his bow and arrows, and most of all – the precious claws of the bear he slew. He deserved to wear the necklace he would make out of them, for everyone to see and know how great and fearless he was.

The tears were back, threatening to take her again, to reduce her into a trembling heap of limbs. She clenched her teeth and looked at the sun, trying to greet the benevolent deity against her will. Father Sun was not to blame.

As it gained power, she watched it, smiling upon her, spreading its warmth, bringing her frozen limbs to life. He would come as he promised, she told herself, beginning to believe again. Two Rivers maintained that the wild boy was capable of even greater, more impossible deeds, and now, as the darkness receded, she began to believe in that as well. He was truly an outstanding man – Tekeni, the wild boy from the lands of the savages, her chosen mate. He would do this and many more outstanding things. Be the part of Two Rivers' mission, but with her by his side.

Smiling now, she remembered coming back to the shore, carrying the heavy bag and the weapons. It was a miracle that no one had seen her, a miracle that no one had wandered outside the town's fence on that particular night: no grief-stricken people from either of the mourning clans seeking some privacy, no couples seeking some love, no playful, mischievous children even.

No one was there to see her staggering under her cumbersome burden, or to find the bodies of four people not far away in the woods. The town seemed too busy with itself, minding its own business, for a change. Or maybe those were the Great Spirits, divine powers, or good *uki*, casting their spell, making everyone blind and deaf for one critical night. *Was Two Rivers' mission that important?*

She remembered her relief, finding them still on the shore, with Two Rivers immersed in examining a narrow, strangely bright canoe he already had dragged all alone toward the shore line, and Tekeni curled upon the sand, absorbed in his pain or the ways to deal with it.

She had knelt beside him, dropping her cargo carelessly, making Two Rivers frown, as Tekeni came back to life, pushing himself into a sitting position, his face twisting.

"Don't get up," she whispered, putting her arms around him, supporting, but also enjoying the touch, giving him her warmth. "You need to rest before your journey."

"I'm not going!" he said sharply, the words slipping with difficulty through his cut, swollen lips.

"Of course, you are going. You have to." She peered at him, her stomach suddenly light, fluttering with anticipation, with the suddenness of her hope.

"I don't have to. I'm not leaving you. We'll find the way to deal with this."

Oh, it was music, a wonderful music of the most beautiful flute!

She took a deep breath. "Do you think we can? How? I'm not sure there is a way, and Two Rivers said—"

"I don't care," called out Two Rivers tersely, turning the canoe over and examining its bottom. "The moment this thing is ready, I'm sailing, with or without your gallant warrior." He spat into the water. "You can try to talk him out of this madness, but remember that you don't have much time."

She let her breath out, torn. If he left, she would lose him forever. If he stayed, she may have him for herself for some time, but the price might be too high, more than she was prepared to pay. Two Rivers was right. Four people were killed, and he would be blamed for their deaths, no matter what truly happened. She wouldn't be able to make them listen.

Heart twisting with pain at the sight of his cut, swollen face, she leaned closer, to kiss his lips carefully, anxious not to hurt him. The more passionate kisses would have to live in her memory only now. Until he came for her!

"You won't break your promise to me," she whispered,

swallowing the knot in her throat. "We promised, and we sealed our love this afternoon, but our plan was silly. It would never have worked anyway, even without the filthy lowlife Yeentso. My Clan Mothers are stubborn; they would not see the reason." Another knot in her throat swallowed, she went on, praying for her voice to remain firm, not to break. "But it doesn't matter. We will just have to achieve our goal differently now. We have to be more cunning, more patient, that's all."

She peered into his eyes, feeling his arms enveloping her, although his body tensed with an effort, his forehead glittering with sweat. She pressed closer, taking some of his weight.

"If you stay, you die. If you leave, you do have a chance. And then, after you have helped Two Rivers, after you two have established yourselves somewhere, anywhere, come here and take me away, too. I will be waiting for you. I will not belong to anyone, I promise. I promised you that already, but I now will be repeating myself. I'll belong to no one but you, and if you come and kidnap me back to your lands of the savages, I will come gladly. Even if it means that I'll have to cook people for your evening meals and to kiss you while watching the snakes twisting in your hair."

She felt his laughter, and the way his body tensed, dealing with the pain the laughter brought.

"Oh, you would deal with that, would you?" he muttered, his lips twisting slightly, but his eyes smiling, happy and unreserved.

"Yes, I would," she said, satisfied with the effect. "Do your people's women work the fields at all?"

"No, they hunt people for meals, instead. And they tend their husbands' hair, to make the snakes happy. That's all they do."

"Then their life is easy, and I will be happy to lead it, as long as you make love to me the way you did this afternoon."

His gaze deepened, taking her breath away. "I will come for you. Unless I am dead, and maybe even then. I will not break my promise. You will be mine, and it won't take me long summers to come, either. I will not make you wait, I promise you that."

And then they sat silent, holding each other, sad and happy at the same time, until Two Rivers declared that the boat was ready, poring through the contents of her bag, nodding his approval.

"So many useful things! And my bird's trap," he exclaimed, as happy as a young boy. "You are quite a woman, Seketa!" Straightening up, he faced her, smiling into her eyes. "I hope to see you again, and soon. This young man will make it happen, never fear." He grinned. "I almost wish we could have taken you along now. You have more common sense than the whole female population of this town put together. And many males thrown in the pile."

"Maybe she should come," said Tekeni, pausing to catch his balance before attempting to step into the boat.

She felt her heart missing a beat. To leap into their canoe and sail away? Was it not the best of solutions? And why not? Why couldn't she come along, into the wonderful, most exciting of the adventures—

Two Rivers' snort cut her daydream short. "You want to drag your girl across the Great Lake and into the lands of the savages, to an unknown destination, in this small canoe and almost no supplies? Oh Mighty Spirits, why don't you think sensibly for once?"

He was right, of course, he was right. She bit her lips, knowing that had Tekeni been in a better condition he would had argued, quite forcefully at that. He would have done exactly as he felt fit, refusing to sail again, maybe. As it was, he just muttered angrily, hugging her shoulders with force, promising even with this hug to return for her, no matter what.

She had stood upon the shore for a long time after they disappeared from her view, reluctant to go back to the town and its people. And when she came, she didn't go home, but went to sit under Iraquas' tree, to wait for the sunrise, and to think.

She was not in any particular danger, she knew. No one would think to question her about the death of Yeentso and his friends when the bodies would be found. They would scream murder and try to reach the fleeing culprits, launching an expedition that would fail, of course. Two Rivers was a resourceful man, with plenty of experience and more clear thinking than any man she had ever met. And with Tekeni for a partner his chances were even better. They wouldn't be caught, and they would manage not to get killed on the other side of the Great Sparkling Water as well. This town would yet hear about this pair, she suddenly knew, and only good, outstanding things.

Smiling back at the friendly sky deity, she felt her tears drying, going away, for good this time. Oh, those two were destined to make great things, to stop the war, maybe, yes. And she would be a part of this happening. She would not let them leave her behind, to come and fetch her when it all was done and ready. She'd find the way to reach him if he didn't appear to kidnap her soon enough.

AUTHOR'S AFTERWORD

Around the 12th century, the lands of the people known to us today as Iroquois were torn by ferocious warfare, with every nation fighting each other, raiding one another's towns, seeking revenge against offenses, imaginary or real. Five sister-nations caught in the web of violence and retaliation, unable to escape the hopeless loop. To settle their differences and make them talk, someone with courage and unusually broad thinking was needed. Maybe a prophet, maybe just an outstanding man, he was an outsider, on that all the versions of the legend agree.

The Great Peacemaker, indeed, according to most sources, came from across Lake Ontario and the lands of the Huron (Wyandot) people, present day southeastern Canada, near the Bay of Quinte. For unknown reasons, his own country folk did not deign to listen to his message; however, the people of the current day's upstate New York turned out to be more open to new ideas.

Most recent studies place the formation of the Great League at around 1142, basing their conclusion on the oral tradition, archeological evidence, and specific events such as the full solar eclipse that was most clearly mentioned to occur above a certain site.

The Five Nations' wise, complicated, incredibly detailed set of laws survived for centuries, and more than a few scholars agreed that the later day USA constitution was influenced to this or that degree by the Great Law of Peace that, needless to say, was very prominent in the area at the times when the dozen or so English colonies were struggling for their independence.

Benjamin Franklin was the most interested person, closely acquainted with the ways of the Great League of the Iroquois. Deeply impressed, he printed many pamphlets, wrote many letters, citing the League's incredibly elaborate set of laws. In 1754, on the famous Albany conference, he spoke openly about creating a union that resembled that of the Iroquois. Thomas Jefferson, John Adams, and George Washington, while being less ardent supporters of the Five Nations' model of democracy, were recorded to speak with admiration about Iroquois' concepts of liberty and political organization.

In fact, in October 1988, on the occasion of the 200th anniversary to the signing of the United States Constitution, the US Congress "... *acknowledged the historical debt which this Republic of the United States of America owes to the Iroquois Confederacy... for their demonstration of enlightened, democratic principles of government and their example of a free association of independent Indian Nations...*"

However, at the times that this novel is dealing with, the bulk of the work was yet awaiting the Great Peacemaker. To cross Lake Ontario was a brave decision. However, to convince the five warring nations living across it to listen to his message and accept the Great Tidings of Peace was an infinitely more difficult task to accomplish.

The continuation of his story is presented in the second book of The Peacemaker Series, "**Across the Great Sparkling Water.**"

The story continues with

ACROSS THE GREAT SPARKLING WATER

The Peacemaker Series, Book 2

CHAPTER 1

Little Falls,
Harvest Moon (mid-autumn), 1141 AD

Onheda shielded her eyes and watched the sun, which was blazing unmercifully in the afternoon sky. The heat was still unbearable, the humidity more so. It clung to her skin in a sticky veil of sweat, permeating her breath.

Picking her basket up, she balanced it over her shoulder with an effort. May the Left-Handed Evil Twin take this place and make it rot, she thought, forcing her way between the swaying stacks of maize. The ground crumbled under her feet, dry after the long summer moons. She hadn't been around to plant those crops, but now here she was, forced to harvest it, curse their eyes into the realm of the Evil Twin's minions.

"Is that the best the Onondaga women can do?" called out a familiar voice behind her back.

She didn't have to turn around to recognize the speaker. As always, Anitas — tall, merry, outspoken, not missing a chance to make jokes at the expense of everyone, the foreigners being the best target, of course. Onheda pursed her lips and proceeded to ignore the remark.

"Oh, don't die on us just yet." Laughing loudly, Anitas caught up with her, treading around the stacks of the harvested corn. "Your people must have been truly lazy, you know? Our women work until the Father Sun is about to kiss the top of the trees. No wonder our people always win."

Your people are nothing but bloodthirsty beasts, thought Onheda. *And they could not tell maize from a squash, either. All they can do is to raid our lands and wave their flint clubs with such persistence one may think they have nothing better to do.*

"No wonder your men are always away, raiding someone else's lands," she answered sweetly. "If you women spent more time at home, they might have found it more alluring to stay. But you would rather work the fields, keep your legs crossed, and let them look elsewhere."

Anitas' broad face lost its color. "You filthy rat," she hissed. "How dare you?"

The man who was supposed to become Anitas' husband had moved to live with a girl from another town. Onheda knew all about it, although the affair was hushed. There were no secrets inside the Turtle Clan's longhouses. In that aspect her life was no different among the People of the Flint than among her own Onondaga people.

While Anitas seemed as though debating with herself what to do with her heavy basket before seizing a chance to punch the stinking foreigner in the eye, Onheda watched her opponent with sheer enjoyment, making sure her gaze conveyed her derision, willing her palms to stop trembling. *Just do it already,* she thought. *Attack me, so I can punch you hard. It'll be such a pleasure to tear your pretty hair out.*

"Stop quarrelling, girls." A familiar voice broke upon them. Kwayenda, a member of the Turtle Clan's Council, and the head of Onheda's longhouse, eyed them sternly, with an open disapproval; always there to make sure the work had been done properly, especially with so many young girls around. "Off with you both. There is still much work to be done."

"I'm not done with you, you stinking rat!" hissed Anitas, burning Onheda with her gaze before storming off, swaying under her loaded basket.

"What were you two arguing about?" asked the older woman.

Onheda shrugged with her free shoulder, bestowing upon

her new opponent a dark glare.

The woman shook her head. "Find me after the evening meal," she said in a voice that brooked no argument. "I wish to talk to you."

"I didn't do anything wrong," muttered Onheda. "I didn't start this argument."

The elder woman sighed. "I wasn't referring to that, either. I have another matter to discuss with you. Don't forget. After the evening meal."

Uneasily, Onheda resumed her walk. What now? she asked herself. What could they possibly want from her now? She was doing her duties and not complaining. Whether in the fields or around the longhouse, she did whatever she had been told to do, never failing to accomplish her tasks. After her first unsuccessful attempt to run away, she was a model of good behavior, wasn't she?

She shivered. What had she been thinking back then, trying to escape, assuming she'd be able to find her way to Onondaga Lake and the lands of her people, crossing vast territories torn by ferocious warfare? She could have starved to death, or been killed, or captured once again.

Or, she thought stubbornly, she could have made it. There was no reason to assume she would not have been successful. She was young and strong, and she could survive in the woods. And by now she would have been back home, harvesting the second crop, living in the pretty town that sprawled not far away from Onondaga Lake, speaking a normal people's tongue and not this strange dialect the Flint People called a language. She could understand them with just a little effort, but their way to pronounce words was unpleasantly twisted. And they were the people who had killed her husband and many of her cousins and friends.

She ground her teeth. She was forced to live among the murderers of her family, among the sworn enemies of her people. Moreover, she was expected to become one of them, like the countless women who had done it before her and countless women who would have to do it after her. This was the custom. Some people were killed, others – adopted. She should have been grateful. It could have been worse. She could have been killed; or forced by some bloodthirsty warrior and then killed. Instead she was brought to their attackers' town, and then honored by being chosen by the Mothers of the Turtle Clan to replace a missing member, a woman who had died a few summers ago, in the winter sickness that carried away so many people. And she was expected to feel grateful about that. The rest of those captured in that raid were not so lucky. No clan had claimed them, and so they were killed. Quickly and painlessly, as there were no warriors in that particular party.

The warriors, Onheda knew, would have been honored to the highest degree; they would die neither quickly, nor painlessly. She had witnessed many such ceremonies, excited and horrified at the same time, strangely aroused by the warriors' courage and stamina. And it's not that everyone was brave up to their very end, of course. There were those who would lose their courage at the beginning of the ceremony and would beg for their lives, dying as painfully but also amidst the deepest contempt of their captors.

Oh yes, not every warrior of the Flint People was brave, she thought, grinning with satisfaction. Far from it! And her people had had the pleasure of raiding many of the enemy's settlements. The ceaseless warfare was a way of life, as long as she could remember herself. It seemed as if it had started from the beginning of times, but there were some who claimed it had not always been like this. They said the war should have been stopped. They said it would do no good to continue raiding each other's villages. They said the towns would perish one by one and not necessarily as a direct result of such warfare. They said all the involved nations were killing themselves.

There was such a man among her people, she remembered. Hionhwatha, a prominent leader of Onondaga Town, the largest town of her lands. Three summers ago, he had called a meeting, trying to bring together as many leaders as he could, from all over their towns and villages, to sit and smoke and talk. His oratory skills gained him a fair audience, and some leaders did listen.

It was an unheard of affair that everyone talked about, remembered Onheda, who had not been such a young girl back then, having seen close to eighteen summers. Her man had traveled there, too, accompanying the leaders of their settlement. Many young warriors like him went, mostly out of curiosity, although her husband said there was something about Hionhwatha and what he had said.

He had turned more thoughtful upon his return, telling her all about the strange ideas of putting a stop to the feuds among Onondaga People, uniting them under some sort of a mutual management. It sounded ridiculous, but she loved to hear her man talking. He had a beautiful way with words, so she argued only mildly, to work him up into telling more.

His friends were dubious too, even those who had traveled with him. They went there out of curiosity more than anything else. It relieved the boredom of hunting and raiding the enemy's lands. It gave them something to laugh about.

However, the results of the meeting were not good. Those who opposed Hionhwatha interrupted the peaceful gathering, not above using violence, and even witchcraft, some said. The meeting disintegrated into a hopeless affair of flying insults and threats, and some people were killed before the present left for their homes, their hearts full of anger. They even heard that one of Hionhwatha's daughters had died, murdered some said, while the meeting was still on. A wild rumor, but a persisting one.

Onheda shrugged. The stubborn leader did not give up, trying to bring his ideas to life by calling more meetings. Then somehow, his other family members died, and crazed with grief, he had left his town, to disappear into the mists of Onondaga Lake. Some said he was living there now, alone, an outcast, a deranged, violent man with whom no reasonable person would come into a contact. She remembered the rumors. They said he was now feeding on human flesh.

Well, some people were strange, and unlucky, was Onheda's private conclusion. The Right-Handed Twin had clearly given up on the struggling leader, but what could one do about it? And anyway, there was no wrong in their way of life. As long as one didn't let herself be surprised and captured, or killed. And she had been foolish enough to get captured, may they all rot for all eternity.

Atiron panted his way up the hill, struggling under the weight of a deer carcass. Sweat rolled into his eyes, and he could barely see the path ahead of him.

Not that he had a cause to complain, he reasoned. If one could wander outside the safety of the town's fence in order to clear one's head and return burdened by fresh meat every time he did this, life could have been made into a bearable affair. Actually, life could have been more pleasant, if one could just walk out every time one needed to clear one's head, instead of being expected to keep oneself either within the boundaries of the fence or surrounded by others, even when needing time alone.

However, this morning's council meeting turned out to be such a depressing affair he could not resist the temptation, slipping through the opening in the double row of poles, taking a trail leading toward the river, a few hundred paces down the hill; not strolling leisurely, taking all the precautions, of course, moving silently, his senses alerted. Outside the safety of the town's fence one could never be too careful, not with the enemy lurking, all these groups of foreign warriors on their way to raid this or that settlement, or even heading for Little Falls itself. People did not venture out unless in large, well-armed groups, yet, from time to time, one just had to have a gulp of fresh air and some privacy.

The Harvest Ceremony was nearing, usually one more happy

celebration, but this time the amounts of the harvested corn were pitiful, creating a problem. Reasons and explanations kept mounting, as they did now in the beginning of every fall, plenty of reasonable excuses, but their mutual nature was difficult to overlook. It towered menacingly, indicating the farmers' state of mind and even the lack of manpower. Women in the fields were busy keeping their watch, ready to sound alarm at the sight of approaching enemy, so the rest could make it safely behind the town's fence. However, for every justified warning, there were quite a few false ones and those pointed at the disoriented state of the people's minds. Nervousness and lack of confidence had been mounting for decades, reaching for all aspects of life, growing with every summer, steadily, imperceptibly.

If only someone could put his finger on a particular event, to recollect how it had all began, thought Atiron, struggling up the hill, listening to his heart that was thundering in his ears. Then the solution might also present itself. However, who could explain how they had come to this?

Although, since the dreadful winter three summers ago, when so many people had died from disease, and after the ill-fated raid of the late War Chief on the following spring, the situation had definitely worsened. The town had never recovered fully, although tremendous efforts were made to get back to normal life. More raids were sent, more captured enemies adopted, still the ranks of the clans were thinning, undermanned. There were simply not enough warriors to send out and not enough food to equip them with.

Sighing, Atiron remembered the War Chief, the closest of his friends. What a man he had been, imposing, intelligent, fierce, a good leader and a great companion, blessed with a beautiful wife and a pair of boisterous twins, a miracle in itself. Grinning against his will, he remembered the boys who had looked absolutely alike and yet different, easy to tell apart, because while one, Tekeni, was vital and handsome, having inherited the temper and the strength of his father, the other, Oni, was quiet and thin, closemouthed, a thoughtful sort of a child, much like his mother.

The boys were always together, and while it might have looked as though the smaller boy was following his impressive brother, the closer inspection showed that the opposite was true. The quiet, thoughtful twin was the one coming up with all sorts of ideas, ideas which the other boy, the boisterous one, was only too happy to implement. They balanced each other perfectly, and the whole town watched them, amused and expectant, remembering the prophecy concerning these boys. Like the Celestial Twins, they were destined to do important things, to better their peoples' lives, to change it dramatically in some unknown, unexplained way. They would lead their warriors to great victories when their time came, whispered the elders of the town.

A prophecy that was cut short by that terrible winter three summers ago. The War Chief's wife and the quieter twin died, leaving the great leader deranged with grief. Deaf to the words of the condolence ceremony and the consoling whispering of his friends and the devastated neighbors, the man spent the rest of the winter alone, talking about the raid he would organize with the coming of spring. A raid into the mists of the Great Sparkling Water, no more and no less; a reckless, unnecessary adventure, but there was no reasoning with his old friend, although Atiron did try. However, all he got was a cold grin that never reached the leader's clouded, distant eyes, and the short, cutting words, suggesting that he should bring his objections before the Town Council if he felt this projected raid was so ill-advised. Where had his friend gone?

He remembered getting to his feet, angered, hurt, offended, to encounter the anxious yet expectant gaze of none other than Tekeni, the surviving twin, huddled in the far corner, listening avidly. According to the decision of the War Chief, the boy was to come along, but by that time, Atiron had given up.

He shook his head, his sadness welling. The man had convinced the Town Council, and the Mothers of the Clans had given their blessing and a considerable amount of food supplies, and so the party of two dozen warriors sailed, never to return. None of them. Not even Atiron's own son, who had insisted on going along, a promising young warrior, his only son. They had all died on the other side of the Great Lake, and the grief stricken town accepted it, trying to get on with their lives for two more hopeless summers of less raids and deteriorating conditions in general.

Sighing, he shifted his burden, searching for a place to hide his catch before entering the town and proceeding along the twisted alleys, washed by the late afternoon sun, spreading the aroma of evening meals being heated upon the glimmering fires that doted the walls of the longhouses.

"Father!" As he neared, Kahontsi, his youngest daughter, burst from under the facade of their building, slowing down reluctantly. The smile she bestowed upon him shone. Tall and pliant, her movements as graceful as those of a young doe, her face a perfect oval, her eyes changing their color from strikingly bright to a very dark brown according to the light, Kahontsi was held to be the most beautiful girl, according to the judgment of the entire town.

Atiron could not fight his smile. "*She:kon*, Daughter. Back home already?"

She shook her head and her braids jumped, sparkling with drops of water, still damp from the wash up that sealed the day in the fields.

"No, not really." Kahontsi's eyes glimmered as brightly as her wet hair. She knew of her father's affection. He could never resist her charm. "Mother is resting. Ehnita had to be taken home this morning. She didn't feel well, and anyway, she is getting too heavy to be of use. I don't think she'll be back in the fields before her baby is out. She is also resting now. I was just visiting her." It all came out in a gush, with no pause for breath. The girl was obviously anxious to be on her way.

"Wait, don't run away. I might need your help. I'm going in to talk to your mother." He grinned at her open disappointment. "Well, you don't have to, of course. Who wants freshly broiled meat for one's evening meal?"

Her eyes widened. "You are not saying…"

However, Atiron was already inside, crossing the storage space of the outer room, heading for the long passageway.

"You just wait and see," he called out, satisfied with her reaction.

"*She:kon.*" His wife's smile flashed somewhat tiredly, as she perched on the edge of the lower bunk, brushing her hair. "What a day! We are almost done with the last of the maize. Might be able to finish harvesting it by tomorrow. Ehnita scared us, though. She became dizzy and almost fainted on us. Had to sit her in the shadow until she felt better, then two girls took her home. I'll talk to our Clan Mother today. I believe she should not be coming to the fields anymore."

"Will they agree?" asked Atiron doubtfully. "She has one more moon or so to go."

"They had better!" Her hand tore at the tangled hair impatiently. "There are other tasks a pregnant girl can do, without working to death harvesting maize."

"Look, I need your help, but if you are too tired I'll take Kahontsi. I bumped into her just outside."

The woman's eyes widened as she listened to his story, flooding with surprise and joy, yet spiced with a fair amount of reproach.

"You should know better than to wander outside unprotected," she muttered grimly.

Her nimble fingers finished braiding her wet hair, tying it behind her back with a thin leather strap. From under the bank, where the kitchen utensils were stored, she fished a pot and a flint knife, tossing them into a big leather bag, talking as she worked, "I had better come with you. You say it's just outside the fence? We can cut it there, so it won't be necessary to drag the whole carcass with us. I hope you hid it well. Wouldn't want any of the other greedy mouths claiming it for themselves. We will invite people for our meal, but it is still our catch."

Atiron grinned. Yes, this was his wife, the epitome of

efficiency. By the ancient tradition, when a man hunted in his spare time, and not as a part of an officially organize hunting party, his catch would be hidden within a fair proximity of the town, while the successful hunter would rush back home to summon his wife, or a daughter, or any other female relative, to accompany him to the hidden treasure, as the meat carried into the town by a woman would become her personal property, not to be shared with the entire community.

Kahontsi was still outside, shifting her weight from one foot to another. At the sight of her mother, the girl's pretty face flooded with relief. "So you don't need me, I suppose?" Broadly, she smiled at Atiron, mischievous and pleading, knowing well which of the two could not resist her charm.

"Be back in time to help me with the meal!" called out her mother sternly, watching the girl's well-shaped shins disappearing down the alley. "This one is a handful. Running around, going wherever she pleases. Careless. Indifferent to her duties. Anxious to finish whatever she does and be off. I wish I knew where she is wandering and in what company. In the fields, it's just the same. We have so much trouble with the young girls. They have to be placed far apart from each other, otherwise they are gathering in groups, laughing and chatting, doing nothing productive. We weren't like that when we were young!"

Atiron shook his head. "It's the war."

"There was war in our time, too!"

"But not like now. Things are worse now. Everything is falling apart. Look at the town's mood. It comes to expression in the young peoples' behavior. They feel the end is nearing and are trying to take the best out of life. I'm afraid to think what it'll look like in another few decades, in what world Ehnita's child will be living."

"Here you are again, plunging into that gloomy mood of yours," complained his wife. "Full of dark prophecies."

It was an old argument, and they made the rest of their way in silence.

Kahontsi rushed toward the southern entrance, elated. Smiling at the afternoon sun as it caressed her shoulders and arms, she breathed the aroma of cooking meals, thinking about their dinner. A broiled meat, of all things! Many would come to share their meal tonight.

Several fires were gleaming near the longhouses, and the women were busy with pottery bowls, stirring a porridge of mashed corn that was prepared from the morning, and now needed to be warmed and spiced with berries and dried meat. Nothing to rival a fresh stew, of course.

Narrowing her eyes, she saw Anitas strolling beside the poles of the inner fence, pacing back and forth, impatient.

"Good that it didn't take you a whole moon to appear," called out the tall girl, rushing forward, speaking as she ran.

"I'm sorry. It's Father. He burst upon me, looking for someone to come with him and get this delicious, pretty little deer he just hunted out there. Luckily, Mother volunteered." Kahontsi waved happily. "Would you believe that? He was wandering out there – don't ask me why he would do something like this – and he ran into that deer. Just like that! And then, whoop, one good shot and we are having a fresh meat for our evening meal." Her braids jumped as she tossed her head and laughed. "I don't suppose you'll be coming visiting tonight."

Anitas' eyes widened. "Wild bears would not manage to stop me. In the name of the Right-Handed Twin, how long has it been since I've eaten a fresh meat! When did the last hunting party leave? Five dawns ago? Weren't they supposed to come back already?"

"Not a chance. Give them another five, if at all." Kahontsi's face darkened, and both girls proceeded in silence for a while. In these war times, the hunting expeditions were as dangerous a business as a raiding party.

"Look at her!" exclaimed Anitas, pointing at the slender figure of the Onondaga girl, as she stormed out of the second Turtle Clan's longhouse. Stumbling into the cooking facilities spread beside the building's wall, the foreigner cursed softly and rushed on, paying no attention to the watching eyes.

"What about her?"

"The most annoying piece of rotten meat I ever met. Never smiles, never speaks to anyone unless it's something nasty. They should never have brought her here, if you ask me. They should have killed her with the rest of her filthy people. Or adopt into another clan, as far away from mine as possible. Stupid fowl!"

Kahontsi shrugged. "I guess it's not that easy to get used to a new place. Think about it. You and I could do no better, maybe. I'm not sure I would be all smiles if forced to live in one of her former settlements."

"Oh, how nice of you." Anitas raised her eyebrow and sneered. "Why don't you go over there and befriend her, if so?"

"I may, when I have time."

Anitas laugh. "But you never have time, do you? That's the catch. And I have to see her ugly face every day, all day long. Today, in the field, I wanted to punch her, I swear. She has such a dirty mouth."

They reached the end of the fence and glanced at the ceremonial grounds and the children running around it, throwing sticks at improvised targets. No adult appeared to be walking by. Relieved, they sneaked out and made their way along the outer side of the inner palisade, crossing tobacco plots.

"Did you bring everything?" inquired Kahontsi eagerly.

Anitas waved a small pouch, in which warriors and hunters carried their sacred objects. Dropping to her knees, she brought out a tiny pottery jar, which Kahontsi took reverently, peeking in, eyeing the glowing coal. In the meanwhile, her friend brought out a pack of corn husks wrapped around the smaller, brownish ground leaves. Next came a pipe – an old, cracked, unpainted affair. The amount of tobacco was hardly impressive, enough to fill only half of a pipe, but the girls went to work on it diligently, excited but cumbersome, lacking the experience.

"This time I had to take it from my brother's cache," murmured Anitas. "Father was beginning to wonder why his stockpiles were melting away."

They laughed.

It took them even longer to light the old thing. They puffed and blew and panted, fiddling with the coal, until the thin line of smoke appeared. By that time, Anitas relaxed and leaned against the warm poles, taking a deep breath, calm and confident, in perfect control.

Kahontsi's experience was not as advanced. She inhaled nervously, unsure of herself. Their hide-and-smoke escapades began not so very long ago, but Anitas had done it previously, from time to time.

"No games tonight?" Making a face, Kahontsi passed the pipe back to her friend.

"No, I don't think so." Anitas' lips twisted. "Not enough people to make up the teams. Everyone worthwhile is out there, either raiding some filthy enemy, or hunting, or doing the Left-Handed Twin knows what. There is no more life in this town. In the end only women will be left, to play with each other. Yuck! Let us hope some of the warriors or the hunters bother to come back in time for the celebration."

"Father is upset about it, you know? I don't know why, but I think something is wrong. He wouldn't talk about it, but I know him, and what is bothering him these days is the Second Harvest ceremony."

"What is wrong with that? No! They can't do this to us. No ceremonies, no celebration, no ball games, no nothing!"

"Who are 'they'?" grinned Kahontsi.

"I don't know! I don't know and I don't care. Whoever they are."

"Don't get all warmed up about it. The ceremony will be held, maybe in a smaller form but it will. No one would think of canceling the celebration. The Great Spirits need to be thanked. We can't make them angrier than they are now. Besides, maybe the warriors and the hunters will come back in time, and then wait and see what a great celebration this one will turn out to be."

Anitas pulled a face. "Somehow I don't think they will come back in time. Everything is bleak and boring. The Great Spirits are angry with us, or indifferent."

Kahontsi eyed the pipe, now lifeless and temporarily forgotten. "It'll be well." Trying to make it work again, she talked between the puffs. "Trust me. Besides... what do you think... the warriors and the hunters know very well when the ceremony should be held..." The pipe came to life suddenly and, unprepared, she inhaled too deeply and began coughing and choking. Tears flooded her eyes, but determined to finish her line of thought, she struggled to continue. "...They are waiting for this ceremony just like us..." She swallowed and coughed again, her face burning.

Anitas giggled. "Too bad I didn't think to bring water. For a beginner like you." She winked and took the pipe, resuming her smoking, at peace with the world once again. "Maybe you are right. These boys are not supposed to miss the ceremony. It's not one of the most important celebrations, but still. They would be insane to miss it."

Kahontsi shook her head vigorously to the offered pipe, taking a deep breath of an evening breeze, smelling the aroma coming from the woods just across the outer fence and down the hill.

"I'm going to participate in, at least, two ceremonial dances. Grandmother promised to prepare two more turtle shells for me, to make it up to eight pieces. Last year I was dancing with six."

She remembered the rustling sound the turtle shells made, when tied to the leg with a wide leather strap, preventing the rattle from bruising the soft skin of the thigh. A skilful dancer would make their rattling merge perfectly with the trill of the flute and the monotonous beating of the water drums. It was a challenge to control the heavy shells. The girls had to practice a lot to be accepted into the circle of the true ceremonial dancers.

Anitas shrugged. "All those girls are running around with a rash on their thighs."

"No, they don't. You just have to make sure the leather straps are wide enough to protect your skin. And, of course, you do not forget to rub enough of the bear fat, a little before and plenty after."

"And you think it helps?"

"Oh yes, it does. Last year, my legs were just fine."

"You had only six shells. Now it's going to be eight. A serious weight."

Kahontsi grinned. "Stop whining and come with me to do this. You are dying from boredom."

Anitas pulled a face. "I bet the warriors are having better time than us. The fields are such a bore!"

"Those who survive, maybe," murmured Kahontsi, her sense of well being deteriorating rapidly.

Two summers earlier, her only brother had been killed in a raid. He died far away from his family, somewhere across the Great Sparkling Water, along with the War Chief and the rest of the warriors who went with him. Even that handsome boy, the War Chief's surviving twin son went on that ill-omened expedition. Not to return, any of them. Oh, how the people of Little Falls were devastated, how reluctant to reconcile themselves to the bitter reality.

Yet, none suffered as she did, she knew, no one! Her brother was the best boy ever, her invincible hero, strong and funny and always there, solving her childish problems, knowing everything. He had a great future, everyone had said that. And somehow, somehow, she knew he did not approve of the way the war was going. He and Father had talked about it often, deep into the nights.

She had seen close to fifteen summers back then, never recovering from the shock of his death. She never talked about him anymore. Neither did Father. But on the rare occasions, when she allowed the bittersweet memories of him to enter her mind, she knew for certain that if he had managed to survive, he would have found the way to make things better. Some way that was unfamiliar to her, or even to Father.

Her mood spiraling downward in a way she could not control, she sprang to her feet.

"What happened to you?" asked Anitas, startled. "Do you feel bad? Because of the smoking?"

Kahontsi shook her head violently. "I have to help Mother. I'll see you there."

As she rushed away, she could imagine Anitas gaping at the place she was sitting just a heartbeat earlier, thinking that her friend had gone completely mad. She didn't care. All she wanted was to be left alone now, truly alone, at least for a little while.

Onheda stared at the small fire, watching the shadows bouncing off the walls, creating strange patterns.

"Sit down, girl," said the heavyset women, indicating the low bank opposite to her.

Sitting down obediently, Onheda did not take her eyes off the fire. *Come on*, she thought. *Just get on with it already.*

She could hear the clamor coming from the longhouse next to this one, its dwellers gorging on the fresh meat, happy and unconcerned. Some simple-in-the-head council member, she knew, had gone outside and hunted a deer. As though there was no danger in doing so; as if no raiding parties were likely to wander about. Would serve him well to get captured or shot, she thought, raising her eyes and meeting the gaze of the older woman.

"So tell me, how do you feel now that almost two moons have passed since you joined our longhouse?"

Oh please, you are not expecting me to pour my heart out, are you? She cleared her throat and tried to keep such thoughts off her face.

"I feel well," she said, clutching her palms tight.

"Are you happy here? Is there anything that bothers you?"

Onheda shook her head, her uneasiness mounting, the scrutinizing gaze of her interrogator making her stomach tighten.

"What happened today between you and Anitas?"

"Nothing."

"It didn't look like nothing to me."

She shifted uneasily, perching on the very edge of the bunk, where blankets and pelts did not cover the hard, wooden surface. It felt uncomfortably harsh against her legs.

"We were just arguing about things, that's all," she said finally, wishing to be outside, away from the suffocating dimness and the threatening pictures the dancing shadows were painting upon the wall.

The stocky woman sighed. "I know it's not easy to get used to a new home. I know it takes time. We are making every effort to accommodate you, to make you feel at home, but with no cooperation from you, we cannot make a good progress, can we?" She paused, and the silence that ensued became heavy, pregnant with meaning.

Onheda dropped her gaze, suddenly finding it difficult to breathe. This compartment truly did not have enough air. They ought to have kept the smoke hole in the roof opened. Glancing at the ceiling, she saw the opening gaping into the night sky, not covered at all.

"I... I'm doing my best," she said, surprised to hear her voice ringing steadily.

"It doesn't seem that way."

The fire flickered as a gust of wind swept through the corridor, making the shadows on the walls jump.

"Look at me, girl!"

The older woman's voice rang sternly, full of authority, not friendly anymore. The flinty gaze held hers. Onheda bit her lips and tried to look calm, and not like the cornered animal she felt.

"I know what you are going through, girl. You are not reconciled to your new life, not yet. You are fighting it. But it's time you made up your mind. Our clan does not need resentful members. We are patient, and we don't change our minds easily. But we can't wait forever for you to adjust. You will have to make up your mind soon. Do you understand me, Onheda? You were offered a chance of a new life. But the question is, what are you going to do with this offer?"

Out there, in the clear evening air, someone was beating on a drum, slowly and mournfully.

Onheda swallowed. "I... I do everything I'm asked. I give no trouble."

The penetrating gaze held hers. "Is this your model of a good behavior? To do as you are told? Have you been as good of a girl in your previous life?"

She licked her lips. "I don't know."

"Is that how you plan to go through your life? Doing as you are told and giving no trouble? You have many moons to go yet, many summers, many hunting seasons. Your life is still in its very beginning, girl, even if it did not go the way you had planned. Are you prepared to give up on everything? To do as you are told until you get old?" The narrowing eyes were now like a pair of dark, glowing coals. "Or do you plan to change your life once again? Are you cherishing ideas of running away to your former people? Would you help them attack us, having a chance to assist? Are you still our enemy, Onheda?"

Shivering, she stared at the woman, unable to answer, unable to shift her gaze. It was a nightmare. The annoying hag was reading her thoughts.

"Like I told you, I understand what you are going through." The stocky woman got up, a look filled with a certain amount of pity creeping in her eyes. "But it is time you made up your mind."

She turned and began rumbling through the clothes piled upon the bunk. Onheda clenched her hands to stop them from trembling.

"It's time you took yourself a husband," said the older woman without turning. "There is a man of the Bear Clan. His longhouse is just across the ceremonial ground. A good man; good hunter, good warrior. He should make a fitting husband for you."

"I don't want to take a husband," whispered Onheda.

"Why-ever not?" The older woman was still busy arranging the clothes. "You are free, and you are of a right age. Why wouldn't you want to take a husband?"

She clenched her palms tight, feeling herself back on the banks of Onondaga Lake, on that horrible day of the early summer, with her cousin killed, her friends dying, and herself tied and hurt, and for the first time realizing that she could do nothing, nothing at all, to fight back and take control of her life – a feeling unfamiliar up to that warm summer day.

She took a deep breath. "I don't want to take a husband," she repeated, voice firm. "Not yet. I will let you know when I'm ready."

Her adversary turned around, losing some of her composure; the sight that pleased Onheda, in spite of her plight.

"You know that the last word in this matter belongs to the Clan Council?"

"The clan's member is also privy to such a decision." Her anger welled, banishing the last of the fear.

"The clan's member, yes."

"I am a clan member!" She stared at the older woman, almost welcoming the developing confrontation. *I know my rights.* Her thoughts raced through her mind, frantically, fervently. *I will not be intimidated.*

The eyes in front of her took a different shade. "No, you are not." The voice of her tormenter was soft, almost compassionate. "Not yet."

Onheda felt her heart coming to a halt. It missed a beat, then began racing wildly, unevenly.

"But I am," she said breathlessly, the sensation of helplessness returning. "I was adopted... I... I would not be here otherwise."

"You didn't go through the adoption ceremony, yet. You didn't receive your new name. You are not officially a member of the Turtle Clan. You are allowed to live in this longhouse, you are allowed to work our fields, but you are not a member of our clan, yet. Nothing is decided."

The emphasis put on the word *live* was unmistakable. It bounced off the wooden walls. *Live, live, live. Do you want to live? Are you ready to die?* There had to be a way out of this nightmare.

"You will be adopted should you show a proper attitude. Not by doing as you are told; or pretending to do so." The woman reached for Onheda's shoulder, pretending not to notice her wincing, recoiling from the touch. "You have to make up your mind, girl. You have to understand that your past does not exist anymore. You have to reconcile yourself to this reality. This clan is your only family now. This town is your only home. This is the only life you can have. Either this or nothing at all."

The face in front of her was so blurry she could not make out its expression. She fought the welling tears.

"I'm certain the council will be willing to give you a few more dawns. Maybe half a moon. Maybe a whole moon, even. You will have to show this clan it will be poorer without you. Work as hard as you have worked so far, but do it cheerfully. Make friends. Take a husband. Either this or there will be no adoption ceremony. Do you understand me? Your time is limited now."

Oh, Mighty Spirits! She stared at the fire stubbornly, remembering the other small flame, the one she would light in this pre-dawn time when everyone was asleep and she would sneak out to make her secret offering to the Great Spirit, the Right-Handed Twin himself. She had done so several times, with no one to notice, no one to know. And if no one had noticed so far...

She almost shut her eyes, as another thought hit, swelling inside her head. She had not been formally adopted, not yet.

The woman said so, thinking to intimidate her further, but actually, doing her a great favor. She was free to go. She could have done this every night, every time she had sneaked out. The Right-Handed Twin was showing her the way, but she had been too blind, too cowardly to see it.

CHAPTER 2

The river sped ahead, flowing strongly, wider than any waterway he had seen so far. Two Rivers narrowed his eyes.

"Impressive," he said, having difficulty seeing through the grayish pre-dawn mist. "So that's *the* river?"

"Yes, that's our Great River." His young companion nodded impassively, with no sparkle brightening the dark eyes, no expression crossing the closed up face. It remained sealed, cold, indifferent.

Used to the sudden spells of gloom in his companion's moods, Two Rivers still raised his eyebrows, surprised. Wasn't the youth happy to see his homelands?

"Well, we had better make ourselves comfortable somewhere in there," he said, glancing at the trees adorning the low bunk. "Before your country folk run into us, entertaining the idea of dumping my juicy parts into their stews before we have prepared our explanations."

"My country folk will not run into us here," said Tekeni, coming back to life all of a sudden. "Onondaga, the People of the Hills, will be the ones feasting on your juicy parts. Or maybe the People of the Standing Stone. Our river begins somewhere between their lands."

"What? When you said 'your river' I thought you meant your lands, too. Weren't you bragging that your Flint People were the most powerful on this side of the Great Lake?"

"They are powerful, but not that powerful." A grin stretched the generous lips, lifting the scars that were crossing them now.

"Unless too many things changed through the last two summers."

The defiant spark was on, bringing back the boy Two Rivers remembered. Regardless of the circumstances of his people, the youth himself had changed into something unrecognizable. Whether because of the scars adorning the handsome face now, painting a strange pattern upon it, or the way it had thinned to look older, losing its youthful look, the change was there, deep and subtle. The boy had grown to be a man.

"And they will be as happy to dispense with my body parts as with yours, so there is no need to feel threatened by me just yet," the youth was saying, his grin challenging. "In a few more dawns? Maybe. If we make good progress."

"With the flow of this current and the moon getting thinner and thinner, I may be safe for longer than that," said Two Rivers, studying his companion with his eyebrows lifted high. *You cheeky cub*, he thought. *You are growing too sure of yourself.*

Careful to conceal their tracks, they carried their canoe along into the safety of the woods, then made a quick meal by mixing the remnants of the sweetened powder Tekeni's girl had been shrewd enough to toss into their bag. In these foreign woods it was not wise to try and spread the traps in order to enjoy some fresh meat, but after a whole moon spent in the uninhabited lands on the northeastern side of the Great Lake, they could not complain of being underfed.

Stretching and stifling a sigh of relief, Two Rivers stared at the brightening sky, remembering the past moon, the first moon of the Shedding Leaves season, and the wonderful days spent at leisure, resting and talking and hunting, preparing their plans.

The youth needed time to recover, and he himself welcomed the delay, enjoying the tranquility of the woods with no people. Five days of sail separated them from his homeland's bay, five days into the wilderness of the abandoned parts of the great water basin. A safety at long last. A wonderful opportunity to relax and to think. His plans needed to be formulated, or maybe just aired aloud. He had never dared to face his ideas fully, to put them into words with no gnawing doubts or misgivings. Not until now. The luxury of it made his head reel, and so he had taken his time in the wonderful loneliness the uninhabited woods provided.

The youth did not argue, needing this time to recover his former strength. His cuts were deep, not healing as fast as expected, and his cracked ribs needed the benefits of full rest. Not to mention his spirit, which needed to recuperate as well. His moods changing interminably, the youth seemed to be constantly torn between spells of rage and depression, one moment hopeful, busy making plans to get his girl back, the other growling, full of anger at everyone, from the men who had made their flight necessary, the men who had tried to kill him in humiliating, painful ways, to human beings in general.

"I wish Yeentso were still alive," he would murmur from time to time, eyes glimmering eerily, telling without words what he would have done to the man now if he could. Not a pretty sight.

"Yes, the filthy lowlife got an easy death," Two Rivers would agree, shrugging. "But he is dead, and this is the main thing. Stop living in your past."

"I'm not living in my past. I'm thinking about my future," the youth would maintain stubbornly, face sealed. "I'm making plans to come back and take Seketa away from them. It is my future."

"Oh yes, it is. But it's not your near future, so stop wasting your time thinking about it. When the time comes, you'll get her."

The gaze shot at Two Rivers was as dark as a stormy cloud. "We should have taken her along!"

"Where? Here?" Glancing at the clearing they had been staying at, a pretty pastoral place, Two Rivers lifted his eyebrows. "Yes, I'm sure she would be happy to live in the woods, skinning rabbits from our traps."

"She might have liked it. She would have taken care of our needs."

"*All* of our needs?" With a murderous glance being his answer, Two Rivers laughed. "Forget it, wolf cub. Forget your girl for some time. She'll wait like she promised. She seems to be a serious young woman, not a lightheaded little thing. So if she chose you, then it's done. She won't be looking at other men."

"She may be forced to take a man. The Mothers of her Clan are mean hags, every one of them. They may be angry with her for being involved with us." The youth sat up abruptly, hugging his knees, his mouth pressed tight, the healing cuts glaring. "What if they know about her helping us? What if someone saw her when she brought us things?"

"No one saw her, and she is capable of taking care of herself, this pretty Seketa of yours. If you didn't notice, she was a good girl, a respectable member of our society, before you drew her into the wild whirlwind that is called your life. So she will be back, working the fields, grinding maize, dancing through ceremonies. Maybe breathing with relief, eh?" Meeting another dark glare, Two Rivers brought his arms up in a defensive gesture. "Oh well. But all the same, she is not the person to be intimidated easily, and she is better off in the town for now. When we cross the Great Lake, you will be happy you didn't bring her along. The adventures that await us are not for a woman, upright or wild. You had no right to risk her life and her well being in this way."

A grunt was his answer.

"So, what will we do when we cross the Great Lake?" asked the youth after a while.

"We'll go to your Little Falls."

"And?"

"And we'll see if they are prepared to listen."

"Why would they?"

Disregarding the defiant, openly challenging glance, Two Rivers shifted closer to the fire, making himself comfortable.

"The situation must be as bad in your lands as it is in mine. So any of your people's settlements can be a good start. But in

Little Falls, we might have a better chance due to your old connections. Even though you were no more than just a mischievous boy back then, they must still remember your father, if he was as great a war leader as you claim."

"He *was* a great war leader, you can trust me on that!" called the youth hotly, forgetting his previous cause of gloom. "He was a great leader, and no one will forget him in a hurry, no one! He led his warriors for many summers, men from Little Falls and from the surrounding villages. He was always victorious, and they always listened to him."

"He must have been a good orator," commented Two Rivers thoughtfully, glad that such an opponent would not be standing in his way. A warrior of this vast influence might have proven a real obstacle.

"Oh, yes, he was. They always listened to him. He could talk passionately but reasonably, so even those who disagreed found nothing to say."

"Where there those who disagreed with him? On what subjects?"

"I don't know. Some raids were less advisable than the others, I suppose." Frowning, the youth narrowed his eyes, as though trying to remember. "His closest friend, Atiron, also from our clan, was always arguing with him. In a friendly manner usually, but sometimes they would grow angry with each other." Reaching for a small branch, the youth threw it into the fire, watching it thoughtfully, concentrated. "Their conversations would last well into the nights, in our compartment, or outside by the fire. They worried about our town and our people. And about our enemies, who grew stronger and fiercer with each passing moon. My brother used to sneak closer and listen. He didn't think it was boring, what they were talking about."

"This man, your father's friend, was he a leader too?"

"Well, he was a member of the Town Council and very esteemed and respected." The youth grinned. "He liked to disagree with my father. He enjoyed listening to his passionate speeches, defending his views and our way of life. My brother said so. He said the man was doing it on purpose. But they were great friends, so Father did not get angry for real, not usually."

"I do hope this man is still there in Little Falls," muttered Two Rivers, his mind racing. He forced his thoughts to slow down, studying the youth, pleased to see the large eyes clearing of shadows. "Your brother might still be there, you know."

But the handsome face closed again, abruptly at that. "He is not."

"How would you…" The rest of the question died away, answered by the empty, sealed eyes staring at the fire, refusing to look up.

How did the other cub manage to die? he wondered. Was he also a part of that raid that the oh-so-highly-praised War Chief decided to drag his underage sons on? What a stupid decision it was, and across the Great Sparkling Water, too. Into the very heart of the enemy lands.

"He died three summers ago, of a winter disease," said the youth quietly, his voice hardly audible, ringing eerily in the thickening dusk.

Two Rivers sighed. "I'm sorry to hear that."

The silence hung, uncomfortably heavy, unsettling.

"Anyone else of your family still alive?"

It took yet longer for Tekeni to respond, and Two Rivers thought he would not hear the answer at all.

"No, no one."

He threw more branches into the fire, then got to his feet, intending to check the traps. Their evening meal needed to be attended to, he knew, welcoming the opportunity to busy himself, to escape the heavy silence. Life could be too cruel at times.

He glanced at the youth, his heart going out to him. So young and yet so disillusioned already, having been forced to face more than some men would see in a lifetime. His own life seemed to be sheltered and uneventful when compared to this boy.

"So what will you do if my people agreed to listen?" asked Tekeni after a while, getting to his feet to fetch the rabbit Two Rivers brought back. Businesslike, he took out his knife and began cutting its back legs off. "Besides a lot of talking."

"Well, besides a lot of talking…" Shooting a direful glance at his younger companion, Two Rivers stirred the glowing embers, to make it ready for the cooking. "We'll be busy organizing your people and their neighbors, and later on, my people too, in a way that will enable them to work together, without the need to war on each other."

"How would you do that?"

"Through councils, of course."

"Town Councils?"

"No. The Town Councils cannot control the whole nation, can they? There are too many of them." Receiving the legless rabbit, Two Rivers sliced its stomach, emptying its contents into the hole he'd dug in the ground. "There will be the need to form a council of a nation, where chosen people would be responsible for dealing with troubles between the towns and villages. Just the way the Clans or the Town Councils are working, but on a larger scale."

The youth was peering at him, his eyes full of curiosity and again free of shadows. "And the trouble between the nations?"

"What do you think?" Two Rivers hid his grin, pleased with his companion's quick thinking.

"Councils too, on an even larger scale."

"Yes, but not many of them. Only one general council, comprised from a group of representatives from each nation." Slicing the fresh, dripping meat into neat pieces, he frowned, sensing his companion's doubts filling the silence. "It will work, because it works on a smaller scale. Our people are living this way, they are familiar with this sort of arrangement, so all they need is a cause to stop warring and get organized."

"And there will be no wars and no warriors?"

"Oh, that I can't promise you. It depends on the amount of nations that would be willing to listen. Not all of them will be able to open their minds, to overcome their prejudices."

"I'm not sure one single nation or person will do that," muttered the youth, picking a bowl Two Rivers carved earlier through the day out of a solid piece of wood. "I'll bring water."

"Yes, do that." Grinning, Two Rivers busied himself with impaling the meat on the sharpened sticks.

The cheeky cub was learning, he thought. And he was gaining confidence. Which was a good thing. He'd make a good partner.

ABOUT THE AUTHOR

Zoe Saadia is the author of several novels on pre-Columbian Americas. From the glorious pyramids of Tenochtitlan to the fierce democrats of the Great Lakes, her novels bring long-forgotten history, cultures and people to life, tracing pivotal events that brought about the greatness of North and Mesoamerica.

To learn more about Zoe Saadia and her work, please visit www.zoesaadia.com

Printed in Great Britain
by Amazon